Street Ends No Outlet

Tales of Marvin Also -Short Stories and Novella

Lee Anians-Mueller

PLAYEDWELL

PUBLISHING

ISBN: 13 979-8985850062

For Marlene

Then we will no longer be little children, tossed and carried about by all kinds of teachings that change like the wind.

— Ephesians 4:14

Contents

Introduction

Thank you very much for purchasing this book. *Street Ends No Outlet* continues with stories featuring the character Marvin Milstead. As I was getting ready to publish my first collection called *Idle Essence -Tales of Marvin*, I had an extra story called *At The Crest* that was not completed in time. The problem was the story grew as I wrote it, taking on a life of its own. This particular adventure threw off the confines of a short story and moved into the novella neighborhood. You see, a method I have employed in writing these Marvin stories is to consider a particular memory--however fuzzy or clear it may be--and work from there. Some authors start at the end of a story and write backward, sometimes I start in the middle and work outward. I will think to myself, well, in order for the reader to understand this I will need to tell them that. And to understand this character, I will need to provide that background and how it relates to something that will happened later... and well, the narrative grows and the story expands.

I've received good feedback on *Idle Essence* which was a surprise since I'm known for writing comedy mystery plays.

Here was a clutch of short stories about a kid growing up in the 1970s and peopled enjoyed it. Many readers asked; *Will you be writing more stories about Marvin?* Well, actually I do have an extra story, a leftover if you will, it's a tad longer than the others. *Great! When will it be out?* Oh, well, I'm not sure it would stand on its own... *So, write some more stories to go with it. Write another book.*

So, here is another book. Yes, I did have more stories floating around.

As with *Idle Essence,* most of these stories hold a kernel of truth and come from real-life experiences but are fleshed out with fictional filler. As an example, *Lunch With Miss Flossie* is a true tale. I remember having lunch with a family who lived in the basement apartment of our building but could not tell you any more than that. I know I sat at a table and ate a sandwich. I had to build around that simple memory.

Whistle Through the Fence contains a true event that I did not witness. It happened on the periphery. I fleshed it out with other matters and people from that time period to give it depth.

The stories that take place when Marvin is older hold a bit more truth. The story *Pollywogs On The Moon* was a suggestion from my mother who wanted me to write about the summer vacations we took at a place called Black River Lodge. There were dozens of memories I could have used but she requested the one that had to do with some tadpoles I brought into our cabin. I blended that with some others along with a poignant memory of watching the Apollo 11 moon landing in a crowded basement of the rec lodge.

Finally, *At The Crest* probably is the most autobiographical story here. As I stated earlier, this started as a simple tale that grew into something larger. When I jogged my memory during this time period, the floodgates opened and I thought, what the heck, let's see where it takes me. It took me back to school, back to my old neighborhood with my old friends, and most importantly, it took me to the movies.

I hope you enjoy these tales.

-Lee Mueller

Lunch with Miss Flossie

The pressure of the water from the garden hose against the concrete created a mist that looked just like smoke rising up from the wall. Just like smoke from a fire that a fireman used a hose to put out. Not a small hose for watering grass but a big hose for fires. If he could pretend the mist was smoke, he could pretend it was a large hose. He could be standing next to a blazing building and not in the basement landing of the apartment building.

Marvin Milstead had come down the back stairs to check for any holes his dog Skippy might have created in the yard. His mother wanted him to check because a neighbor had said something to someone so his mother said something to him. He did not find any holes but he did find a garden hose laying near the steps going down to the basement that lead to a subterranean concrete area; one of Marvin's favorite, secret areas. It was under the back porch and resembled a bunker he saw in all those old war movies.

After 10 minutes or so of *pretend fire* time, he decided the building was safe. He dropped the hose, walked over to the spigot, and turned the knob. His shirt was slightly damp, along with his shorts, but his tennis shoes were soaked to the socks. Not good.

"What're you doin' down there, kid?"

He looked up. A small boy had squatted down in the yard, a few feet away, and must have watched what he had been doing. He looked like one of Miss Flossie's kids. Miss Flossie did things for the building; swept off the porches, fixed things when they were broken, and called a repairman to fix the things she couldn't. His dad called her the *Super Lady* even though she didn't wear a mask or a cape. Miss Flossie and her children lived in the basement apartment of the corner building.

"Nothing," Marvin told him.

"Sure enough?"

"Yep."

A measure of silence passed. Besides an occasion bird chirp, intermittent water drip, and the gurgle of water going down a drain. The two boys sized each other up. The squatting kid wore blue corduroy pants and a white button-down shirt. Why was he dressed up? Marvin wondered. Church? School maybe? It was warm to be dressed as he was. This was *t-shirt and shorts* weather. It was what he wore on these summer days. It's what his dad wore.

"Ain't your name Marlon?"

"No. I'm Marvin."

"That's right, Marvin."

"What's your name?"

"I'm Alprentice Davis." He stood up and straightened his pants. "So, why you shooting water all over?"

"I dunno," Marvin said. "I was pretending there was a fire. I was a fireman putting it out."

"Pretending?"

"Yeah." He took a few steps forward and his sneakers squeaked with water. "I pretend stuff sometimes."

"Sure enough?"

"Yeah. Isn't Miss Flossie your mother?"

"That's right," Alprentice said. "Ain't your daddy's that policeman?"

"Yeah."

"And you got that dog. The one that digs all them holes."

"She doesn't do it anymore," Marvin said. "When she was a puppy she did it."

"What do you call that's dog?"

"Her name is Skippy."

"Like the peanut butter?"

"Yeah," Marvin said.

"I seen a cat round here earlier. Only had three legs."

"Really?" Marvin walked up the steps from the lower landing. His tennis shoes squished with small bubbles. "Where did you see it?"

"Seen it by the gate goin' to the alley and seen it up there on the walkway," Alprentice said pointing to the second-floor balcony.

"Only three legs?"

"Sure enough. Two in the back and one up in the front," he said. "Ain't much trouble gettin' round. My sister tried to catch it, but it ran. Ran real good."

"Where did it run to?" Marvin asked.

He pointed to a short staircase to the first-floor landing. "Up under them steps." Marvin had watched Skippy inspect that small space below those stairs and knew there wasn't much room. It was an ideal hide-and-seek spot for a small animal.

"Think the cat is still there?"

"Beats me," Alprentice replied. "You can go look if you want."

Marvin pulled his lower lip as he considered it.

"You sure got yourself wet," Alprentice said. "Specially them shoes of yours."

Marvin shrugged. He knew he could now ask Alprentice why he had on nice clothes which could lead to a long conversation about good clothes and wet clothes but he would much rather see a cat with three legs, so he tossed it away with a simple response; "Yeah, I know. I'll get dry soon."

"I never played fireman before," Alprentice said. "Sounds fun."

"It is," he said letting his lower lip smack back into place. "Hey, you know, sometimes fireman rescue animals. They get cats out of trees."

"Sure enough?"

"Yeah. Maybe we could rescue that cat."

"Maybe," Alprentice replied. He looked over at the stairs and then back at Marvin. He squinted with concern and said, "I can't get my clothes dirty though."

"You won't. You could be like the fire chief. They just stand around and tell people what to do. They never get dirty. Or wet even."

"Sure enough?"

"Yeah. Are you ready, Chief?"

ALPRENTICE TOOK a position on one side of the stairs while Marvin knelt down on the other side to look below. "I can't really see anything... much," he told Alprentice.

"I seen him run under there. Never saw him run out."

Marvin moved closer and bent down further. He was used to peering under the porches and balconies to locate his dog or holes she may have dug.

"What in Heaven are you children doing over there?" a woman's voice echoed across the yard.

"Ain't doing nothing mama," Alprentice answered. "Marlon is lookin' for some cat."

"Who?"

Marvin stood and stepped out onto the grass. "It's me, Marvin."

"Well hello there, Marvin!" Miss Flossie was poised on the top step from the basement landing. She had on her usual gray dress, gray apron, and white scarf on her head. "How are you doing child? You know, I just spoke with your daddy the other night."

"His daddy is that policeman," Alprentice said. "We were just playing fireman."

"Alprentice, I need you to come in and change outta them good clothes and wash your hands. We're gonna have lunch soon."

"But we didn't rescue the cat yet."

"You can rescue it after lunch."

"Ah, mom!"

"You heard me now," Miss Flossie said with a stern tone. She stepped up onto the sidewalk that ran down the yard. "Look here, Marvin sugar, you had your lunch yet?"

He reflected for a moment. He had Malt-O-meal at some point this morning but didn't recall anything since that point. "I don't think so."

"You like cold cuts?"

"I'm not sure," Marvin replied. "I don't know what coal cuts are."

Miss Flossie chuckled. "It's sandwich meat, darling. Like ham, turkey, and such. Mr. Mecurio got a whole mess of cold cuts from Millers' deli round the way. There is more than plenty."

"Yeah?" Marvin considered the offer. He had never had cold cuts nor had he eaten any type of meal, cold or otherwise at a table other than the one in his apartment. Would his mom let this happen? "I dunno."

"I'm the chief," Alprentice said. "And I say that you have to eat your lunch here!"

"You hush up now," Miss Flossie replied, "You let Mister Marvin decide for his own self."

Marvin looked from Miss Flossie to Alprentice who looked at the ground. Using the time he was given to decide for himself, he considered the area Miss Flossie emerged from; the steps and concrete landing below the porch were just like his war bunker. The door at the bottom of his space opened into dark musty laced rooms with storage lockers, boxes, and an old crank-style washing machine. The door at the bottom of their steps opened into a space where they lived. What did it look like? Dark and musty?

Alprentice sighed and kicked at the air above the ground. "Bet he don't want be around us, that's all."

"I said hush your mouth son."

"Yes, Ma'am," he replied with another kick.

Marvin wasn't sure what Alprentice had meant but it must have been something his mother didn't like. "Can I ask my mom?" he asked.

"Why sure you can," Miss Flossie said. "That's the proper thing to do."

"Yeah. I don't think she was making anything. She's been talking on the phone a lot today."

"Well, you tell your mama I said *Hello* now, will you?"

"I will."

"And Marvin," Miss Flossie said, "you might want to change into some dry shoes."

"Yes, Ma'am," he replied as he ran up the backstairs.

His mother wasn't on the phone when he came through the back door, she was on the couch in the front room talking to the neighbor lady from the apartment below. When Marvin's presence was realized the conservation shifted to a whisper. He waited until it moved to silence.

"I didn't find any holes," he said.

Skippy who was lying in a pool of sunlight on the floor in front of the window lifted her head as if she understood Marvin referred to her misdeeds.

"Good. I'm glad," his mother replied. "Why don't you go play in your room while I talk to Doreen?"

"OK. But um... Miss Flossie asked if I could eat lunch with them. She's got coal cuts. Ham and stuff."

"Miss Flossie?"

"Yeah. Me and Alprentice were playing firemen out in the yard. Miss Flossie came up she asked me. And then I said I would ask you."

"Oh. I uh... well," his mother blinked a few times.

"Miss Flossie?" Doreen asked with a furrowed brow. "Isn't she..." She paused and looked at Marvin.

"Kind," his mother said as she glanced at Doreen who relaxed her face, and then back to Marvin with a smile. "Isn't she *kind* for asking you? What would you like to do? Would you like to have lunch with Miss Flossie?"

He thought for a moment. He looked at Skippy who had peacefully gone back to sleep. He could hear the theme of *The Andy Griffith Show* coming from a distant television somewhere. "Yes. I'd like to."

"All right. So, why don't you get cleaned up? At least wash your hands."

"I need to change my shoes too."

"OK, change your shoes too," she replied.

He washed his hands, changed into his newer, dry Converse tennis shoes, returned to the front room, and waited a few minutes for a lull in the whispering to say goodbye. Marvin's stationary presence in the archway prompted Skippy to rise and trot over to him.

"You can't go with me Skip," he whispered as he bent down to scratch her head. "I'll bring you some cheese if they have any."

"Are you ready to go?" his mother asked.

He nodded his head.

"You washed your hands and face?"

"My hands. My face wasn't really dirty," he said. "I changed my shoes."

"I wish you would have changed that t-shirt. It looks damp."

"It's pretty dry now."

"Were you playing with the hose again?"

"A little bit," he replied. "Then we looked for a cat with three legs."

Whatever tension had been present in the room conjured by the whispers had now cracked. Doreen laughed loudly. "A what?"

"All right, Marvin," his mother said. "Why don't you go ahead and go? Have a nice time. Tell Miss Flossie thank you for me."

"OK." Skippy followed him through the kitchen to the back door. "Stay there. I'll be back." She barked a few times at the door as he walked across the balcony and down the stairs.

ALPRENTICE SAT on a concrete bench in the corner of the yard under the sporadic shade of a mimosa tree. Marvin saw him wave his arms as he made his way down the sidewalk. Alprentice stood and saluted.

"Glad you came back private," Alprentice said. "At ease soldier."

Marvin studied Alprentice. He had changed into a t-shirt from his button-down but still had on the corduroy pants. "Not sure what that means. What I'm supposed to do?"

"Don't you watch *Combat* on TV?"

"Yeah," Marvin replied. "I don't remember them saying that."

"Well, they do. It's army talk."

"Yeah? Did you find that cat?"

"Not yet," he replied. "Mom made me wash up."

"Yeah. Mine did too."

"Guess we can look after while."

A small girl in an orange dress materialized in Marvin's periphery. She stood on the sidewalk with her arms folded. "Mama said for you all to come on in now."

"K," Alprentice replied. "We will."

Marvin nodded at her, she smiled, turned, and skipped away.

"That's Shirley. My little sister."

"Oh."

"You got sisters?"

"No," Marvin said.

"Brothers?"

"No. It's just me."

"You lucky," Alprentice said. "I got two sisters and two brothers."

"That's a lot," Marvin replied. A slight breeze stirred the humid air. Shadows thrown by the branches of the mimosa tree bounced around their faces. "I don't ever hardly see anyone outside playing."

"Yeah. We stay with our dad. But he had to go in the army. We had to stay here," Alprentice said as he squinted over toward the apartment building. A screen door slapped on the 2nd floor. They both looked up at the balcony and could hear Mrs. Richardson coughing. "I guess we should go in now."

THEY WENT DOWN the stairs of the walk-up basement. Alprentice grabbed the door handle, twisted it, turned sideways, leaned out, bumped into it with his hip, and the door popped open. Marvin expected the traditional aroma of damp concrete to greet him but instead was met with a smell similar to his grandmother's vegetable soup.

"Now you boys have a seat at the table," Miss Flossie's voice carried above the chatter of other children's voices and music from a radio.

Marvin stepped inside. It did not resemble the basement on his side of the building. There were no musty stone walls but instead wood paneling on the walls and photographs on the paneling. There were cabinets, credenzas, and shelves instead of storage lockers. Large quilts and blankets were suspended from clothes lines which divided the space into various rooms. A box fan hummed from the floor in the far corner while a small round fan looked from side to side on a shelf.

"Come on over here. Sit by me," Alprentice said as he motioned Marvin to follow. He walked around the long table where an older boy and girl were already seated with sandwiches on their plates.

Alprentice pulled out a chair at the end of the table and nodded to the spot on the other side. "You can sit there soldier."

"Soldier?" The girl smirked as she looked at Marvin. "That boy ain't no soldier."

"We were just playing," Alprentice replied.

"Denise?" Miss Flossie said as she appeared from behind a quilt. "You leave them alone, ya hear?" She held a large serving plate. "Marvin is our guest. He don't need your lip."

"Yes ma'am," Denise said.

"Shirley?" Flossie called out.

"Yeah mama?" her voice answered from somewhere in the room.

"Bring that loaf of bread on the sideboard in here." She set the plate on the table. "Now Marvin honey, what we got here is ham, we got salami, turkey, pastrami, and if none of them strike your fancy, we got us some baloney in the ice box."

"That's my baloney," the older boy spoke up.

"It ain't your baloney," Flossie replied. "It's for everybody."

"Yeah Rodney, it's for everybody," Denise said.

"I don't know how you take your sandwich Marvin, we got mayonnaise, mustard, catchup, whatever you want."

Shirley entered and placed the bread on the table.

"Mayonnaise is fine."

"He say, *Mayonnaise is fine.*"

"Hush up Rodney," Shirley said. "We can hear him."

"Yeah Rodney," Denise added.

"Children!" Flossie snapped. "Where are your manners? You may act a fool at your daddy's house but not when you are here with me. Not with a guest at our table. I will not have it, you hear?"

"Sorry mama," Rodney replied.

"Now, Alprentice? Before we get started, would you like to give thanks for these gifts we are about to receive?"

"Yes, mama." He folded his hands and lowered his head.

"God is great, God is good, let us thank him for our food. By hands we are fed, give us Lord our daily bread."

"Very nice." Flossie screwed off the lid from the mayonnaise jar and set it by Marvin's plate. "Now, what would you like for your sandwich?"

He studied the slices of meat fanned around the plate. "I like ham."

"He wants ham mama," Alprentice said.

"Hush up Alprentice," Rodney said, "we can hear him."

"Very well, ham for Mister Marvin."

He wasn't sure if it was the breeze from the fans or the excitement of a new environment but his skin tingled and goose bumps rose on his arms. On an average day, during lunchtime, he sat at the table; sometimes with his mother, and sometimes by himself. The only sounds or voices came from conversations on the television. In Miss Flossie's place, there were many sounds and many voices. Brothers and sisters were teasing and laughing. Marvin was mesmerized and overwhelmed but enjoyed it.

"Now see here," Miss Flossie told him, "I'll just let you fix it up yourself." She moved the bread within his reach. "Unless you want me to make it for you."

"No, thank you," Marvin replied, "I can do it."

"He'll do it, mama," Alprentice told her.

"I heard. Just you mind yourself."

He set two slices on his plate. He picked up the jar of mayonnaise and a butter knife and slathered each piece. He could feel his every action being observed. Perhaps he was doing it in an unusual way they had never witnessed. Marvin glanced over at Alprentice. He had piled up slices of cold cuts on the bottom half of his bread and was now coating the top with mustard.

"Here's something nice to wash it down," Flossie said as she set a glass in front of Marvin and poured lemonade from a pitcher.

"Thank you."

"You're welcome."

Marvin closed up the bread around the ham and took a bite. Not bad. His mother usually made his lunch but on occasion, he tried out his sandwich-making skills. As he chewed he glanced around the table; Rodney and Denise were focused on their area of the table. The novelty of the new kid must have passed. He looked at the pictures on the paneling. There was a painting of Jesus with a gold circle around his head. Next were family photos and a picture of a man that looked familiar. It looked like that president. The one who had been shot.

He could see a hint of a couch just beyond one of the blankets and the flicker of television on the tiles below. He took another bite. His mother usually cut them in half. Sometimes diagonal. But whole was good. Everyone else at the table was eating theirs whole. Just over the hum of the fans, he could hear baseball scores coming from the radio.

A tall teenager wearing glasses entered from one of the blanket rooms. It must be Alprentice's other brother Marvin thought. The oldest one. He had an angry look on his face as he surveyed the room and his eyes stopped on Marvin. Marvin looked down at his plate. It was the kind of plate his mother would call China. It had a dark green ring around a flower pattern near the rim. It was the type of plate he had to be careful with because if it fell, it would break.

"What's that boy doing here?"

"This is our guest, Antoine," Flossie said, "This is Marvin Milford."

"He's my friend," Alprentice said.

Rodney and Denise looked at their older brother and then turned to Marvin as if to await his reply.

"Milford?"

Marvin considered his sandwich while he felt the tension rise around him. The sandwich was difficult to hold as one solid object. If he held it too far down, it would yawn open. He had to hold it near the center.

"He that's cop's kid?"

"That's right," Alprentice said, "his daddy's the policeman. Marvin and me was playing firemen out in the yard."

"Were you?" Antoine chuckled. "Out there playing Watts were you? You know about Watts kids? How about you Marvin?"

"Nah," Alprentice replied, "We was playing rescue."

"Would you like a sandwich?" Flossie asked. "There's plenty here, as you can see."

"We got cold cuts," Alprentice said.

"Turkey is good," Shirley said.

"Salami's better," Rodney replied.

"Where'd you get that spread?" Antoine walked to the table, studied the plate, picked up a slice of salami, and rolled it up like a cigarette.

"Mr. Mecurio. Up on second," Flossie told him. "He got it from Millers, around the corner. Some function I guess. He gave the rest to us. What was left over."

"Leftovers?" He sighed. "You mean charity."

"Have a seat son. Let me fix you something."

He pulled out a chair. "I'll have seat. But I don't want no hand me down food."

"I got baloney in the ice box," Rodney said. "You can have some."

"Don't want no baloney." He placed the salami roll in his mouth and chewed. "Got no cheese?"

"No cheese, son."

"Shirley ate all the chips," Rodney said.

"I did not!"

"Man," Antoine said. "No cheese. No chips. No good."

"Children? Be still," Flossie told them.

It stayed silent for a few moments. Marvin could hear the song playing on the radio above the whir of fans. It was one he knew called, *I'm Your Puppet.*

"Hear about Chicago, mama?" Antoine asked as he rolled the salami grease around on his fingers. "They threw a rock at Dr. King. Struck him in the head."

"Lord have mercy," Flossie replied as she sat down.

"They say he does," Antoine said. "Just not for everybody."

"Hush now," Flossie said to him.

The song on the radio ended and a series of commercials began.

"I saw a three-legged cat," Alprentice announced. "Me and Marvin was trying to find it."

"A three-leg cat?" Rodney asked. "That's crazy."

"I seen it," Denise replied, "it was next door. By that garage. Day before yesterday. Saw it eating crickets out of the weeds."

"Crickets?" Rodney scrunched up his face and stuck his tongue out. "Blah!"

"Ain't nothing wrong with that," Antoine said. "Every living thing has to do what it needs to survive."

"I seen him under the stairs," Alprentice said. "That was this morning. We want to rescue it."

"Lord has mercy on the three-legged cat," Antoine said, "But not our brothers up north."

"Antoine," Flossie snapped. "That's enough."

"I'm just telling it like it is," he replied. "There's more talk about a damn crippled cat than…"

"Son." Flossie's voice stilled the air and deflated Antoine. She didn't say that one word loudly or forcefully, but it carried a warning buried in her tone that her children recognized. They all looked down. Marvin's eyes stayed up. He watched Miss Flossie as she placed her fists down on the table and pushed herself up, her chair squeaked backward across the linoleum. "Now, I said enough of this kind of talk at this table, did I not? These here children don't need this type of nonsense right now. There'll be plenty of worldly business to meet them when they get older and get out there. Let them be children a while longer and just enjoy this bounty and fellowship here with one another. Let them have this time with this boy Marvin right now. Things are about to change. Let's keep it pleasant for the time being. Please."

"Alright." Antoine rose from his chair, regarded the meat plate for a moment, shook his head, and retreated behind the blankets. The kids finally looked up from their plates.

"Don't mind your brother," Flossie said. "His mind is full of worldly matters right now."

The commercials ended on the radio. The Disc Jockey announced it was half past the hour, it was 92 degrees, and here were the Walker Brothers with *The Sun Ain't Gonna Shine Anymore.*

"What things are about to change mama?" Denise asked.

"What's that?"

"You said, *things are about to change.* What things?

"Be still," she replied. "Don't you worry none right now."

"I know," Rodney said. "She means daddy. Goin' to that war."

"Like *Combat* on TV," Alprentice told him.

"I said you kids be still," she replied. "Finish your lunch."

Shirley sighed. "I wish we had some chips."

"You ate them all," Denise said. "Didn't have no mercy on the rest of us."

"Tell me more about this kitten," Flossie said as she eased herself back down.

WHEN EVERYONE HAD FINISHED EATING, Denise and Shirley cleared the table, Rodney excused himself saying he wanted to finish going through his new comic books. Marvin thanked Miss Flossie, and he and Alprentice returned to the backyard to resume their rescue mission.

They looked under the stairs once more and walked around the narrow yard peering under the walkways and other hiding places.

Alprentice sighed and wiped his forehead with the back of his wrist. "Man! It's sure getting warm out."

"Yep," Marvin replied. "Hey, do you wanna go up on the second-floor balcony and look? Maybe it's hiding up there somewhere."

Alprentice looked up and thought about the proposal for a moment. "Nah. I don't like goin' up there much."

"How come?"

"Mrs. Richardson. She don't like me much. She yells at me."

"Oh," Marvin said. "Yeah, she's not very nice. I think she's the one that complained about Skippy digging holes." He glanced up to make sure Mrs. Richardson wasn't listening at her back door. "So, what do you wanna do?"

Alprentice shrugged. "Maybe we can try later. Or even tomorrow."

"Yeah." Marvin looked down at the sidewalk. He kicked at a broken piece of concrete and sent a chip out into the meager grass area.

"Mama's gotta enroll us in that school across the way."

"The school on the corner?" Marvin asked.

"Yeah."

"That's where I go."

"What grade are you gonna be in?" Alprentice asked.

"First."

"Me too," he smiled. "Maybe you'll be in my class."

"Well," Marvin said as he rubbed the back of his neck. "I think we're moving."

"Moving?"

"Yeah. But just me and my mom. I'm supposed to start another school. Not the one on the corner but this other one that's by my grandparents."

"By your grandparents. Where your grandparents at?"

"They live a ways from here." Marvin kicked another chip from the sidewalk. "They live in a house. They got their own trees, grass, and stuff. A big yard with a fence for Skippy to run around in."

"Really? A house? Is it nice?"

"Yeah. And they live on this street that ends with this big circle."

"A big circle? Whatcha mean?"

"Well... it doesn't go anywhere. Like the streets around here do. They all go places. The one they live on doesn't. When people drive down their street... they have to turn around and go back."

"Huh," Alprentice said. "Why would you wanna live someplace that doesn't go anywhere?"

"I don't know," Marvin replied. "I guess I'll find out."

"I guess. Maybe you'll turn around and come back."

"Yeah, maybe."

Alprentice and Marvin made a half-hearted check for the cat before they called off their rescue mission.

"Alprentice!" Flossie's call reverberated from the concrete walls. "Need to come in now and get cleaned up. You hear?"

"Hear you, mama," he called back. "Well soldier, until next time."

"Next time," Marvin replied.

They saluted each other and went their separate ways. Marvin climbed the stairs up to the second floor and walked toward his back door. He stopped for a moment and looked over the rail down at the yard. From above it was just a green and tan spotted rectangle with a brown line that ran down the middle. Not a fire station. Not a battlefield. Not a playground, ball field, or what he could imagine. It was a yard. Miss Flossie lived in the basement. It wasn't a musty-smelling place, it held furniture, photos, and a family. He never imagined he would see inside or have lunch there or make a new friend. But things were about to change as Miss Flossie said.

Just as Marvin turned to go he heard a sound. It came through the background hum of cars outside on the street and the usual neighborhood murmur; it was a soft plea. It was a kitten calling out. Marvin saw the orange fur hovering near the railing between Mrs. Richardson's and Mr. Mecurio's back door.

Marvin squatted down and snapped his fingers. The kitten trotted toward him. He could see it only had one front leg and two in the back. It stopped about a foot from Marvin. He held out his hand. The kitten sniffed.

"Hey little guy," Marvin said. "Would you like some milk? Do you want to come inside? Have lunch? Meet my family?"

Whistle Through The Fence

"How have you and your mother been?"

"Fine," Marvin said.

"That's good to hear." The elderly man sat back in his chair which seemed to consume his whole form. The dark green material with tree and windmill designs inflated around him. Marvin wasn't sure how old Grandpa Milstead was but he was certain he was older than his mother's parents. Everything about him was gray; his hair, his skin, and his teeth. And when he smoked, his breath.

"I understand you're staying over there with your other grandparents"

"Yeah," Marvin replied.

"They treat you all right there?"

"Yes. They treat me good."

The ceiling above them creaked as someone moved around on the second floor. Marvin looked up toward the sound and then let his attention ease down the wall and explore the room around him. The Milstead home was old and furnished with old things. Old furniture, old pictures, and old people. Grandmother Milstead had excused herself to help Marvin's dad with some tasks upstairs, which allowed Marvin time to visit with his grandfather. He sat patiently on a creaky wooden folding chair next to the quilt-covered couch to pass the time. *Don't you want to sit on the nice big davenport? No, thanks. I like this chair.* It was the easiest way Marvin could say the couch smelled strange without using words that might hurt someone's feelings. When he did sit there, the musty-wet-dog-mothball smell sank deep into his clothes and followed him all day. The creaky wooden chair didn't share an odor, only a sound or two.

"What grade will you be going into?" Grandfather Milstead asked.

"First-grade."

"Is that right? First huh? " He rubbed his chin. "Wouldn't be nice to keep going where you were? Go into first grade at your same school?"

"Yeah," Marvin replied. He shifted and his chair moaned. "Wish I could."

The ticking of a mantel clock perched on top of the television console set filled in a significant pause.

"Had a lot of friends there, didn't you? At the old school."

"Yeah, I did."

The dogs in the backyard began barking at something they saw or sensed that needed a state of alert raised. Marvin looked toward the back of the house; through the series of archways that lead to the back porch.

"Ah!" The old man said and waved his hand in deprecation of the racket. "Lady Bird's getting old." He was referring to the matriarch of the beagles in the back. "The wind comes along, whistles through the fence, and it sets her off, Gets the other two riled up. Her hearing's going."

"Do you want me to go and see what they're barking at?" Marvin asked.

"What's that?"

"Want me to go take a look out there?"

"It's nothing," Grandfather Milstead said. A twinkle came to his eye and then with a smile said, "You know what it could be Marvin? Could be... somebody came to do mischief. What do you think? Maybe a burglar. Do you think you could handle him if you went out there?"

Marvin looked toward the back of the house again. "I don't know." The shades were drawn over the windows. He couldn't see outside, he could only see shadows from tree branches moving across yellow squares.

"Tell you what, I have my old service revolver around here somewhere if you want to take it with you." A grin tried to challenge the seriousness of his tone. "Ever shot a gun before, son?"

"Well... not a real one," Marvin told him. "I shot a BB gun a few times. At a can."

"That's good enough. Same principle. Different results," he said. "It might be in that old roll-top in the hallway. Bottom right-hand drawer. Metal box. It should have a couple of rounds in it. I would think that would be enough."

Marvin chewed on his bottom lip as he thought. He didn't believe his grandfather was being serious. His tone was very serious but his eyes were laughing.

"I don't think I'll need that," Marvin said.

"Are you sure?"

"Yes."

"I guess you're pretty strong, huh? You eat your spinach like Popeye the sailor"

"Sometimes," Marvin said.

"It might be a big dangerous fellow."

"I will be fine."

"All right, then." He laughed. "When your dad comes down, I'll let him know that you went out to investigate."

Marvin rose from the chair. "Thank you." He moved

through the rooms quickly, the floor creaked with each step. He didn't know what it was about the Milstead house but it felt spooky to him, even in the daytime. There were countless dark corners where things could hide. Old paintings with old people who looked angry as if they had been trapped there and wanted to leap out of the landscape and hide in those corners. If he had to spend time there, time was better spent outside where there were no paintings nor darkness.

The yard in the back of the Milstead house was large. It was bordered on one side by hedges and a wrought iron fence. There was a small squeaky gate at one end for people that opened on the street side and a large wooden gate at the back for vehicles. A tall wooden fence ran across the back that ducked behind a makeshift horse stable. Most of Marvin's friends were stupefied to learn he had a grandfather who had horses. A grandfather who did not live in the country on a farm but instead lived in a section of the city everyone called *Dogtown*.

How can he have horses? There's no way. Liar liar pants on fire.

But he did have horses. Marvin was told it was because his grandfather had been a police sergeant for many years. *Your grandpa knows the right people,* his dad told him. *He could have giraffes if he wanted.*

So, why didn't he get giraffes? Marvin had asked. *Too tall,* his dad said. *They could lean way over the fence and it would frighten the neighbors. Horses were just the right height.*

MARVIN STEPPED out into the sunshine leaving the scent of old dust for the fragrance of a backyard. Lady Bird wagged her tail and barked a greeting. The last two of her pups that had not been bestowed, named Jackie and Bobby, ran to him as he came down the steps.

"What's going on out here?" He asked as he sat on the bottom step. The pups wrestled to claim space in Marvin's lap. Bobby wiggled, squeezed, and pushed under his sister to stake his claim. Jackie resolved to perch on the high ground of his thigh.

"What were you guys barking at?" He rubbed each of their heads as their tails slapped against him in approval. Bobby had been promised to Marvin as his first official pet. What better way to learn responsibility than pairing a boy with a dog? But when the family circumstances shifted from their traditional course, it was decided Bobby, should remain at the Milstead house—it would still be Marvin's dog—but they would keep it for him. He could see the dog when he came to visit; the weekends his father brought him over.

He looked around the yard and did not see a large, dangerous fellow lurking anywhere. Off to his right was a vegetable garden that claimed a large patch of dirt. Nothing seemed out of place. Next to the garden was an old maple that held a wooden platform complete with railings and steps; a treehouse Grandpa Milstead had built for him, Marvin preferred a *tree fort*. No one was hiding in the tree or the fort.

To the left was a long stretch of grass that buzzed with insects and a row of shrubs that hugged a wrought iron fence. Beyond the fence was a side street that the Milsteads called *the alley*. It was a narrow lane that gave up after two blocks and ended at a guardrail. In the summer the guardrail was swallowed by bushes and weeds; it looked like the street ended at a green wall.

The coast or at least the yard was clear. Lady Bird must

have taken issue with a sound the wind had made or maybe one of the horses made a noise.

Marvin eased the puppies onto the grass as he stood. If he was going to investigate, he should do a thorough job. Bobby and Jackie followed as he walked toward the large outbuilding that had been a garage but was now what his dad called an urban barn. He raised the latch and opened the door which skidded across the dirt and gravel. "You guys stay back," he said to the pups. Marvin pretended to throw something and they ran after the foil.

———

It was cool and dark inside the building, except for one shaft of dusty sunlight coming through a side window. Marvin wrinkled his nose at the smell of manure. He pressed the crease below his nose and above his lip, the button that held sneezes as the fine floating soot tested his allergies.

He surveyed the horses and what he saw appeared as it should be. There were three horses in three stalls; a brown one on each end and a white one called Casper in the middle. Casper was the only one he was warned not to touch. *He's a bit feisty*, Grandpa Milstead had told him, *He's apt to snap your fingers off and chew them up like carrots.* Grandpa Milstead had also passed along the warning that *if a turtle would ever bite your finger, it wouldn't let go until it thundered.* Every mammal and reptile in the world seemed to be after your fingers.

———

The horses blinked a few times through the dusty haze. Casper shook his head and kicked the door of his stall. Isabelle, the brown mare at the far end snorted and twitched as a few flies buzzed her head. Marvin felt another sneeze trying to gather power, so he stepped back out and closed the door.

"No one in there," he said. The sound of a metal clank responded. It wasn't the door latch or anything nearby, it was a distant noise. It seemed to result behind the tall back fence. There was a house next to the Milsteads on the side street, just beyond the fence. it must be someone over there making the sound Marvin thought. He heard a voice followed by a response. A kid speaking to an adult. There was an older boy who lived there, Randy, Billy, or something with a *y* at the end. He had met him about a year ago when Marvin and his parents were at the Milsteads for dinner. A pudgy boy came to the back door and asked if he could give some carrots to the horses.

Not right now, Grandfather Milstead told the kid. We have company.

Hello Benny, Grandmother Milstead had said. (That was his name, *Benny*) *How are your folks?*

They're OK. Benny replied.

Come by tomorrow, Benny. We'll see about the carrots.

MARVIN HAD SEEN him another time, riding his bicycle on the side street. Benny would glide by and glance over at Marvin as he sat in the new tree fort. *Did he want to come in and see the horses or maybe sit in the fort?* He would ask but a memory halted the idea. A kid came to the gate one day while Marvin was in the yard. Before the fort lived in the Maple. The kid claimed that his name was *Marvin* also.

How crazy was that? Your name is Marvin and so is mine! We should be pals, the kid said. Do you mind if I come into the yard? What a great yard! Do you have soda in your house? Why don't you get your pal a soda? Marvin went in and asked

Grandma Milstead. She mentioned it to Grandpa Milstead who promptly came outside and chased the other Marvin away. *That kid's no good. You stay away from him. Don't let him anywhere on this property.* There was only room for one Marvin here.

THE SPACE between the slats in the wooden fence was tight and didn't allow much of a margin to peek through. Benny must be in his yard and could be responsible for the *clank*. Perhaps that's what made the dogs bark. They were used to natural sounds like birds, bugs, and neighborhood sounds, such as cars, trucks, lawnmowers, or people talking. Odd sounds made Marvin uneasy so it might be possible it was true for dogs. He could go back in the house and let them know what he found out--which wasn't anything--or he could remain outside for a while. He found a soft patch of grass below a little tree with an odd name —his grandmother called a mimosa.

Lady Bird rose from her patch of dirt near the shrubbery and trotted over as Marvin sat down at the base of the tree. Once again the beagle pups vied for a spot in his lap. They pawed and chewed on each other until Marvin had enough and put them on the ground. He walked over to the grouping of shell chairs near the barbecue pit, selected one that wasn't too rusty and pulled it over to the tree, and sat down.

"You guys stay down there," Marvin said as the dogs jumped and tried to climb up. "You're going to hurt yourselves. Stay down!" A command that echoed of a protective parent. It was something a father or mother would say at some time to a kid. Someday he might, but today it was a 6-year-old talking to adolescent dogs.

Marvin pulled his feet up onto the chair and wrapped his arms around his legs and rested his head on his knees. He imagined he looked like a roly-poly or pill bug as his dad called them. After a few minutes, Bobby and Jackie gave up the struggle to ascend and settled on rooting up crickets from the grass.

Maybe because the chair had been near the barbecue pit there was a faint scent of lighter fluid. Marvin raised his head and took a breath. It was in the air. There was another metal clang from behind the fence. It must be Benny's family. Maybe they're cooking out. His stomach growled at the image of hot dogs or hamburgers sizzling on a grill. He had cereal this morning but its value was diminishing. Grandma Milstead had some type of stew on the stove. Marvin saw potatoes, corn, peas, and carrots swimming on the surface. *Doesn't it look yummy, Marvin? She asked. Yeah, I guess. Vegetable soup? He asked. Why no honey, it's what they call Mulligan.*

Shifting in the chair Marvin thought he'd rather call Benny over the fence and ask what they were having for lunch.

"Are you doing all right, sport?"

Marvin looked in the direction of the question. His dad stood at the back door, his hand cupped as a sun visor on his brow. In his white t-shirt and white shorts, he looked like a sailor searching for land.

"Yeah, I'm fine."

"Swell," he replied. "Say listen, I have to go out to the car and move some of that stuff in. So, I'll be out front or upstairs in case you need to find me. OK?

"OK."

"We'll be having lunch in a little while."

"OK," he told his dad and swatted at a fly that buzzed his ear. It had probably followed him from the horse stable. He wanted to tell his dad to let grandpa know there were no burglars around but his father had gone.

A yelp coaxed Marvin's attention. It came from under the shrubs near the side street fence. He slid out of his chair and went over to look. Bobby had wedged himself between two bottom branches. His small back legs worked for leverage but only pushed against air. Marvin reached under and lifted him out of the V he occupied, his legs paddling as if he were swimming until the soft grass met his paws once again did he cease his struggle.

"You're going to be all right," Marvin said as he brushed off bits of mulch. "You need to be careful. Who's going to save you when I'm not here?" Bobby rolled on his back and Marvin rubbed his belly. He was up again in no time and set off under the bush to locate the insect that got away.

An odd sound came from behind the fence. It was similar to the metal clank but more involved—it was a metal crash. If they were cooking hot dogs and hamburgers, based on the noise, it should be all over the ground. The racket spooked the dogs. Lady Bird barked which invited her offspring to sing along.

"Quiet! Lady Bird, stop it," Marvin said. "Quiet!" The dogs ran toward the back fence and continued the clamor. Grandfather Milstead would not think he was doing a good job. As he chased the dogs toward the fence the chemical smell was strong; similar to gasoline. Marvin scooped up the puppies and carried them to the center of the yard. Lady Bird lingered to consider the fence with its sounds and smells.

It was as Marvin dropped the dogs off near the mimosa there was another sound, similar to a strong gust of wind but nothing reacted; the spindly arms of the tree did not shiver, the grass did not flutter, he felt nothing brush against his hair or shirt sleeves. It was as if a giant exhaled nearby or a dragon. Godzilla or Puff the magic dragon, only this dragon claimed a victim because Marvin heard the screams. Where was it coming from? From beyond the fence?

Lady Bird began barking. Bobby and Jackie followed the prompt. The scream circled the yard, crawled under the stable door to disturb the horses, and traveled down the side street to the guard rail.

Above the pealing bleached wood of the fence, smoke spiraled skyward. Not the clean white billow from grilled meat, but an unhealthy dark mist like the wicked witch of the west exiting. The scream continued and Lady Bird's bark persisted. Marvin tried to imagine the scene behind the fence. A scene that involved screams and smoke. He recalled a night years ago when he was awoken by a flurry of sirens. He followed his dad down the stairs of their apartment out to the sidewalk and around the corner.

The evening sky, usually a mix of dark and light blue from the city lights, was bright orange. His father said a factory a few blocks away was on fire. He picked the pajama-clad Marvin up for a better perspective above the on-lookers. The view gave him a sense of wonder at first; the towers of flames and the moun-tainous smoke that looked like giant monsters rising from the broken bricks, but his wonder turned to worry. *Will that fire come over here?* He asked his dad. *No,* he replied with a laugh. *It's two blocks away and they have it contained.* Marvin wasn't sure what *contained* meant but it sounded safe for the moment and calmed him. Later as he tried to sleep, the sense of calm crept away and unleashed nightmares of melting buildings.

MARVIN HEARD other voices now above the screams. Shouts were coming from all directions, not just over the fence. There was ringing from somewhere, a phone maybe. So many sounds it was difficult to focus on just one. Casper was kicking the boards in his stall. Other dogs in other yards were answering Lady Bird's signal. May he should alert his dad or his grandfather. He turned toward the house just in time to see the door open.

"Marvin! Get inside," his grandfather commanded as he ran toward the gate to the side street. He had never seen his grandfather run before. His dad also came out of the house in rush.

"Go inside, son. Do what I say," his father said. "Right now." He ran across the yard and out of the gate.

Marvin watched as his father and grandfather ran down the side street toward the house behind the fence. He trotted over and up the steps into the porch. He hesitated a moment to walk any further into the darkened house on his own.

"Marvin honey," his grandmother called from the kitchen. "Why don't you come in here? I have some butter cake if you would like some. It's the gooey kind that you like."

"OK," he replied.

"I'll get you a nice glass of milk also," she said. She stopped stirring the stew and shifted herself around from the stove. Grandma Milstead was a short, heavy-set woman with gray hair. She reminded Marvin of Aunt Bee from the *Andy Griffith* show. "Go ahead and take a seat there at the dinette.

Marvin sat down. She cut a square of the cake, placed it on a plate, gathered a napkin and fork, and brought it to him. "I'll get your milk."

"Do you know what's happening?" he asked. "I heard some noises over there."

"Well," she sighed as she went to the cabinet. She grabbed a stack of aluminum cups. "What color do you want?"

"Red," Marvin replied.

She pulled the cups apart to get to the red one. "I believe something may have happened to the boy back there. You remember Benny, don't you?"

"Sort of." He dug his fork into the cake. "I only ever saw him a few times."

She opened the refrigerator for the bottle of milk and

brought it over to the table with the cup. As she poured it Marvin could hear sirens rising in the distance.

Grandma Milstead put the bottle of milk back in the refrigerator. She went over to a metal cabinet that held a bread box and a radio. She had it on a station she liked to listen to—what she called band music.

"Did Benny... do something wrong?" Marvin asked.

"No sweetie," she replied and turn the volume up. "Why don't you just enjoy that cake for now? It's not every day you get dessert before your supper. Don't suppose your other folks allow such a thing."

"Probably not." Marvin noticed cardboard boxes stacked in the hallway. His father's police uniform was draped over the top along with other clothes still on hangers. The sirens were louder now. The radio was not drowning them out.

"I'm pretty sure there was a fire over there," Marvin said.

"Is that right? Well now, I'm sure your father and grandfather will tell us about it when they get back."

"Grandpa was running."

Marvin took a bite of the cake. A siren moaned to a stop outside. He wanted to look out the window but remained at the table and took a drink of milk.

"You know, they like to help people where they're needed," she said as she returned to the stove and turned the burner off. "Sometimes people need help... things will happen, sometimes bad things. Some people run away from bad things and some people run toward them."

Two more sirens dominated Mitch Miller on the radio. Marvin could see lights flashing through the windows. He took another bite of cake. Grandma Milstead remained at the stove. She stared straight ahead at the wall. Not blinking. It almost appeared that she was not breathing. He looked away and watched the red lights bounce off the ceiling and the gray walls.

The flashing lights erased the darkness in the corners. The old people in the paintings who appeared angry before now appeared concerned. Right now Marvin thought, being inside the Milstead house wasn't as unsettling as it had been a while ago.

"I guess a bad thing happened out there," Marvin said.

She sighed. "I think it has."

Pollywogs On The Moon

Sunday Night - Sugar Bread

The room was stuffy and dark. It didn't seem as if too many more could fit. A few people opened the door, saw how many were already inside, gave up, and walked away. It was nice when the door opened he thought, the temperature in the room dropped a degree or two. Between watching the door open and watching the flickering images on the television, more was happening at the door. He and his mother had only arrived one day ago. It would be nice to watch this on this TV at home but they were here now. This was their vacation. Standing in this room watching the events unfold on the screen was a special treat. So he waited.

"THAT'S ENOUGH. NO MORE," his mother said. "You'll ruin your dinner."

"But I already have it started."

Marilyn smiled at the Schnurbrytes who sat across the table.

She intended her correction to be soft and only perceived by her son's ears. The chatter inside the Lesterton River Lodge dining hall was at a resonant level and she thought if she spoke just a notch below it, it would be covered by the din. A side glance at Gerald Schnurbryte and his tooth-filled grin made her believe otherwise. She adjusted to a level softer.

"OK Marvin, since you have it started but that's the last one."

He finished spreading the butter, set the knife across the plate, scooped up a spoonful of sugar with a spoon, and shook it across the surface of his bread.

"Gee whiz," Gerald said, "if that doesn't look like a confection I sure could go for."

"Right," Virginia Schnurbryte smirked, "you go for that Jerry and I'll have to *go* for your insulin."

"See here, it might be worth it," he said with a chuckle. "How about it young fellow, is it worth it?"

Marvin glanced up at Mr. Schnurbryte. He looked like a television dad. Not a new one. Not Darrin from *Bewitched* but an old TV father. Black and white style. Like Ward Clever or Mr. Wilson from *Dennis The Menace.*

"I think it's worth it," Marvin said.

Gerald chuckled. "I thought so."

"Is it your first year down at Lesterton Lodge... Mrs. Milstone?" Virginia asked.

"It's Mil*stead.*"

"Forgive me, *Milstead.*"

"Actually, this is our second year. We love it here. Last year they had us paired up with the Donaldsons for the meals."

"Ah yes," Virginia replied. "Lovely couple."

"I heard the Donaldsons tried the Ozarks this year," Gerald said. "It's not unusual to see the same people, the same week, every year. The McNamaras over there by the pillar have been coming here for 10 years. The Ruzickas over in the corner, same story. Same week. Creatures of habit I believe is what they call us."

Marvin turned to survey the room. Some of the faces he recalled from a year ago. He met eyes with a boy at a table across the room. He had one of the familiar faces. The boy waved at him. Marvin waved his sugar bread back at him.

"But really," Virginia said, "this place is truly slanted for kids, you know. The activities have a youth orientation."

"True," Marilyn replied. "Marvin really enjoys himself."

"He likes the activities, does he?" Virginia asked. "The volleyball and the horseshoes and the... what is it called? Where you push the thing... oh! The shuffleboard."

"Well no, not really those things, he loves swimming. Especially in the river." Marilyn moved the sugar bowl.

"I see," Virginia said as she tilted her head. "Well, sure, some of us old folks enjoy some of the things they offer here but it's better for the young people."

"See here now," Gerald replied, "who are you calling old folks?"

"You know what I mean," she replied.

"Perhaps," Gerald said, "but don't you think it's a great turnabout for the young people? I mean what a marvelous opportunity for the kids to get away. Out from the suburbs and the old idiot box. A chance to get out in nature. Catch a fish. Ride a horse. Assume self-sufficiency."

"Yes," Marilyn replied, "that's just what my dad said. Marvin needs to get outside. Breathe the good air. Explore more than just the rooms of the house."

"Wise words," Gerald said. He picked up his water glass, swirled it until the ice cubes clinked, and then took a sip.

"So, Mr. Milstead couldn't be here?" Virginia asked.

"No," Marilyn replied, "he... well, there is no... Mr. Milstead. We're not..."

"Oh, I see." She raised an eyebrow toward her husband. "I'm sorry."

"You know, I heard quite a few of the July regulars canceled this year," Gerald said. "The moon landing, you know. Everyone wants to see it happen, live on television. "

"Yes, I know." Marilyn looked at her son. He feigned a smile that only appeared on one side of his face. "Marvin was looking forward to that. Unfortunately, this was the only week I had the time off available from work."

"I see," Gerald said. "What do you do, if I may ask?"

"Sure, I work for United Artists..."

"Really? The motion picture company?" Virginia asked.

"Yes, but it's not as glamorous as it sounds. I work on the distribution side. We book the movies into cinemas around the Midwest. We sit in an office. Not a Hollywood studio."

"A shame," Virginia said, "it's a shame they don't have televisions in the cabins. But... it's just as well. I'm sure most of the young people would remain inside ruining their eyes if that were the case. There would be no one for the tournaments and activities."

Marvin sighed and took a bite of bread. A rain of sugar not secured by butter sprinkled across his placemat. Marilyn touched the corner of her napkin in her ice water and dabbed up the debris.

"Well see here," said Gerald, "I have it on good authority that over at the rec lodge, on the lower level, there *is* a television. And what I understand, it will be available Monday for all interested Apollo-watching parties."

"Did you hear what Mr. Schnurbryte said, Marvin?" his mother asked.

"Uh-huh, I did." He heard Mr. Schnurbryte begin with,

'*Well see here*' again. Almost every sentence started that way. He might look like a TV dad but he sounded like Watson in the old *Sherlock Holmes* movies that were on Sunday afternoons after the *Bowery Boys*. Marvin took a bite and used his finger to corral the falling sugar dust into a straight row.

"Ah! Here come the dinner carts now," Gerald said. He picked up his napkin, shook it a few times, and laid it across his lap. "I believe tonight we have pot roast and potatoes."

Marvin rolled his eyes. Pot roast was near the top of his detested food list, a notch below sauerkraut and anything with coconut. Good thing he filled up on bread.

Along with the dinner plates that rolled through the kitchen doors, Dale "Dilly" Overmen also flowed through to make his entrance. Dale was the master of ceremonies at Lesterton Lodge. He presided over tournaments, talent shows, bonfires, float trips, and any event where he could be the face and voice of the Lodge. He was short, stocky, sported a salt and pepper crew cut, a permanent smile, and a twinkle in his eyes as if he just heard an off-color joke. He flipped a wall switch, unfastened a microphone from a stand, and tapped it a few times until he could hear the thuds echo through the speakers in the ceiling.

"Good after-Nooney *rooney,* everybody!"

"After-noon rooney, Dilly," everyone responded--as they had for decades.

"Hey, what a great-looking group! Let me tell ya, ladies and gentlemen, of all the folks that come to Lesterton Lodge, here on the beautiful banks of the Sandy Fork, and I mean this... out of all of the faces I've seen, you are certainly one of them."

A laugh went up in the room as the plates were set on the tables.

"You know why they call him, *Dilly?*" Gerald asked as he watched a young brunette waitress maneuver meals between the guests. "Thank you, Bridgette. Anyway, many years ago, I understand that Dale floated down the river in a raft shaped like a giant dill pickle. Hence the nickname."

"How about that? Marvin wondered about that," Marlyn said. "There you go, Marvin."

Bridgette set the pot roast and potato plate down in front of him and whispered, "There you go, Marvin."

"But seriously, speaking of faces," Dale's voice crackled through the room, "we're having the *get-to-know-you* bonfire and weenie roast tonight by the Pheasant Pavilion. So, come on down around 8 and get to know some people and some weenies."

Marvin looked at the pieces of pot roast on the plate. The meat wasn't bad, it tasted fine; it was the gristle—the solid white lines of slime that taunted him and flirted with his gag reflex.

"Hey folks on Monday, there is a trip scheduled to the *Shut-ins*. Beautiful area if you have not seen it. I recommend it. And a big float is happening Wednesday. You can see Trixie at the rec to sign up. Oh, and Friday night is movie night! That's right. For all the kids and kids at heart, we will be showing *The Incredible Mister Limpet* featuring the very funny, and always apprehensive, Don Knotts."

Marvin pressed his fork into the mashed potatoes allowing the brown gravy to run down onto the shiny plate and form a mote around the meat and green beans.

"That's enough," his mother said.

Sounds of evening

He felt bored. Bored and tired. Bored, tired, and hot. Too many people in this room. They all wanted to watch it happen. But nothing was happening yet. They wanted to stare at the screen but the screen wasn't showing anything interesting, so they just looked around at other people who were searching for something to focus their attention upon. Bored and restless. This would probably be important when it happened. When it revealed itself on the small screen. But for the time being, they were all indifferent to the stuffiness.

THE AFTER-DINNER CONVERSATIONS and reunions moved outside into the early evening air which was flavored with cigarette smoke. Just beyond the aroma lingered cedar, wet leaves, campfires, and a sour musty smell of the river that wafted up the hill.

Marilyn was swept up for a few moments in the social pleasantries; *Glad to see you this year! How have you been? Are you in the same cabin as last year? Are you doing the float trip? Horseshoe tournament? Bonfire?*

Marvin stepped away from the milling conversations and walked to the paved edge where a wooden railing halted any short-sighted stroller from toppling down the hillside to the rocky beach below.

When they first arrived, Marvin wanted to visit all of his favorite spots. He wanted to run down the stairway to the river, see the horses at the stable, and visit the rec lodge, but a late start and a long drive made the time for reunions unwise. They had made it to Lesterton with enough time to check in, unlock the cabin, unload the car, wash up, walk to the dining hall, and discover they were seated with the Schnurbrytes this week without a second to spare.

As they walked back to their cabin, Marilyn pointed toward the distance, "Oh my goodness, just look at that, would you?"

Orange and violet hues blended into the sky--a sign the day was drawing a colorful sunset behind the tree line. "It's beautiful, isn't it? Now that's something we don't see at home," she said. Marvin wanted to say he had seen many *beautiful* sunsets at home but let his mother have the moment and enjoy her discoveries. Perhaps some people don't notice the sky until they're on vacation. "Yeah, it's pretty cool," he replied.

The dimming light of day was also a nod to the nocturnals, insects, and amphibians everywhere that it was time to cue up their evening songs and announcements. The twilight chorus would grow in volume in direct proportion to the darkness and last until dawn.

"Don't you love those sounds?" Marilyn asked as she stopped, tilted her head back, and closed her eyes. "You don't hear that back at home."

Marvin listened. It was pleasant. He was able to admit it now with confidence, but when he was younger, any unidentified sound coming from the dark, especially from the woods was unsettling. However, he would now admit, he never witnessed a werewolf, or a triffid, or saw Boo Radley emerge from the blackness between the trees. So, it was pleasant.

He looked back up at the sky. "Can't see the moon, yet. Wonder if they made it?"

"Made it?" Marilyn opened her eyes. "Who?"

"The astronauts," Marvin replied.

"Oh. I don't know." Marilyn looked up to scan the sky as if she could spot them in flight and answer Marvin's question. "Wonder what they'll find up there?"

"Probably rocks and stuff."

"Maybe they'll find cheese. It's made of cheese, right?"

"No mom, it's not made of cheese."

"It's not?" She laughed. "That's what I always heard."

"How could you believe that? Cheese comes from milk.

And milk comes from cows. So, how could the moon be made of cheese since there's no cows up there?"

"Well..." his mother smiled, "a cow jumped over the moon, right? Maybe it dropped off cheese."

Marvin sighed. "Very funny."

THEY STEPPED into a pool of light cast by a dusk-to-dawn fixture atop an electric pole next to the walkway. On the other side of the pool was a small cabin sporting a cedar log veneer and a hand-painted sign over the door that read *Oriole*.

"Here we are. Home sweet home," Marilyn said. She reached into her purse and rustled the contents. "Now, if I can find the key."

Marvin glanced over at the silhouette of trees in the distance. Emerging just above their jagged canopy vista, he saw a familiar crescent of light forming low in the sky.

"Found it," his mother said.

"Yep. Me too."

Monday Mist

It was difficult to imagine that three men traveled that great distance in a tiny vessel. And now two of them were inside another small vehicle for the final leg of the trip. The man on television said it took three days, three hours, and 49 minutes to get where they needed to be. He found it difficult to imagine because traveling in a small car with a lot of people could be miserable after 10 or 15 minutes. Riding in his aunt's Volkswagen beetle with more than four passengers was not pleasant. It was hard to imagine doing that for three days.

THE NEXT MORNING, the repurposed school bell perched atop the dining hall clanged out a 30-minute notice that breakfast would be served. For those Lester Lodge guests who were not in the habit of opening their eyes before 8 am, especially on vacation, adjustments were in order.

Marvin had been up for an hour. He sat on the front stoop of the Oriole while his mother got ready. He watched the dew rise from the grass like smoke from a smoldering fire. It rose and formed a cloud that hovered below the trees. He could hear the chatter of voices in the fog. Lodgers were slowly making their way toward the sweet smell of maple syrup and bacon. Marvin was eager to make his way down to the river after breakfast, he had a new snorkel and scuba mask that would be initiated in the Sandy Fork.

"WELL, SEE HERE NOW," Gerald said as the omelets landed on the table, "Virginia and I will be taking a trip down to Elephant Rocks State park this afternoon. Have you been there?"

"No, we haven't," Marilyn replied. "We'll have to go."

Gerald coated everything on his plate with pepper and passed the shaker to his wife. "Giant boulders that were formed a million years ago. All huddled in this one area. Fascinating. It's like stepping foot in an alien world."

"That does sound like fun," Marilyn said. "Marvin would love that, he watches those space shows. The *Lost in Space* and that stuff, don't you sweetie?"

"Yeah," he replied as he freed the green peppers from his omelet and moved them to an open spot next to the sausage links.

"Plenty of room in the Country Squire if you are so inclined," Gerald said. "We would love to have you."

"Jerry," Virginia replied quickly, "Don't make them feel obligated. Maybe they have plans."

"Thank you but..." Marilyn looked at her son. "I think Marvin has his heart set on swimming today."

"Well, that's fine," Gerald said as he blew across the eggs on his fork. "Perhaps another time."

"Yes," Virginia concluded. "Some other time."

A click and a shot of static crackled through the speakers. Dale's voice followed in a soft, early-in-the-morning tone. "Wakey wakey, eggs and bakey," he said. "Good morning everybody!"

"Good morning, Dilly," the room replied.

"Sounds like a few of you are... *over the moon* on this beautiful July morning." Dale smiled. "And later on today, there will be a few people *standing* on it." Marvin smiled.

***

AFTER BREAKFAST, Marvin bargained with his mother to make a solo journey to one of his favorite spots--besides the river and the horse riding stables--and that was the Rec Lodge itself.

"I won't be long. Just a few minutes," he said.

"All right. Just be careful."

The Lodge was a log-clad building with a long covered porch that held a dozen Adirondack chairs, an ice machine, and two soda machines.

The spacious interior accommodated a dance floor, a snack bar, three ping pong tables, two pool tables, two pinball machines, and a jukebox that played music from morning till night. As Marvin stepped up onto the porch the current selection was *Spinning Wheel* by Blood Sweat and Tears. Chances were very good the song could be heard for miles based on the volume.

He stood in front of the soda machine and shook the two quarters in his palm. His mother wanted a *Tab* or *Diet Rite* and Marvin wanted a *Grape Nehi*. He had not had a Nehi since the last time he stood on the porch of this lodge. As far as he knew, this was the only machine on Earth that held the Nehi brand and delivered it at the perfect temperature and flavor. Just like the Vess Black Cherry soda only tasted ideal at his grandfather's fishing cabin. Fruit-flavored sodas only seemed to taste good when you were near a river. Maybe it was the position of the summer sun and the musty river air mixed with a fragrance of sun tan oils and mosquito spray. Grape and Black Cherry covered all foul odors.

Floating

The man on television said there were only very thin traces of oxygen on the moon. They could not breathe without helmets. And the gravity is only 1/6th as powerful. On Earth, someone who weighed 500 pounds would only weigh 80 pounds up there. The suits they wore weighed 180 pounds on Earth but only 30 pounds on the moon. The sensation for the astronauts would be similar to being underwater.

THE SANDY FORK is a slim body of water that pushes through the hills of Reynolds county in southeast Missouri. As the river flows by the Lesterton Lodge it stumbles over a smattering of rocks that conjure a minor turbulence that many lodgers refer to as *the rapids*. The mild churning ended 10 feet beyond the rocks and calmly passes below a bridge. Kids were warned to stay clear of the rapids. The concern was more in fear of potential *slip and fall lawsuits* that large wet rocks were prone to initiate but Marvin--like most kids--was drawn to this feature of the Sandy Fork. *Stay clear* was considered more of a suggestion than a serious warning. Marvin had seen real rapids on television and in movies before and this was not comparable. This was a drowsy current that became roused as it squeezed between some rocks, folded in on itself, and moved a tad quicker as it funneled through the interference. It was a brief thrill ride for any kid. You would start a short distance upstream, float along and allow the current to command your navigation, pull you with a minor surge, and then spit you out under the bridge. It was fun for a while until you got tired of making the trek back upstream or an adult warned you to Stay Clear.

Marilyn found a sandy spot near the riverside and planted her lawn chair. She could keep her eye on Marvin and read her book. The beach wasn't crowded in the hours after breakfast. Many lodgers opted for leisure pursuits at this time; horseshoes or other sports-minded activities before lunch. Only a select few lounged around the shore or floated in slow circles on oversized inner tubes along the banks. *Good Morning Starshine* echoed down the hill from the jukebox at the lodge.

"If you're going to play around the rocks be careful," Marilyn said to Marvin.

"I will." He didn't feel like floating through the rapids today like Bogart in the *African Queen*. He wanted to explore the world below with a new mask and a snorkel like the crew in *Voyage to the Bottom of the Sea*.

"Don't wander too far where I can't see you."

"I won't."

He took a few steps out. The water sent a chill through him as soon as it rose above his tennis shoes and surrounded his shins. He stood in one spot for a few minutes to allow the goosebumps to subside. In the shallow areas, the water was clear and you could see small fish darting around the rocks. On the other side of the river, Marvin watched some kids shimmy up a tree, grab a long rope tied to an upper branch, and swing out over the water. It looked like fun but he would play Tarzan some other day.

He trudged against the current toward deeper water and away from the loud conversation that had started on the beach. It had something to do with one of the Kennedys, an accident, and a lady who died from drowning inside the car. Death and dying seemed to be a popular subject for older adults. Maybe because it was closer to them now and talking about it was a charm that kept it at a distance. And then someone changed the topic *Oh I see you're reading The Godfather. Is it good?*

Marvin secured the mask over his face, sucked in the mouth-piece, folded his hands, and dove into the water. It took less than a minute for his system to accept the sudden switch from warm and dry to cold and wet. A few body shivers and all was well.

Below the horizon of the river, it was a drab olive-colored world. Besides the hushed shimmering sounds of water being stirred by his arms and legs, Marvin could only hear his breath moving through the tube of the snorkel. As the silt settled the visibility became sharper. He could see the contours of the sandy riverbed. A shadow of something swimming by—maybe a fish, hopefully not a snake—it was an exciting mystery below the surface of the Sandy Fork.

Marvin traveled a little further upstream and discovered a deeper pocket where he was able to hover vertically like the frogman on the TV shows, *Sea Hunt* and *Flipper* or imagine drifting in space like the Russian cosmonaut or the American astronaut who both walked in space. *Was this what it felt like?* He wondered. To explore a strange new place. To know you were far from home, floating around above it all like some crazy dream.

He swam further upstream. The current didn't put up

much resistance. How far away had he traveled? He broke the surface to take a look. There was a splash to his left. He saw legs kicking inside a column of bubbles. A small wake from the motion caused him to bob up and down. He raised his mask above to look as if someone broke the surface. It was a girl. She flipped her long black hair back over her head which sent an arc of water into the air that seem to pause before raining back down. Where did she come from? Marvin wondered. Did she jump in from the wooded bank? Fall from the sky?

"Sorry kid," she said spitting water from her lips, "didn't mean to scare you."

Marvin pulled the snorkel out to speak. "It's OK."

Her brown eyes blinked before she rubbed them with cupped fists. Marvin thought she looked familiar. Not like anyone he knew but someone from the movies or television. She had a dark complexion and sharp features like an Indian maiden from some western. He wasn't sure how long he stared at her but finally, she nodded to him and said, "As long as it's OK. Then it's cool right?"

"Yes, it's OK and... cool."

She smiled and sank below the water. A moment later her feet broke the surface as she kicked to propel herself down; the splash rained around Marvin.

Laughter echoed from the sandbar upstream. Marvin looked and saw two kids throwing rocks or something at each other. Marvin glanced back downstream and saw there were more people on the beach now. It took a minute to spot his mother. It looked like she was reading again. The chit-chat must have ended.

He'd been treading the same spot for a while. The meager current hadn't moved him very far. He looked toward the bank and recognized the same sycamores and determined he had only drifted a foot or two at most. It had been a minute or two since he saw the black-haired girl. Did she not come back up for air? Maybe she did and he didn't see her. Did she leave as mysteriously as she appeared? He decided to take a look. He pulled his mask down and lowered his vision under the surface. It took a moment but he spotted movement. There in the shimmering hazel depths, he could see branches of her black hair expanding outward. She was closer to him than he realized. Her eyes were closed, and her face was peaceful. Her arms were outstretched, moving back and forth while her legs cycled slowly; it was a dance to maintain a fixed position between the surface and the bottom. It was beautiful to watch.

Something skidded across Marvin's head that startled him. An involuntary sound escaped his mouth and shot up the snorkel. It emerged as "Gah!" He lifted his head from the water. He wasn't sure how loud his exclamation had been but the kids at the sandbar must have heard it because they were looking toward him and laughing. He saw one of them throw something toward him that splashed down a few inches away. It wasn't a rock; it had a tail and swam away.

"A TADPOLE?" Marilyn asked.

"Yeah," Marvin replied. "It was big. Huge. I thought it was a fish at first but it wasn't."

She sipped her iced tea as she considered his story. "So, I don't understand. Why did they throw a tadpole at you?"

Marvin shrugged. "I don't know. Because they're stupid." He picked up his glass of chocolate milk and took a drink.

"Strange," Marilyn said. "I guess kids do some... strange things down here."

"They even threw some of them straight up in the air and let them fall to the ground. On the gravel."

"On the gravel?"

"Yeah. Just splat!"

"That's awful!"

"I know," Marvin replied. "The girl yelled at them."

"What girl?"

"The one in the river with the black hair. The one I said looked like a movie Indian." Marvin replied. "Or like that Mexican lady in *High Noon*."

"OK. I remember. Anyway..."

"Anyway, she used some bad words and chased them. They ran away."

The speakers crackled overhead in the dining hall. "Good Monday Monday afternoon, everybody!"

"Good afternoon, Dilly."

"Hey, what a terrific day folks!" Dale said. "Hey if you haven't heard, it looks like Armstrong and the boys will be making footprints on that gray ball in the sky! Hope they wipe their shoes when they come home. If they don't, I hope they *Apollo-gise*." The lunch crowd chuckled. Most of them were used to Dilly's routine, even the cadence of his voice. The jokes had a rhythm they knew where to laugh even if they weren't listening. It was two jokes followed by announcements. When they heard times and dates, the jokes were done. "Hey, I hope they don't bring anything home with them," Dale continued, "like bugs. But you know, up there, they call them *Lunar Ticks*." They laughed.

Marvin noticed there was no bread on the table. Maybe they don't serve it at lunch. He nodded at the vacant chairs. "Where are the Schnurbrytes"

"They were going on a day trip, remember? To that place... the rock place," she said. "They'll probably be back at dinner-time. It's nice to be on our own for a time, isn't it?"

"Hey, speaking of dirty shoes," Dale said as he consulted his clipboard, "we still need some Robin Hoods for the archery tournament Wednesday at 1:00 and a few more for shuffleboard Thursday at 2:00."

"Did you hear that?" Marilyn asked. "You like shuffleboard don't you?"

"Yeah," Marvin replied, "I like to play it but I'm not the tournament type."

"Oh, I see," Marilyn chuckled. "Would you rather watch them play?"

"Not really. It's boring if you don't know the people playing," Marvin replied. "It's not like watching baseball with Bob Gibson, Lou Brock, and Julian Javier. Plus it's usually the old folks playing anyway."

"I see."

"I wonder why he doesn't say anything about watching the landing?"

"The what?"

"Landing. The Moon landing," Marvin said. "Mr. Schnurbryte said they had a television at the lodge for people to watch it. But they haven't said anything about that."

"Well, maybe they don't want everyone to know. It might be by invitation only."

"Oh," Marvin turned and watched the lunch trays make an appearance through the swinging doors.

Polliwogs on the porch

They were just killing time right now. The reporters were repeating things. Everyone was waiting. It took so much time to get there, it seems like they would jump right out and explore. But they didn't. They had to wait. There were safety lists and other lists. Things needed to be double-checked to be sure they didn't miss something on the first check. But it felt like they were just killing time right now. They were repeating things. But it was to make sure everyone was safe. Everyone had to wait. Instead of watching the television, some looked at their watches. Some looked at other people. Some studied the floor and some the ceiling. Someone declared there were 42 tiles above our heads.

AFTER LUNCH, Marvin wanted to don his trunks and explore the river again, but his mother rebuffed his ambition.

"It's Monday," Marilyn said, "we have all week. And I really don't feel like climbing those steps again."

"You don't have to," he replied. "I can go by myself."

"I don't feel comfortable with you going down there by yourself."

"Why? I'll be fine. I'm not going in the rapids."

"I don't mean the rapids. It's the... look, just... no more today, OK? " she replied. "We'll go tomorrow. We can go over to the pool for a while if you want to swim with your mask."

Marvin considered the blue-chlorinated realm for a moment. The pool was a fine substitute but he dreaded the unpleasant conditions: the gallery of older adults shining with lotion sitting in deck chairs staring through sunglasses worn under straw hats. Gesturing with cigarettes and paperbacks as they complained about things older people complain about. You could hear the music coming from the lodge or someone's radio but it couldn't top the volume of conversation about politics, the war, and *these damned kids running around and splashing in the pool.*

"Is it OK if I go to the lodge to get a soda instead?" he asked.

"I guess. As long as you go straight there and back."

THE JUKEBOX PLAYED *Crystal Blue Persuasion* as Marvin settled down into an Adirondack chair with his grape Nehi. The Lodge porch was a good place to loiter and watch people pass by on their way to where ever. There went the Ruzickas carrying towels, their flip-flops slapped as they walked. Probably on their way to the pool. The afternoon unpacked more heat than it had brought in the morning. Sweat was forming across Marvin's face and on the cold glass bottle that he held. There went the McNamaras carrying tennis rackets.

As he wiped his forehead with the back of his arm he felt the sting of sunburn. A horsefly buzzed close and landed on the arm of an empty chair a few feet away. He studied it for a moment and then his attention jumped to the motion of a girl in a waitress uniform—like the ones from the dining hall—as she walked up to the soda machine. He wondered which one she would pick.

The screen door of the lodge popped against the frame as someone came out. Marvin glanced over and saw a kid standing there holding a bag of chips. He wore a yellow t-shirt that said *Baldknobbers* that hung over his green plaid shorts. The boy smiled at Marvin. There was a considerable space behind his lips and he saw that only one of the kid's two front teeth had started to descend. The transition gave an odd appearance and caused a whistle when he spoke.

"Hey," the kid said, "I seen you at dinner last night. I waved. I 'membered you. Last year. From the float trip. And the hay ride. Ain't your name Melvin?"

"Marvin."

"I'm Kenny. Kenny Clopton. 'Member? From last year?"

"I think so."

"Sure," Kenny said as he tore open his chip bag and walked toward Marvin. "Hey, member my brother, Denny?"

He thought for a moment. "Sort of."

"Well, anyways... he and some kids that he knows... Brett and Micky Malone from the Sandpiper cabin... well, they're gonna do the *bridge drop* today. You wanna watch?"

Marvin knew about the bridge drop from the previous year. Kids walked to a certain spot on the Sandy Fork bridge, climbed over the railing, lowered themselves to hang from a girder, and then dropped to a specific spot, 30 feet below into the river, clear of rocks and just deep enough to accommodate a falling object without serious injury.

"Maybe," Marvin replied.

"Ya know, I heard that a boy died doin' it," Kenny said as he placed a pinch full of chips in his mouth.

"It's just a tale," the girl at the soda machine said.

"Huh?" Kenny asked.

"A legend they perpetuate to keep kids from trying it." Martin glanced over at her as she stuck the top of the bottle into the slot to pry off the cap. He noticed her brown skin. Her long black hair was pulled up. It was the girl from the river.

"It's propaganda. Just stories to scare little kids like you. It's the same agitprop that states meat and potatoes make you strong. Spinach gives you muscles. That's the consumerism side. On the flip side, there is conservation. Keep humans from having too much fun. Stop signs and warnings. Add a bit of terror and they can keep you in check. Tell you there's a troll under the bridge. A snake in that garden. Beyond here be dragons. Little Johnny Jones died doing what you're doing."

"OK," Kenny said. He held up his bag of chips. "Anybody want some?"

"No thanks," Marvin replied.

The girl took a drink of her soda and winked at Marvin. "Peace, you polliwogs." She stepped off the porch and strolled away.

"What a weirdo," Kenny said. "She must be on drugs." He stuffed more chips in his mouth.

"Why do you say that?"

"I dunno. The way she talked. I seen people on TV that talk like that on drugs. Them hippies. Besides, Popeye's the one that said spinach gives ya muscles." The horse fly buzzed Kenny's head. He ducked and swatted at it. "Dang thing!" Some of the chips fell from his bag. He stomped on them as if they were bugs.

"What did she call us? Polliwogs?" Marvin asked. "What's a polliwog?"

"Ain't ya never heard of a polliwog? Same thing as a tadpole." Kenny chewed for a few seconds. "Ever seen 'em down to the river? Theys all over the place."

"Yeah, I've seen them," Marvin replied. "I never heard them called that."

Kenny stuffed a few more chips in his mouth and said. "I got me a bucket full of 'em at our cabin."

"A bucket full?"

"Yep. Wanna see 'em?"

AT THE SIDE of the Whippoorwill cabin, was a bucket full of tadpoles. They squatted on either side for a view of the alien-looking creatures. They resembled green table spoons squirming with life. Marvin had many questions but tried to narrow them down to the basics.

"Did these come out of the Sandy Fork?"

"Yep," Kenny said. "Got'em this morning."

"Did you and your brother catch them?"

"Nah. Just me."

"Cool," Marvin replied. "I was down there today. At the

river. After breakfast. I saw some of these. Tadpoles or polliwogs or whatever they're called."

"Sure," Kenny replied. "They're all over this time of the year."

"They're so big."

"That's cause they're bullfrog polliwogs. Regular ones ain't so big. Look! Some of 'em in there got legs already. A few of 'em even hopped away."

Marvin watched them spin and roll in the confined quarters. "What're you going to do with them?"

"Watch 'em turn into frogs." Kenny wiped his lips as some chip remains escaped with his answer. "Then maybe set 'em loose. Or maybe..." He reached into the bucket and grabbed one. It wriggled in his hand. Marvin hoped the rest of Kenny's statement and action did not hold an act of cruelty. "We got us a pond back home," Kenny continued, "I can take 'em and turn 'em loose. Love to hear bullfrogs croakin, don't you? Sounds like an ol' fat man belchin' Like my dad when he drinks his beer."

"Yeah," Marvin said with a sigh. "They are kinda cool."

"My brother Denny likes to go giggin'.'"

"Gigging? What's that?"

"It's this big ol' fork he pokes 'em with. He likes to catch'em and cookin' 'em. Said they taste like chicken but they don't."

"What do they taste like?" Marvin asked.

"More like quail."

"Oh." Marvin decided not to ask what quail tasted like. "I saw some kids throwing them up in the air today."

"What for?"

"I don't know," Marvin replied. "Maybe they were trying to send them to space."

"That's funny. Frogs in space."

"Yeah. Maybe they'll find them up on the moon tonight. Are you going to watch?"

"Watch what?"

"The astronauts. Landing on the moon."

"Didn't hear nothin' bout it," Kenny said. "They're puttin' people on the moon?"

"Yeah. They're in orbit now."

"Really? How'd they get up there? In a spaceship or somethin'?"

"Yeah." Marvin sighed. Some kids knew about the space program and some kids knew what frogs tasted like. "I heard there's a TV in the basement of the lodge. They're going to have it on."

Kenny shrugged. "Oh lookie!" He dropped the tadpole he was holding and plunged his hand back into the bucket. "I seen one." He lifted one with primitively formed legs. "Told ya some of 'em had legs!"

"Oh yeah."

"You want some of 'em?" Kenny asked. "I gotta sand pail you can use."

Appollosa

It was called Columbia which was named after Christopher Columbus. Parts of the Wright Flyer were inside the ship. The lunar module was called the Eagle. Michael Collins was the pilot of the command module that orbited the moon. If things did not go well, Michael Collins would have to return alone.

"I THOUGHT YOU WANTED A SNOW CONE," Marilyn said.

"I did," he said to his mother. "But there's a bunch of wasps in that trash can over there." He pointed to a small building with a sign that read *Snack Shack*. She could see insects flying in and out of the trash barrel.

"I think those are just sweat bees. They won't hurt you."

"I'll try it later. I want to see the horses." He walked across the gravel toward the stables with a sense of urgency. He felt he had pushed his luck to visit his third favorite spot. He needed to move before his mother changed her mind.

It's only the second day, Marvin, his mother had said earlier. *We have all week.*

I know but… last time we were here, it took me all week to find things I liked. I just want to see if the appaloosa is still there. I don't want to go for a ride. I just wanna see the horses. And they have snow cones.

But it's only a few hours before dinner and it's quite a walk down to the stables.

Let me go then. I'll go by myself.

Marvin knew that one day he would be able to venture out on his own and looked forward to it, but for now, his insistence was a means to an end.

Marilyn believed it would be best if she would oversee the journey—in case the nefarious tadpole tossers made an appearance at the barn and found new material to throw. She walked with her son along the dirt path next to the drive that led out of the lodge grounds, over the side road to another dirt path that led to the putting greens and horse stables.

"Do you see her?" Marilyn asked. A few horses were in the pasture, but none of them sported the familiar brown spotted coat.

"No."

"She could be on a ride."

A man dressed in dusty denim and a white cowboy hat led a sorrel from the stables. Marvin recognized him, everyone referred to him as *Reverend Jeff*. He learned last year, over dinner with the Donaldsons that Jeff became a *Reverend* to avoid the draft. Marilyn explained to Marvin—as simply as possible—what the *draft* was and how some young men preferred a different path.

"Excuse me, sir?" Marvin called out. "I was wondering... is Polka Highness still here?"

Reverend Jeff glanced up. "She sure is," he said as he cinched the straps. "She's in her stall at the moment. Resting. Was she expecting you?"

"No," Marvin laughed. "I was just asking cause... I rode her last year."

"You signing up for a ride?"

"Yeah," Marvin replied. "But not today though. It's only my second day."

"We might tomorrow," Marilyn said. "I told him it was too late today. Too close to dinner."

"Is that your mom?" Reverend Jeff asked with a wink at Marvin.

"Yeah."

"What's your name?"

"Marvin."

"Well Marvin, do you listen to everything your mom tells you?"

He looked at his mother. She smiled. He looked back at Reverend Jeff who eased himself up into the saddle.

"Most of the time," he said. He wondered if another lesson was coming; like he got from the floating waitress: *Stories to scare little kids.*

"Well, you should," he said. "*Hear the instructions of your father and do not reject the teachings of your mother.* How old are you?"

"I'm eight."

"Eight? That's a fine age to be." Reverend Jeff replied.

"You're almost there kid. No need to hurry to nine and ten. Be eight right now. Ain't that right, mom?"

"That's right," Marilyn replied.

"Well, Marvin, will I see you tomorrow? On the trail? I'll tell Polka Highness you're coming. I'll set her aside."

"OK. Thanks!" Marvin said.

Reverend Jeff made a clicking sound, flicked the reigns, his horse turned, and they rode away.

"Wasn't that nice?" Marilyn asked. "He's going to keep her for you tomorrow."

"Yeah, it was. But don't Reverends have to be nice?"

Marilyn smiled. "No, they don't have to be nice. Most of them are though."

"But some aren't?"

"A lot of people aren't."

"Like the ones that go into the draft?"

"We can talk about this later. Let's see about the snow cones."

Astronauts on the bridge

The man on the television said they would be on the lunar surface for about 22 hours. They would require sleep. While the world slept comfortably in their beds, they would be sleeping on the moon.

WHEN THEY GOT BACK to the cabin, Marvin felt withered. The patches of pink on his arms and face were stirring a warmth as their hue turned red. It was a while before the 30-minute dinner bell but the day's activities gave him a late-in-the-evening tired.

It was very much like the *tired* he would get near the end of *The Tonight Show* with Johnny Carson.

"Why don't you rest for a little while?" His mother asked as she dug through a small travel bag. "You've had a busy day."

"Maybe. Just for a minute."

"We should get something on that sunburn. I have some Solarcaine."

"Maybe," Marvin replied. He pried off his shoes as she rubbed the lotion on his face. He eased back on the bed and watched the popcorn-plastered ceiling grow dim as his eyes closed. One of the last thoughts to cross his mind was of the bucket of tadpoles by the bush next to the cabin. He should probably mention it to his mother.

HE WAS PERCHED atop one of the large rocks that held court in the rapids of the river. There was an odd noise floating around his ears; it wasn't the sound of water or an insect. It was a voice. It was someone speaking in the distance--the voice crackled through a loudspeaker--somewhere above his head. Marvin looked up. He saw people standing on the bridge. They were dressed in costumes; large outfits with helmets of some sort, like deep sea divers or astronauts—that was it, they were astronauts. They were standing at the railing of the bridge pointing down. He saw kids hanging from the girders just below waiting to drop. Marvin sensed that the astronauts weren't pointing to the hanging kids, they were trying to indicate something farther down, something in the river.

He stood up from his spot and saw an object in the water. It created turbulence similar to the rapids around the rocks but it wasn't rocks, instead, it appeared to be four tires that peaked above the surface. The tires of an overturned car. Marvin could see the muddy undercarriage grasping a muffler and long tailpipe resembling a snake coughing out brown water.

The kids suspended from the girders were yelling out something. They couldn't drop into the river because the car was in the way. They were stuck in a gravity stalemate. Their voices were being drowned out by the radio static loudspeaker the Astronauts generated. One moment it sounded like human voices and the next moment it sounded like a chorus of crickets and cicadas in the trees along the shore. A bell clanged in the distance.

Marvin felt movement. A vibration under his sneakers. The river around him rose. The rock below him sank. The current tugged at him and urged him to float away, downstream toward the car below the bridge. He called out in panic and it was as if his cries caused the kids to let loose from the girders and plunge into the space beneath. A cloud of tadpoles flew into the air from where they landed. The submerged car started up. The exhaust coughed and belched out steam, the tires spun arcs of water into the air. The astronauts now pointed to him.

"Marvin?"

The astronauts stepped off the bridge and hovered in the air. Slowly they floated upward. The current of the river was strong. He was being pulled toward the overturned car. He couldn't swim around it. He braced himself for the impact.

"Marvin sweetie, wake up."

The popcorn ceiling came back into view. He lifted his head. "What? What is it?"

"Almost time for dinner," his mother said. "You better get cleaned up. Wash your hands and face. And I laid out a shirt for you to change into."

He laid his head back on the bed.

"Are you feeling alright?"

"I'm fine," he replied. "Had a weird dream."

"What about?"

"I was in the river and... there were astronauts on the bridge and kids hanging down. And a car that wrecked."

"A car that wrecked? On the bridge?"

"No," Marvin replied. "In the river. It was upside down."

"You probably got that from the news," she said. "Now get up and go get cleaned up."

HE STOOD in the bathroom and observed himself in the mirror for a few minutes. His forehead and cheeks displayed the shortcomings of sunscreen lotion. He felt groggy with a hint of a nap headache. The simple task of walking and moving felt as though it took more effort than normal as if after two days of vacation Marvin's age had jumped from 8 to 80. Might as well sign up for the shuffleboard tournament.

He turned on the faucet and held his hand under the cold water. It sent a shiver through his system, made him feel more awake, and cleared some of his cloudy thoughts. He soaked the washcloth and pressed it against his face. There was a slight stinging sensation on his forehead and cheeks. He wiped the areas that didn't protest a terry cloth touch. The sound of water as it ran and gurgled in the sink motivated Marvin to close the door and lift the toilet seat. Might as well take care of it now. His mother would ask if he needed to go before they left. He could say he did.

"Hey Marvin?" she called out over the hum of the air conditioner.

"Hang on. I'm almost ready."

"I wanted to tell you, there's a little boy here. He said his name is Kenny."

Marvin pondered for a moment. *Why is he here? I wonder what he wants?* "What does he want?"

"What?"

"I said, what does he want?"

"I think he wants to walk with you to the dining hall."

"All right," Marvin replied. "I'm almost done. I'll be out in a minute."

He finished, flushed, rinsed his hands, opened the door, and walked into the bountifully air-conditioned room. He expected to see his mother, purse over her shoulder ready to go but instead found Kenny sitting in the chair at the table by the window.

"Where's my mom?"

"She said she was walkin' on up," Kenny replied as he swung his legs back and forth. "The folks from the Bluebird was passin' by, she was goin' with them. Said she'd see you there. Oh! Change your shirt. She said to tell you. I had to change mine too. It was pretty ripe. "

Marvin peeled off his t-shirt and scooped up the new one before the cool damp atmosphere elicited more shivers.

"This room's a lot like ours. 'Cept our beds are on the other wall." Kenny picked up the paperback from the table. "Is this any good?"

"I'm not sure. My mom's reading it."

Kenny studied the cover. "Is it about a puppet or somethin'?"

"No. It's about gangsters," Marvin replied. "So did your brother drop from the bridge?"

"Nah he got in trouble for sneakin' one of dad's beers. He's goin' tomorrow." He scratched a mosquito bite on his arm. "What're doin' tomorrow?"

"We're going on the trail ride."

"We're supposed to go Friday. Dad said it makes his keister sore. We gotta wait."

"So, we should get going to the dining hall."

"Yep. I'm gettin' hungry." Kenny slid off the chair and tossed the book on the table. "Hey, where'd you put the tadpoles?"

"They're on the side of the cabin. Next to that bush out there."

"I meant to tell you, a coon or somethin' got into mine. Knocked over the bucket and ate a bunch of 'em. You oughta put yours someplace safe."

Marvin thought for a moment. His nap headache still lingered through his reasoning. *Where could he put them? Why did he even have them? Why were they in a sand pail and not at the river where they belonged? What was he going to do with them?* He thought of the movie *Born Free* where they have to let the lion go. His mom cried and cried at the end of that movie. Not sure she would cry if he released the tadpoles; she didn't even know he had them yet. "Where could I put them?"

"I don't know," Kenny said. "My brother wanted to flush 'em down the toilet. Said they'd end up back in the river that way."

After Dinner thinks

To keep the viewers informed and interested, the television network had a re-creation of what they believed was occurring 238,856 miles above their heads. If anyone crowded in the lower room watching the TV mounted to the wall did not know better, and had the words CBS News Simulation not flashed at the bottom of the screen, they may have thought they were witnessing the sharpest, clearest images this side of the stratosphere. People dressed as astronauts moved around inside the simulated module which sat on an artificial lunar surface. The scene was bleached underneath studio lights as a demonstration of what may be happening. A restless audience wearing stale summer clothes watched and waited in a swampy crowded room. They waited for something genuine to happen. Something real; such as the hatch to open and for men to step outside and find dirt and rocks and not cheese.

"The rocks were extraordinary, otherworldly," Gerald said as he blew the steam from his cup of coffee. "It was as if we were standing... on a distant planet. These large stones, rounded and curved in nature... worn by nature's erosions and time... surround the landscape."

"Teenagers climbing all over them," Virginia said, "no regard for safety. Surprised someone doesn't fall to their death."

"See here, most people are cautious," Gerald replied.

"I heard a teenager was seriously injured down at the Shut-Ins the other day," Virginia said, "jumping from a cliff into the river."

Gerald sighed. "Anyway, despite the misfortunes in the world, there are natural wonders for the eye to behold out there. And to see these geological oddities is well worth the trip." He took a sip of coffee and let a sound of satisfaction out.

"Well, it does sound interesting," Marilyn said. "I'm sure Marvin would enjoy seeing that place."

"If you enjoy walking in circles for long distances," Virginia said, "then that is the place for you."

"See here," Gerald began setting his cup down, "we did get

slightly turned around along the trails and had to backtrack some distance."

"We had to walk two and a half miles back to the car."

"I'm not sure it was that far, Virginia."

"It was probably more, Jerry," she replied. "We had to travel clear around the perimeter, down these narrow blacktop roads just to get back to the parking lot."

"It was a bit of an excursion but overall... as I stated, it was worth the journey."

"Sure, if you want to see a bunch of boulders that resemble humongous petrified poop. What the Jolly Green Giant may expel, then yes, it's worth it."

Marvin tried to suppress a laugh.

"Virginia, really," Gerald said, his face turned slightly flush. "The analogies you use..."

"Oh it's fine," Marilyn said, "my son has heard far more... colorful language."

"Oh really?" Virginia raised an eyebrow.

"Oh sure, sometimes my dad allows him to tag along and they visit some interesting places. There's a tavern they go to on Saturday afternoons, Marvin enjoys this bowling game they have. And the pinball machine."

"I love pinball," Gerald said. "A wonderful means for a young man to develop hand-eye coordination."

Virginia cleared her throat. "And I would imagine a means to learn an extraordinary vocabulary."

Marvin smirked. He could illustrate by repeating some words he had heard but was warned by his grandfather *never to repeat them in mixed company*. The Schnubrytes were probably what he meant by *mixed company*. Virginia droned on about the sad state of affairs with the youth of today, Marvin tuned out and glanced around the dining room. The conversations at all the other tables mixed into a soothing vibration that drowned out the Schnurbrytes. He saw Kenny and his family across the room. Mr. Clopton scratched the side of his crew cut as Mrs. Clopton leaned in close to him. She seemed to be upset based on the deep lines on her forehead. Kenny held a fork above his head. He studied it against the ceiling tiles until his mother said something to him and it became a plane that flew a circle eight back down to the tablecloth. Across the table, his brother Denny spun his butter knife in circles, and his long hair eclipsed his face. Occasionally he would swat at it as if it were a fly. Marvin wondered what Kenny would think if he looked over at his table. He would probably think; *there's the rotten egg that was the last one here.* The race was declared a few feet from the cabin. By the time he had realized what Kenny had shouted, there was no point in trying to catch up. Let him have his victory. Marvin would walk by himself.

"Did you hear what Mr. Schnurbryte said?" his mother asked. Marvin turned back around. "He said there was one of those bowling machines on the lower level of the lodge."

"Now mind you… this was a few years ago," Gerald said, "It was in the lodge but they moved it to make room for the new ping pong table."

"Below the lodge?" Marvin asked. "Where the TV is?"

"Why yes. The very same."

"Young people always know where the televisions are, don't they?" Virginia asked with a forced chuckle.

"I think he was asking because of the moon thing tonight," Marilyn said. "Weren't you sweetie?"

"Moon thing?" Virginia's eyebrow arched again.

Marvin wanted to speak but the confused look on Mr. Schnurbryte's face brought his words to a halt. Disappointment set in. Static crackled from above.

"Good evening everybody!" Dale's voice bounced around the room.

"Good evening Dilly," the response rolled back.

The dinner carts bumped the kitchen doors open and the smell of fried chicken entered with the servers.

"Well, well," Dale said, "it looks like the good folks in the kitchen outdid themselves tonight. But hey folks, don't let them fool you. They just sent a couple of the kids over to *Kentucky Fried Chicken* in Centerville and picked up dinner for you tonight. Hey and how about some Moon Pies for dessert?"

Marvin watched the dinner plates land on the tables around the room. He looked for the dark-haired girl but didn't see her among the servers.

"This just in," Dale said. "Benjamen Laturno and Francis Dole were our champions at the horseshoe tournament this afternoon. They will receive a coupon for five dollars off of blinker fluid. Hey folks, that stuff comes in handy let me tell you."

He spotted her. She was serving the table next to the Cloptons. Denny Clopton said something to her but she ignored him. He spoke again and she turned to him with an angry look. Denny lowered his head and allowed his hair to cover his face. He must have said something she didn't like. One of those things you shouldn't say to girls or in mixed company. She put the last plate down and pushed her cart away.

"Marvin, forgive me," Gerald said. "When you get older, former thoughts and intentions, well, they can get... annexed by the day's nonsense and lulled into submission by prattle. What I mean to say is... would you like to join me this evening to watch our fellows walk upon the moon?"

Marilyn beamed a smile at Marvin as Virginia rolled her eyes at Gerald. "How bout that? Would you like to watch that with Mr. Schnurbryte?"

"Sure. That would be cool," he replied.

Gerald laughed. "Would it be? Yes. See here now, I think it will."

"Well," Virginia said, "if these astronauts go walking around up there, I pray they remember where they parked."

Geronimo from the fingertips

On the television, we saw a large room with people who were watching smaller televisions. Some voices sounded as if they were coming through walkie-talkies. They spoke to mission control and a place called Houston. It was the astronauts. We could hear them clearly. Mr. Schnurbryte said the room they showed on TV was mission control. It was located in Houston. The astronauts were now sitting inside the module that was on the moon and the people in Houston were talking to them. They were getting ready. After all the waiting they were getting ready to open the door. The door out onto the moon.

OUTSIDE THE DINING HALL, the social conversations were taking longer to conclude. As time had allowed the lodgers to rekindle old relationships and branch toward new associations, the casual after-meal conversations were not as quick to scatter from their circles. Marvin stood a few feet from the group his mother was involved with which included the Schnurbrytes, the McNamaras, and some other familiar dining room faces. He looked around at the other congregations whose chatter was starting to be matched in volume by the cicadas, crickets, and Creedence Clearwater from the distant jukebox. He spotted the Clopton family who stood away from everyone else. Kenny was running laps around his parents as they blew cigarette smoke toward the sky.

"Marvin, why do you go over and see your friend?" His mother asked.

"I don't know," he replied. "I've already seen him. He's... I don't know."

"He's what honey?"

"He's not that... I mean he doesn't even know about them landing on the moon tonight."

"Is that what you're worried about? You know you have plenty of time," Marilyn told him. "Gerald said the watch party doesn't start till 7:oo. We have an hour."

"Oh," Marvin said as he thought for a moment. "Are we going back to the cabin first?"

"Well, not just yet."

"What are we doing?"

"Some of the people from the Cardinal and the Blue Jay cabin are playing horseshoes. I thought... you know, it would be fun to go watch... for a while," she said. "And then we'll go over to the lodge later. How does that sound?"

"OK. I guess," he answered as a roar of laughter swept his mother's attention back into the group. He didn't want to watch adults throw objects back and forth for an hour but it was doubtful his mom would allow him to pursue his own adventure; he had tested those waters, and there was a sign posted.

"Hey Marvin," Kenny's voice called. He was running toward him. "Hey Marvin, whatcha doin'?" He asked as he leapt and came down a foot away which spooked a few adults.

"Nothing much, Kenny. Just standing here right now."

"Cool. Hey, wanted to tell you, Denny, my brother, he's goin' to the bridge."

"He's going now?"

"Yeah. Him and some others."

"They're going to drop?"

"Yep," Kenny replied. "Right on top of the fishes and the

frogs and the pollywogs." He jumped up in the air and landed into a squatting position to illustrate his point. "Splish splash!" He laughed and stood back up. His face flinched as a thought occurred to him. "Oh hey! Did'ya tell your mom yet?"

"Not yet. I was going to, but we were eating," he said. He glanced at his mother. She was smiling and she rocked from side to side; a movement that usually meant contentment. As if moving to music only she could hear. "I thought I would wait," he said to Kenny. "Till we got back to the cabin."

"So, do you want to go watch?"

"Well, we're supposed to go watch some people play horse-shoes. My mom wants to watch them. I guess I have to go."

"Oh," Kenny said as he pulled on his ear lope. "Can't 'cha ask if you can go with me instead?"

Marvin considered. *Excuse me, Mom... would you mind if went with my friend here to watch some teenagers take their life into their hands by jumping from the bridge into the river? I know it sounds dangerous and is probably against the law but... what do you say? Please?* He looked up at his mother who had just turned to him as if she had heard his thoughts.

"Oh, there's your little friend," Marilyn. "I'm sorry, what's your name?"

"Kenneth, ma'am," he told her. "Kenneth Clopton."

"Right. You were here last year, weren't you?"

"I was. I 'membered Marvin from the hayride and the float trip."

"That's right. I am so glad that Marvin has found a friend."

"It sure is," Kenny forced a smile and bowed for some reason. "I was just askin' Marvin if he'd like to kill some time with me. But he said he's fixin' to play some horseshoes."

"I'm not playing," Marvin spoke up. "I'm watching."

"Sure, sure," Kenny replied. "Sounds like fun. I wish you could go with me. It'd be fun too."

"Why not, Marvin? That's a great idea," Marilyn said. "Why don't you go with your friend for a while? Have fun."

An urge to question what she said almost broke the surface but was held back. What he heard was very plain; she implied he was free to travel on his own—with Kenny of course—without any particular rules, restrictions, or explanations. Why question? Why not act? "OK. Come on Kenny, let's go." Marvin began walking. He wasn't sure where he was going, he just walked. Kenny's shoes slapped the asphalt as he ran to catch up.

"Hey, you're headin' the wrong way!" Kenny said.

"I know."

"We need to go the other way."

"I know. I thought about getting a soda first."

"Marvin!" his mother call out.

Here it comes. The mind change. The follow-up questions. The reconsideration. He could continue on as if he didn't hear her over the Jukebox but he stopped. He turned around. She was smiling. Still swaying. "Yes?"

"Don't forget about the moon tonight," she said pointing up.

"I won't."

THE SUN WAS in the first stages of its final approach. It had moved into an angle that allowed the golden and purple light to shine down. The dull maroon steel of the Sandy Fork bridge appeared to be glowing with an orange sheen. Marvin and Kenny walked halfway down the stairs to the river and decided the steps would be the best place to sit. They had a decent view of the bridge and could avoid getting sand and silt in their shoes. Glen Campbell's voice dreamed of *Galveston* on the jukebox in the distance, accented by the clank of horseshoes clipping the stakes.

"I think they was gonna park on the other side then walk to the spot," Kenny said. "We should be watchin' for 'em over there." He pointed to the far side where the road and guardrails exited through a curtain of oak and sycamore trees.

"What kind of car is it?"

"I ain't sure," Kenny told him. "Why?"

"Well, I've seen a tan station wagon and a green mustang cross over. I just wondered."

"I ain't sure."

They watched the bridge for a few minutes. Kenny rubbed at the few dozen or so chigger spots on his ankles. An older couple holding cans of beer came down the steps. Marvin and Kenny scooted over to give way.

"How are you boys doing this evening?" The man asked.

"Doin' good sir," Kenny replied.

"Good to hear"

The couple stepped off onto the beach and into a large gnat cloud that floated in sunlight. The man failed his arms and jostled streams of beer while the lady bellowed, bowed her head, and jogged away chanting a string of curse words. Kenny bit into his knee to suppress a laugh while Marvin pulled his lower lip. The man recovered and attempted to wipe the damp spots from his shirt and pant leg. "Ah, fudgesi-cles!" He said.

Marvin looked over at the lady. She was sweeping the gravel around with her flip-flop. She cupped her hand over her eyes and looked at her husband. "When you get done fussing," she said, "look for small pebbles for the fish tank. I mean small."

"I know, I know," he replied. "For Chrissakes."

Marvin focused his attention on the bridge to prevent a laugh. "So," he said to Kenny, searching for a diverting topic, "they drove a car to the other side... and they're walking back?"

"I guess."

"Why not just walk from the lodge on this side? It would be easier."

"Dunno," Kenny said as he scratched at a new mosquito bite on his arm. "Didn't want to be seen walking there... from here, I guess."

"I see." Marvin nodded. "Didn't want your parents to see him?"

Kenny laughed. "Nah. My parents don't care what we do."

"They don't?"

"Heck no. Last year Denny drove his minibike straight outta the hay loft. Broke his collarbone. Dad didn't say nothin'. Not *be careful. Don't do such a thing.* Nothin'." Kenny squinted at the distance and stood up. "Hey, lookie! I think that's them over there."

Three figures appeared on the far side of the bridge. Two guys and a girl. They must have been in the Green Mustang Marvin thought. They didn't look like the type for a tan station wagon. As they came closer, Marvin could see one of the boys had a crew cut and the other had bushy red hair. "Don't see your brother in that group."

"Nope," Kenny replied. "That's Brett and Micky Malone from the Sandpiper cabin. They was on the hayride last year."

"Oh yeah." They watched the redheaded kid walk along the bridge rail. He stopped occasionally to look down, searching for the dark green oval smudge that was visible from overhead. The portal below which held enough depth to allow a falling body adequate clearance. A new figure appeared from the near side that drew their attention. "Hey, there's Denny." Kenny pointed for visual guidance. "Must've walked from this side."

The redheaded kid stopped, raised his arm with one finger pointed up, and made a circling motion. Marvin had seen the gesture in movies on TV; it meant to *gather around* in war films or *circle the wagons* in westerns. Denny ran to the group.

"Hey Marvin, you think you'd like to try it? You know, dropping?"

"I'm not sure," he replied. "What about you?"

"Heck yeah." Kenny sat back down on the step. "I done jumped from the high dive at the pool back home. I expect it's a lot like that."

Denny seemed to be first. He climbed over the outer rail and squatted to lower himself onto the lip of a support beam. The others at the bridge party cheered and clapped. The ruckus drew the attention of the pebble-seeking couple.

"What are those kids doing up there?" she asked.

Denny gripped the outer flange of the beam under the bridge and slid down until he hung by his fingertips.

"Looks like they're having fun," the man replied as he took a sip of his beer.

"For crying out loud," the lady said. "That looks dangerous hanging from there."

"That's what makes it fun," he replied with a belch.

Denny inched his way along the beam to position himself above the correct spot. Once he got there he remained motionless for what seemed like several long minutes. Marvin guessed Denny was thinking or praying. The only thing that held Denny was his fingertips; there was no turning back. Denny kicked his legs as if he riding a bike and shouted "Geronimo!" He seemed to hover for only a second before a significant splash went up from the Sandy Fork. A cheer went up from the bridge.

"I still think it's dangerous," the lady said tossing a rock into the river.

Kenny giggled and waved his hand in the air. "See, just like going off the high dive."

One of the girls climbed over the rail next.

"But if you think about it... the high dive isn't really dangerous," Marvin said. "The drop might be similar but... it's not the same."

"Why ain't it the same?"

"I mean... you're not going to get in trouble jumping off a diving board."

"Well, no. Course not," Kenny said. "It ain't as fun either."

"It's not fun unless somebody tells you that you're not supposed to do it."

"Shoot," Kenny said with a smirk, "with me... it's that I ain't old enough or tall enough for stuff. Like the *Tumble and Whirl* at the State fair. It's the only ride that looks like any fun but I'm too young and too short."

"You can do other stuff in the meantime," Marvin said. "Go on other rides till you grow. Jump off the high dive until you can drop from the bridge. Float underwater till you can float in space. Visit a strange place with large rocks till you can visit an alien planet."

The girl yelled *Geronimo* and dropped into the river. The redhead boy climbed over. Marvin sighed. The thrill of watching started to wane. "I guess when you imagine what something will be like, that's what's fun. They probably thought about this bridge all day and in one minute... it's over."

"What are you talking about, Marvin?"

"I don't know," he replied. "It's just stuff I think about once in a while. You might think about this stuff when you get older."

"I hope not," Kenny laughed. "I just want to ride the *Tumble and Whirl* when I get older."

Geronimo! yelled the redhead.

"You think some kid really died doin' that?"

"I'm not sure," Marvin said. "Maybe."

"I knew a kid... I went to school with... died in a wreck." Kenny reached out and tore a leaf from some ivy growing next to the steps. He began to pinch pieces from it and flick them into the air. "Did'ya ever know anybody that died?"

Marvin thought for a moment. "Not really. But I knew a kid that lived behind my grandparent's house that got burned up pretty bad."

"Burned up? How?"

"He was messing around with lighter fluid by a barbecue pit. I didn't actually see it happen. I heard it. Heard him screaming."

"And he lived?"

"Yeah he did," Marvin replied. "I wonder what time it is?"

"Why?"

"I'm supposed to meet Mr. Schnurbryte at the lodge.

"How come?"

"We're going to watch the moon landing."

"Oh," Kenny replied and looked up. "Think there's pollywogs up there on the moon?" He flicked the remains of the leaf skyward.

"No. I don't think so."

Kenny laughed. "Think there's some in your bathtub?"

"I think there is."

Not Cheese

The picture was upside down. They had put the circuit breaker into the camera and we now had a television signal from space. It was fuzzy and shadowy. A few people in the room tilted their heads to the side. If you allowed your imagination to make sense of the image it resembled a shaft of light coming into a dark room. It wasn't a room it was supposed to be the moon. We weren't seeing it right. After a second or two, the image was corrected and the picture flipped over. Some heads remained tilted. The mind could now reassign sense to this new image. The shaft of light appeared to be a surface of some sort; a landscape in the background. The lunar surface. A shadow in the foreground was an astronaut. He was standing on a small ladder just outside the door.

"WHAT DO you think of that young man?"

Marvin heard the question but it took some time to process. His thoughts were cloudy and he had a dull headache. On a typical day at this time of night, he would be asleep. But on this Monday evening, he was not. He was in a hot crowded room for what felt like several days. More people squeezed inside to listen to Walter Cronkite describe the flickering visuals and provide context. Even the cigarette smokers who lurked outside the door were now present with their aroma.

Marilyn leaned down; "Marvin, did you hear Mr. Schnurbryte?" He had but his attention was focused on the sound of the astronauts speaking. It was clear. Not at all like a radio loudspeaker. The images on the TV were still murky, too bright or too dark, but he could hear them.

"I think... it's pretty cool," Marvin said to Mr. Schnurbryte. He wished he had a better response but it would do for now.

"Yes. *Pretty cool* indeed," Gerald replied. "See here now, one must keep in mind the telecast on that television up there... ...that's an old TV we are watching. The last image it probably put forth was the series between the Red Sox and the Cardinals. And that camera they have there... well, it's new isn't it? And it's broadcasting those images from a world away. The factors don't make for remarkable clarity. But the sheer scope of what we are witnessing... it staggers one's mind."

Marvin understood most of what he said so he supplied a

nod to acknowledge it before his mother asked, *did you hear Mr. Schnurbryte?* again. Someone in the room mentioned that *the simulation had been crystal clear* and someone else replied *But it's not actual. Just fake actors in a studio.* Marvin wondered what the simulation people were doing now. Did they get to stop and watch the actual thing? Was the fake Neil Armstrong watching the real Neil Armstrong hover there on the ladder? It seemed as if he remained motionless for several long minutes. Was Neal thinking or praying? Would he shout *Geronimo* and drop down onto the moon? Probably not.

The room went silent as they watched him move down slowly and carefully. Was he there? Did he step off the latter? A collective sigh went up as the words appeared on the television that read *Armstrong On The Moon.* The room erupted with cheers and applause. Marvin looked up at his mother, she had tears in her eyes. Other ladies also seemed to be crying. Mr. Schnurbryte was laughing and smiling. Other men smiled as well. Marvin thought it best to smile, after all, it was pretty cool to think a man was standing on that shiny ball up in the sky. It felt important as if at that moment everyone who was watching saw something meaningful. It could lift all doubt and silence, all the evil for a while. At least until the end of the broadcast.

The smokers stepped back outside and shouted as dug into their cigarette packs. The chatter subsided as they listened to Armstrong describe the surface. A fine powder. Like charcoal. Marvin looked up at his mother and said, "See. I told you. It's not cheese."

It was very late. He was very tired. As they walked back to the *Oriole* Marvin wished he was much younger, much smaller, and his mother could pick him up and carry him as she did long ago. He could close his eyes and listen to the night sounds around the Lesterton lodge grounds, next to the Sandy Fork river, below the occupied moon. But he was too old for that. Instead, he walked next to his mother, her hand on his shoulder which he allowed since his self-conscious side was overtaken by fatigue. He smiled knowing he could sleep soon and wake tomorrow to another day of activity; a ride on Polka Highness, maybe another swim in the river, a float trip, and a hay ride with Kenny. It was only Monday. There was a whole week to fill. He could imagine what it would be like.

"Don't you just love that sound?" his mother asked.

"Yeah. I think I do." He wished he had a better response. And suddenly he remembered there was that matter of the tadpoles in the bathtub.

Crest
WALT DISNEY'S
THE 3 LIVES OF
THOMASINA /
THE BRASS BOTTLE

At The Crest

Norbert, The Fire Drill, and authoritative resistance

Norbert Stiebert had the most unfortunate name in 5th grade at Baymore Middle school which is probably what made him the toughest and coolest 11-year-old kid that Marvin Milstead had ever known. He became familiar with Norbert or *Norb* as he preferred to be called in 4th grade, during a fire drill. Each classroom lined up in an orderly manner, walked down the hall in a systematized fashion, and stood outside-at a designated safe distance-for a short period of time before returning inside.

It was while *returning inside* that Marvin became aware of Norb, not so much his physical presence among the multitude of middle schoolers filing down the hallway, but the sound he made, specifically the sound his shoes made; a clicking-scraping across the tile floors. The percussive taps caught Marvin's attention above the muddled drone of voices, he turned his head to figure out who was responsible. Whoever it was, was not too far behind--somewhere in the single file row behind Mrs. Penrodski's hulking figure.

Each group stopped outside their classroom door so the teachers could make sure the number of children huddled nearby equaled the number they started out with. Marvin leaned forward from his line to study Mrs. Penrodski's line which was now losing formation as attention spans spun away. Slumped against the wall was a kid with disheveled brown hair —two strands hanging down in his face-wearing an oversized army jacket, red t-shirt, jeans, and brown harness motorcycle boots. Marvin learned this kid's name was Norbert Stiebert. He learned it when Mrs. Pedrodski shouted it. Norb had pulled a Zippo lighter out of his pocket, flipped it open, and waved the flame around for the amusement of his peers. She lunged forward, grabbed his arm, and shouted, "NORBERT STIEBERT!"

"What?" he answered with an annoyed tone. "It's a fire drill isn't it?"

"OK, Mister smart mouth! You can come with me!" Mrs. Pedrodski jerked him by the collar with one hand and snatched the lighter with her other hand.

"Hey!" Norbert protested, "That's mine!"

"Not anymore!" she said and turned toward Marvin's group, "Miss Langford? Would you please watch my students while I take Mr. Stiebert to the office?"

"Of course, Mrs. Penrodski."

As she Norb him away Marvin heard the clicks and scrapes generated by Norb's boots. He saw metal strips attached to the heels, similar to taps that dancers wore. He doubted that Norb Stiebert was a dancer.

"All right class, listen to me," Miss Langford said, "the show is over. I need everyone to listen up, *my* class, please go quietly into our room and take your seats." Chirps of disappointment and dissent were expressed. "Quietly, I said."

The muttering fell to a whisper. "And Mrs. Penrodski's class? I need you all to go quietly into your room and take your seats. Quietly I said."

As Marvin quietly went back into the classroom, a fascination formed in his mind. Sure, he'd been intrigued by new movies, actors, singers, TV shows, plastic model kits, and things he saw on the news, but there was something about witnessing an ordinary kid, same age, same grade, and same school; cause such a commotion through his simple actions. Like a real-life Eddie Haskel or even like the Franko character in the movie *The Dirty Dozen*. This was real. This had unfolded before his very eyes in t

he hallway of Baymore Middle school, not on any screen.

This was Marvin's first introduction to Norb and authoritative resistance.

Friday Night at The Crest (A madhouse)

The second encounter was during a showing of *The Abominable Dr. Phibes* at a neighborhood cinema called the *Crest*. Most of Marvin's friends had seen the movie and didn't want to go again-they were saving up to see *Big Jake* in a few weeks—so, he could find no one to tag along. His final option was his mother. She could be reliable to take him to the Crest, especially to see a monster movies. A favorite ritual he shared with his mother was staying up late watching the Creature Feature on television. It was his last hope but if he played up the scary factor, it might work. She resisted his pleas but finally relented. The only night she could possibly take him was Friday.

He had heard rumors in school about Friday nights at the Crest and discovered much of it was true. The audience was mostly high school kids, none of whom were interested in watching a movie. They roamed the aisles looking for friends, maybe someone to *make-out with* in the back row, perhaps anyone who sneaked liquor inside, or any variety of amusements that would enhance an evening in a dark auditorium. Whatever movie happened to be on the screen, really did not matter.

Twenty minutes into *Dr. Phibes,* Marvin's mother said, "This is ridiculous." She wasn't referring to the plot or Vincent Price's makeup. "It's like Grand Central Station in here. Why are they all walking around?"

Marvin shrugged. He had not been paying attention to the movie but rather he had been watching a couple sitting one row up who seemed to be trying to swallow each other's faces. A sight he would have pointed to as disgusting a few years ago, but now, this Friday night, it was impressive.

The girl he knew. She was one of the library helpers from school, she was in fifth or sixth grade. He didn't recognize the boy. "I know," he replied to his mother. "No one's watching the movie."

"If it's going to be like this the whole time, I'm not sitting here," his mother said. "We might as well go. Might as well just leave. Watch it on TV when it comes around." She sighed. "I'm sorry. I know you wanted to see this but..."

"It's fine, mom," Marvin said. "It is kinda stupid. We can go. But can I go to the bathroom first?"

"Yes. Sure. Of course," she said. "But just be careful. There's some rough-looking characters in here. Go straight there and come straight back."

"I will."

"And then we'll go. Don't dilly-dally."

"I won't." Marvin moved down the row to the main aisle

just as Dr. Phibes exacted revenge upon another unfortunate person in the plot. He rounded the corner at the back partition, which was a half wall appointed with yellow curtains. Patrons could pull back the material and peek through into the auditorium. Tonight the curtains were opened to a rouges gallery of older kids leaning against the wall. As Marvin passed by they made odd noises at him. He kept walking and kept his head down-avoiding eye contact; until just outside the restrooms when a figure emerged at a fast clip, ran into him, and almost knocked him down.

"Sorry, kid."

Marvin looked up to see a furious exodus from the men's room. Kids of all sizes and ages dashed out of the door. The movement carried with it a cloud of smoke. He stood there for a moment unsure whether to proceed forward. A figure emerged from the haze, it was Norb Stiebert. A cigarette dangled from the corner of his mouth and a very large police officer held onto the collar of his coat.

"Man!" Norbert said with disgust. "Come on, man!" He tried to pull away but the officer pulled back. He snatched the cigarette from Norb's lips and held it up. "What did I tell you about this?"

"About what? I don't see nothing."

The officer dropped it to the ground and stepped on it.

"Hey, you're littering," Norb told him. "That's against the law."

"Come on, James Dean, let's go." He jerked Norb's collar and pulled him through the doors to the lobby and out of sight. Dr. Phibes' victim screamed in terror as something bad happened to him on the screen. Marvin stood in place to take in all that happened there in front of the restroom. Did he want to go in there now? It probably smelled like cigarettes and other bathroom fragrances. Was it safe? The policeman had chased all the delinquents out so it would be safer now.

Just then, a succession of loud pops erupted that didn't come from the movie playing through the little curtains behind him. It came from inside the auditorium. Marvin saw flashes of light as it emerged through the aisle entryways. Shadows of people in various positions bounced off the walls and curtains. A girl screamed and then another. Someone yelled, "Fire-crackers!" The clatter stopped and the commotion started. The overhead lights came on. The men's room policeman ran back inside. Marvin pulled back the curtain to see. A thin cloud of smoke hovered on a plain midway between the seats and the ceiling. There was the faint essence of gunpowder inside the stench of cigarettes and popcorn.

Marvin decided to forgo the bathroom and made his way back to his seat. The half-wall leaners had scattered. They blended into the gawker groups walking around, it appeared everyone was up now and moving around, including his mother who made her way up the aisle through the crowd.

"Come on Marvin, we're going. It's a madhouse in here. A madhouse." He wasn't sure if his mom was quoting Charlton Heston in *Planet Of The Apes*, or not. He decided not to ask. She appeared quite upset. He followed her through the doors, across the small chaotic lobby, and out into cool night air.

No Sign Of Norb

Marvin didn't see Norbert for the rest of the school year. A glimpse in the cafeteria during lunch occasionally, or outside during recess, maybe the sound of taps clicking out in the hall-way-although many kids joined the tap bandwagon, so it was difficult to tell if it was Norb or not. It seemed that the coolest kid in middle school wasn't around anymore.

Word on the playground was that he had been suspended over the Zippo lighter incident. Others said he had been sent to a military academy somewhere across the river in Illinois. Someone else heard it was an academy in Iowa. Another tale placed Norb into a home for wayward boys. Some had heard he had run away to join the army. He wanted to go fight in Vietnam but when it was learned he was only 11, they shipped him back and he was in a detention center somewhere in Texas.

As the weeks passed the story changed and evolved into ridiculous branches. Norb joined a gang of traveling circus people. He swung from a trapeze while tossing knives at the clown car. He was now a member of the Hells Angels motorcycle club. The youngest member in history. There was a story about him in a magazine.

And then the stories faded. Summer started and the 4th grade stopped. Norb was forgotten.

Summer: Pools and Condensers

Marvin spent his summer days with his friends in the neighborhood on Candle Drive. Everyone who lived on the street called it *Cancel* drive since it ended in a cul-de-sac. The rusty gray asphalt road faded after two blocks and unfurled into a large circle that lead you back the way you came. Candle drive *canceled* any travelers' hope of cutting through to somewhere else. Even though a sign at the start of the street clearly warned all who entered; Street Ends No Outlet. It was referred to as the SENO sign--pronounced *see no*--as in *I see no reason to continue down this street because can I see no way out.*

The street was appointed with two and three-bedroom ranch homes, or tract homes; 8 on each side. Most were adorned with red-cedar ridge siding on the front and gray asbestos shingles the rest of the way around. Marvin's grandparents, Leonard and Irene Wilson purchased one of the homes on Candle drive during the rise of the manifest suburban destiny. They planned to enjoy their golden years there. A short time later, their oldest daughter Marilyn Milstead, brought her son, Marvin, to stay for some time. A few years.

MARVIN's close friends were Ronnie Phegel; who lived across the street and two houses down, and Ryan Heffendorf who lived on the same side of the street but 5 houses away at the curve of the cul-de-sac circle. Ronnie and Ryan were both three years younger than Marvin and attended a Catholic school. They both were reliable for a game of freeze tag, Indian ball, whiffle ball, bike rides, or any other activity that burned through the hours until the sun went down and the porch lights came on. When it was too hot outside there was always television; if nothing good was on, there were swimming pools.

THE PHEGEL FAMILY had purchased a new pool for the summer and so did the Heffendorfs. The Phegel's pool was a 6-foot long and 3-feet deep vinyl affair with *Scooby-Doo* characters on the outside panels. The Heffendorfs had a large round galvanized pool that resembled a spaceship. Ryan called it the *Enterprise pool.*

Perhaps a touch of envy prompted Ronnie to claim the *Enterprise pool wasn't really a pool, but a thing that cows drank from.* Ryan said *the sales guy at the hardware store told his mom it was indeed a swimming pool. He didn't say anything about cows.* On hot summer days, when Ronnie's older sisters monopolized the *Scooby-Doo* pool, he was just as happy to jump into Ryan's cow trough spaceship with no complaints. Marvin decided their soundtrack for the summer was the theme from *The Banana Splits* TV show, prompted by Ronnie's tendency to sing the song at any moment's notice until it was in everyone's head the rest of the day.

ONE POST-POOL AFTERNOON, Marvin, Ronnie, and Ryan sat on the ground in front of the central air condenser unit in the backyard of the Phegel house. It was a large faded green metal unit that was wide enough to accommodate three boys planted in front of its vent. When the air conditioner turned on, each boy held up their towels over their head and secured the bottom with their toes. The strong breeze from the fan inflated their towels like sails on a ship and created small tents of warm wind. It was the best way to keep warm and dry after an afternoon of backyard pool amusement.

"ANYBODY WATCH *Kelly's Heroes* on TV last night?" Ronnie asked as he smoothed the goosebumps on his arms.

"Part of it," Marvin answered, "I saw it last year."

"Me too," Ryan said. "I've seen it three times. I like *The Dirty Dozen* better."

"Yeah," Ronnie said, "I love the end where Jefferson has to run and drop the grenades down the pipes."

"But then the Nazis shoot him," Ryan said. "It's kinda sad

he doesn't make it. Wish they were like the Nazis on *Hogan's Heroes*. The dumb ones."

"You know the guy that plays Jefferson is Jim Brown?" Marvin asked. "The football player."

"I knew that," Ryan replied. "Cleveland Browns."

"I like Joe Namath," Ronnie said. "He's cool."

"Tarkenton is better," Ryan told him.

"Yeah," Ronnie said.

"Yeah," Marvin said.

The hum of the fan-filled the silent space as their thoughts regrouped.

"Anybody see *Fists of Fury?*" Marvin asked. "Bruce Lee?"

"Was that at the Crest?" Ryan asked.

"Yeah," Marvin replied. "A few weeks ago with *Five Fingers of Death.*"

"Nah," Ronnie said, "my mom wouldn't let me go. She says karate movies make me too crazy. They activate my metabolism or something. That's how I broke the credenza." He sneezed.

"Gesundheit," Ryan said.

"Thanks."

"Anyway," Ryan continued. "my sister says that place smells like dirty socks. She calls it the *Crust.*"

"Yeah," Marvin replied with a chuckle. "It does smell pretty nasty in there."

"Can you imagine how many times those seats have been farted in?" Ronnie asked. "Like a million and one probably."

"Who did you see *Fists of Fury* with?" Ryan asked.

"My cousin Brad."

"Wish I had a cousin," Ronnie replied. "All I got are stupid sisters."

"Yeah," Marvin replied. "I used to wish that I had a sister. Or a brother."

"You can have one of mine," Ronnie said. "I have plenty of them."

Ronnie Phegel had three older sisters; Joannie who was 18, Janice who was 16, and Lauren who was Marvin's age. Marvin saw Lauren around quite frequently and spoke with Lauren. She participated in neighborhood games of freeze tag and hide and go seek. The other sisters were mysteries who stayed in their rooms and listened to records or the radio. Marvin caught glimpses of them from time to time. Doubtful he could pick them out of a line-up.

Ryan Heffendorf had one older sister, Linda who was 14. Out of all the sisters his friends had, Linda was the coolest. She could be nice, she could be mean and she could be funny. If he could have a sister, he would pick her.

"Saw *The Abominable Dr. Phibes*," Ryan said.

"Yeah? Me too," Marvin replied. "But only the first part. We had to leave early."

"Leave early? Why did you leave?"

"Well, I was with my mom. We went on a Friday night."

"Friday? Are you nuts? I heard about that place on Fridays," Ronnie said. "I heard there's fights, people getting stabbed and weirdos running around naked on drugs."

"No way Ronnie," Ryan said. "You're making that crap up."

"I am not!"

"I didn't see anything like that," Marvin said. "I did see some people making out pretty heavy. No one was naked. No one got stabbed."

"Did you leave because of the making out?" Ronnie asked. "Cause that's gross."

"No," Marvin said. "We left because we couldn't hear the movie. And everybody was like... walking around and talking. It was loud. And then get this, somebody set off firecrackers."

"Firecrackers? Inside? During the movie?"

"Yep. Inside."

The condenser fan stopped with a shutter and the towels collapsed on their heads. They dropped them down over into their laps.

"Who did it? Did you see?" Ryan asked.

The back door opened Lauren emerged. She had an orange beach towel over her shoulders and a *Six Flags* bucket hat on her head. She glanced over at the boys through her thick glasses. The lenses made her green eyes appear twice their actual size and slightly closer to you than the rest of her face.

"Mom said not to lean back on that, you guys," she said. "She said she's afraid you'll break it."

"We're not doing anything. We're not leaning on it," Ronnie told her.

"Fine."

"Fine."

"Hi Marvin," Lauren said with a smile.

"Hi, Lauren."

Ronnie made a whining sound that mimicked his sister's voice and echoed, "*Hi Marvin.*"

"Stop it you brat!" Her face turned red.

"You stop it," Ronnie replied.

"What did I do?" she asked.

"*Lauren and Marvin sitting in a tree,*" Ronnie began singing. "*K-I-S-S-I-N-G.*"

"Shut up!" Lauren said.

"*First come love! Then comes marriage. Then comes monkey butt sitting in a baby carriage!*"

Marvin reached over and flicked Ronnie on the side of the head with an audible snap.

"Ow! Ronnie yelped. "You butt!"

Lauren pushed up her glasses, turned, and walked toward the plastic chair by the pool.

"Why doesn't she say hi to me?" Ryan asked.

"Why'd you throw her Barbie down the sewer?" Ronnie said followed with a sneeze.

"Gesundheit," Ryan said. "That was a million years ago."

"No, it wasn't."

"Yes, it was."

"No, it wasn't."

Ryan and Ronnie continued their in-depth discussion but Marvin's focus followed Lauren. He didn't look upon her as cute or attractive as he began to see other girls. Lauren was OK. She was plain in appearance, with mousy brown hair and a smattering of freckles. She reminded him of Jane Hathaway from the *Beverly Hillbillies*--if Jane was a 10-year-old girl. He felt connected to her only because they were the same age, she was Ronnie's sister, and he felt sorry for her. Lauren's kryptonite was a lazy eye that drifted toward the center. It prompted some of the neighborhood kids to call her *Clarence,* which was the name of the cross-eyed lion on the TV Show *Daktari.* The name would send her home in tears every time.

Ronnie rubbed his temple where Marvin had thumped him. "I think you damaged my brain, Marvin."

"If you keep sneezing, you'll blow your brains out," Ryan told him.

"Can't help it. I have allergies. And I have to pee."

"What? I don't get it," Ryan said. "Allergies make you pee?"

"No, fart head!" Ronnie replied. "This warm air blowing on me makes me have to pee. The crap that gets blown around in it makes me sneeze.

"Well go to the John, Ron," Marvin said.

"I know but..." Ronnie squirmed. "I don't want to move yet. It feels good right here. Plus, I'm not dried off."

"Why don't you just go here then?" Ryan asked. "Who cares?"

"Go here? What do you mean?"

"He means just pee right here," Marvin said.

"In my swimming trunks? Gross! Are you serious?"

"Very serious," Marvin replied. "You pee in the pool, don't you? And you're wearing your trunks in the pool. What's the difference?"

"Your swimming trunks are wet anyway," Ryan said. "It'll be fine. I did it a few minutes ago."

"You did? *You peed*?" Ronnie moved over a few inches.

"It's the warm air. Makes me pee."

"Well, I'm not sitting here in your pee." Ronnie stood up quickly and wrapped his towel around his shoulders. "I'm goin' inside to use a real bathroom."

"Good for you," Ryan said. "Using the big boy potty."

Ronnie searched for a response but came up empty. He looked and around for a moment, draped the towel behind him, and ran toward Lauren. He raised his right hand and curled at the wrist to fashion a claw. "Lahh-run! Lah-run! I'm Barnabas! Barnabas Collins! Bah-nah-bus!!"

"Knock it off, weirdo! Stop it! I'll tell mom!" She kicked at him as he ran past her. Ronnie circled back and bounded up onto the porch and ran into the house. "I hate *Dark Shadows*," Lauren said as she tossed her towel over the chair, stepped over Shaggy's head, and sank into the pool.

***

MARVIN AND RYAN held their towels and waited in anticipation. They knew when Ronnie went inside, he'd carry just enough warm air with him to cause a slight rise in temperature and trigger the thermostat. Any moment the fan should kick on again.

"There was an 8th grader at Our Lady of Calvary who

flushed a cherry bomb down the toilet," Ryan said. "It cracked the bowl and flooded the hallway by Father Saladino's office. He was so mad he said a curse word."

"Oh wow? Which curse word did he say?" Marvin asked.

"I heard it was the S one. Not *shoot* but the real one."

"Cool," Marvin said. "Did they catch the kid who did it?"

"Yeah."

"What happened to him?"

"He got expelled. He said that someone dared him to do it. But you can't punish someone that dares you. You can only punish the person that does the dare."

"Yeah," Marvin said. "I mean if the dare is something like that."

"Nobody could use that bathroom for a month."

"Everybody would have to S *word* someplace else."

Ryan laughed. "Good one."

The cicadas began harmonizing from the sycamore and oaks around the neighborhood. Lauren flailed at a horsefly that hovered near her. "Leave me alone! Go awaaaay!"

"Don't know if I could do something like that for a dare," Marvin said. "Firecrackers. Cherry bomb. I mean... you might look cool and tough... but... I don't think I could."

"Me neither," Ryan replied. "My last dare didn't turn out very well."

"Which one was that?"

"When Rich Schwartz dared me to jump over 25 *Hot Wheels* on my bike."

"Oh yeah. You almost made it."

"Those were some of the biggest scabs I ever had in my life."

Lauren took off her glasses and laid them on the chair. She sat down in the pool letting an exhalation go as the cold water enveloped her.

Marvin wondered what she could see without her glasses.

What did everything around her look like? How blurry was the world? What did it look like when her eye drifted? Did it even matter to her?

The condenser fan came on and they grabbed their towels and raised them up.

"So, I heard the 8th grader was sent to military school," Ryan said. "My mom said that's where bad kids go."

"I guess your school doesn't have many... bad kids," Marvin said. "All those statues of Jesus and Mary keep everyone good."

"Yeah. Till they leave."

Marvin rubbed the side of his face. A strand of his hair was blowing against his cheek. "Anyone at your school wear taps on their shoes?"

"You mean like for dancing?" Ryan asked.

"No, like... for making noise when you walk."

"They don't allow noise at Our Lady. They don't allow anything." Ryan sighed. "That's why I wish I could go to a normal school."

"How come you don't?"

"It has something to do with the split between my mom and dad. I had to go Catholic school." He tugged on his trunks and squirmed.

"You're not peeing are you?" Marvin asked.

"No. It felt like something was crawling on me." Ryan flicked it away. "A stupid ant."

"They don't eat much."

"What are you doing after supper?" Ryan asked.

"I don't know." Marvin dropped his towel down and leaned his head back against the slated vents. He felt the vibration resonate inside his head. His eyes saw everything in earthquake vision and something inside his ears felt like it was being tickled. He lifted his head back up and said, "I got some new records. Probably listen to those. If you want to come over later."

"Yeah?" Ryan dropped his towel down and squinted as his eyes adjusted to the sunlight. "What'd'ya get?"

"*Indian Reservation.* Paul Revere and the Raiders and *Theme From Shaft.*"

"You got *Theme From Shaft?*"

"Yeah," Marvin said. "You wanna come over?"

Ryan's face dropped the smile it held. "Crap! I can't. My mom's going to her *Parents Without Partners* thing tonight. I'm not supposed to leave when she's gone." He inspected the grass under his legs. "My sister and I have to stay home."

"Oh."

"But why don't you could come to my house," Ryan said and squirmed. "It's OK if I have friends over. I just can't leave."

"I could do that."

Ryan jumped up quickly and began jogging in place as he slapped the back of his swimming trunks.

"What are you doing?"

"Ants! I think I'm sat on their house or something. They're biting my butt!"

Marvin laughed. "It's probably because you peed on them."

Dinner Rush (I can't imagine what it does to floors)

"What's the big hurry? You're eating like it's some kind of race," Marvin's grandfather said.

"Leave him alone, Leonard. He's probably hungry," his grandmother replied. "Kids have been out swimming all day. He's worked up an appetite."

"Yeah?" Leonard picked up the pepper and shook it over everything on his plate.

"Watch what you're doing. You're getting it all over the table."

"For crying out loud, Irene. I'll wipe it up when I'm done." He used the side of his hand to sweep the liberated pepper into a straight line near his plate.

"Where's mom?" Marvin asked.

"Well," Irene said, "she had to stop by the store. She needed something to wear tonight."

"Something to wear?" Leonard asked. "Where the hell's she going?"

"Leonard!" Irene replied with annoyance. "The language." She scooped a spoonful of potatoes, lodged a portion on her plate, and then tapped the spoon on the rim of the bowl as if calling order to the proceedings while clearing the utensil in one gesture. "I've told you and Marilyn told you about this evening."

"Told me what?"

"Told you, that Regina Heffendorf invited asked her to go to that meeting she attends."

"Meeting she attends?" Leonard picked up the serving fork next to the roast and tapped it on the plate before he selected a slice of meat. "What kind of meeting?"

"I don't know what they call it. It's for the single parents."

"What? They go to some kind of bar or something?"

"No Leonard, they meet at a restaurant. It's not a bar."

"Corky's Pizza Parlor," Marvin said. "Ryan told me about it. They sing old songs and stuff. I went to a birthday party there last year."

"Oh," Leonard said as he lined up some more pepper.

Marvin placed his fork and knife on his plate. "Can I go now? I'm finished eating."

"Where are you going?" Leonard asked.

"Ryan's house." Marvin picked up his plate and went to the sink.

"Aren't you going to wait for your mother?" Irene asked.

"No. I'll see her."

"What did you need?"

"I wanted to ask her..." Marvin looked at Leonard and then back to Irene. "Ask her if I could get some taps for my shoes."

"Some... what?" Leonard asked.

"*Taps*." Marvin turned on the faucet and rinsed his plate.

"Are you taking dance lessons?"

"No, not for that." He turned the faucet off. "Kids at school wear them. They don't dance. They just used them to make noise."

"The kids are wearing them?" Irene asked.

"Yeah, he said they wear them for the noise. Not to dance," Leonard said. "Ain't that something? Just drawing attention to themselves I guess."

"Does Ronnie and Ryan wear them?" Irene asked.

"No," Marvin replied. "They're too young. Plus, they don't let kids wear stuff like that at the Catholic schools."

"I should think not," Irene said. "I can't imagine what it does to the floors. Probably scuffs them up something awful."

"So, the boys at your school wear them? Leonard asked.

"Yeah. The girls don't wear them."

"And now you want to wear them?" Leonard let the question hang. Marvin didn't jump at it, he knew where it was headed. A ploy he had heard before. "So let me ask you this, if these same kids with the taps, all jumped off a cliff, would you want to jump also?"

"Oh Leonard," Irene snapped. "Don't be so ignorant."

"I just asked a question."

"No, I wouldn't jump off a cliff if they did," Marvin said. "I'll just scuff up the floors."

Leonard cut his meat. "I see." He allowed the knife to slice through onto the plate to produce a squeak. "Remember last year... what's his name got that mini-bike. Remember that Irene? And because of that, Marvin had to have one. Begged for one. So, Marilyn went out and bought him one. Remember?"

"Yes, well, what's your point, Leonard?" Irene asked.

"The point is... now, the damn thing sits out in the garage."

"That's because there's no place to ride it," Marvin replied, "I can't ride it on the street because you said it's illegal. And you won't let me ride in the backyard because it tears up the grass. What am I supposed to do?"

"Don't get smart with me," Leonard said, pointing a fork full of meat at Marvin.

"I'm not. I'm just telling you why it sits out there."

"And I'm just telling you that your mother has better things to spend her money on than piddly crap. If she got some sort of alimony or support, it'd be different."

"Leonard," Irene interrupted as an alert. Leonard put the bite in his mouth and chewed while he stared at the wall.

"Well," he said.

"Well," Irene said.

The *wells* were an indication that their differences had reached an end or perhaps a stalemate. Tradition dictated a full moment of silence should follow.

Marvin sighed. Silence was a perfect place to leave from. "I'm going now."

"What time will you be home?" Irene asked.

"I don't know. Not late," he said. "I'm grabbing some of my records. I'll just go out through the back."

MARVIN TOOK two steps at a time down the stairs to the basement. An area his younger self had found unsettling and quite spooky. It was a widely held adolescent gospel that monsters and murderers hid in the basement. The mere consideration of traveling downstairs to an area below a home was a knot in the stomach of many children. But one day the knot in Marvin's belly loosened. It was calmed by the logic Leonard proposed one day a few years back;

Now you realize, if there's some crazy damn boogeyman waiting in the dark down in our basement, well, ask yourself, where'd he come from? How did he get there? He would've had to come in the front door, wouldn't he? He would have to walk through the house to get to the basement. We would have seen him already. Right?

Slowly, his grandfather's simple statement began to make sense. It could have been the logic or maybe it was getting older that lifted those mental shackles. Closet creatures, dark room dwellers, and even tooth fairies seemed childish. The basement was now his favorite place in the house. The only monsters down there were the plastic models that Marvin had put together standing on his metal bookshelf next to plastic cars and motorcycles. The Mummy stood next to a Big Daddy's dragster. Dracula protected a Triumph street racer.

Leonard had built a bar against one wall, brought down a couch, a coffee table, and a stereo console; put down a few old rugs over the green and red floor tile to create a space for entertaining, but when Marilyn had moved back home with Marvin, Leonard postponed any further plans for his subterranean area.

Marvin picked up his records, went back up the stairs, and out the back door avoiding further kitchen table conversation.

The sound of the wind chain clanking when the back door opened, was a sign to Skippy of possible interaction or food; she wagged her tail and trotted over to Marvin. He bent to rub her ears. She sniffed at the records he held. "Nope. You can't eat my 45's. It's vinyl. Doesn't taste very good. A bit oily. I'll bring you some cheese later. You want some cheese?" The dog loved cheese and toast for some reason. "See ya, girl." He kissed her on the head and went out the gate and down *Cancel* street toward Ryan's house on the circle.

Records and the Sister (Some friend you are)

Marvin occupied the floor in Ryan's room as they listened to music on his Sears all-in-one stereo unit. Ryan's sister, Linda would check in every 20 minutes or so.

"Hi. Are you guys doing all right?"

"Yeah," Ryan replied. "Go away."

"What are you listening to?"

"Paul Revere and the Raiders," Marvin told her.

"Cool," she said. "Have you heard Black Sabbath?"

"No," Ryan said. "Go away."

"I have," Marvin told her.

"Really? Where did you ever hear Black Sabbath?"

"Last summer. I was at a pool party. It was some people my mom works with. I went inside to use the bathroom and there was this kid... he was older, a teenager, he was sitting in the den with headphones on. He said, '*Hey kid, come here. Listen to this.*' He put the headphones on me. It was something called *Electric Funeral*. Kinda scary sounding. But I liked it. It was different."

"How cool," she replied with a smile. "Different is cool."

He wasn't sure why, but every time she came into the room, his face felt warm, similar to a sunburn. Of all the sisters of all the friends Marvin knew, Linda was the only one to cause a reaction. She wasn't that pretty, not like Rachael Welsh or Susan Dey but she was OK. Linda was 14 years old, tall, thin, and had shoulder-length dark blond hair. Her eyes were large and overshadowed a small button nose. She had hints of acne on her cheeks, yet her presence brought an unsettling hormonal consequence that Marvin became aware of early in the spring. He felt incredibly self-conscious around her. Why? He wondered. She was just Ryan's lanky older sister with buggy eyes that used to annoy him. But something had changed to make matters more difficult. She appeared different also, she wore a puffy white blouse and black slacks, not the usual casual sister uniform. Linda seemed to be aware of Marvin's condition and kept coming back to provoke the occurrence. It would explain her sly smile and why she only spoke to Marvin and not her brother. If he could switch off the part of his mind that was remodeling his imagination he would. As soon as Linda left, he felt normal again. But he wondered how soon she would return.

"Why are you talking to her?" Ryan asked.

"I don't know. She asked a question and... I gave her an answer."

"Are you trying to catch cooties?"

"Come on, Ryan," Marvin laughed, "aren't you a little old for that stuff?"

"Never." Ryan shuffled through his stack of 45s on top of his dresser. "Hey! You want to hear '*Animal*'?"

"Is that the weird one?"

"It's not weird, it's cool! Better than Back Stab-ith." Ryan peeled the last record off the turntable and dropped it on the others. He fit the plastic disk into the center of the record and put it on the turntable. After a few hisses and pops from the small speaker, he turned up the volume. The sound of birds was joined by noises from the jungle; elephants and lions. The wildlife faded into the chatter of people.

"It's kinda loud," Marvin said.

Suddenly, the music jolted into playing short bursts as the singer repeated the word animal over and over in different and humorous inflections. Ryan sang along. The energy of the song infected him. He jumped up and down swinging his arms. He climbed up on top of his bed, bounced a few times, lept off high in the air, and landed on the floor off balance, stumbled into the dresser which sent the needle skidding across the record with a loud scratch. The sudden silence was filled with Linda's voice bellowing from her room. "Ryan! Whatever you're doing... knock it off, you spaz!"

Ryan picked up his record, checked it for damage, and set it down. "You wanna watch TV?" he asked.

"Sure."

MARVIN SAT on the floor against the couch as Ryan sat in front of the television console and flipped through the channels; he stopped on *The Sonny And Cher Comedy Hour.*

"That's good. Let's watch that." Marvin told him.

"Yeah, I guess, but... they just argue. I'm tired of people fighting. It's not funny," Ryan said. "I like Flip Wilson. He's funny."

"Yeah, but he's not on now," Marvin replied. "These guys are kinda funny and Cher... she's not bad to look at." And... Marvin wanted to add: she makes my face warm also, but Ryan would think it was from cooties.

Ryan rolled his eyes, stuck his tongue out, and made a vomiting sound. "Girls are gross." He crawled across the floor and sat against the couch.

Marvin knew it was unwise to say it but let it out anyway. "Not all girls."

"Yeah, all of them."

As if on cue, Linda came out of her room and walked down the hall toward them. Marvin noticed she had changed into sweatpants and a t-shirt. Probably what she slept in. He quickly focused on the television.

"What are ya watching?" she asked.

"None of your beeswax," Ryan replied.

She sat down on the couch behind her brother. "Why do you have to be so rude?"

"Why do you have to keep bugging us?"

"Who's bugging you, turd butt? Mom asked me to watch you."

"You don't have to watch me every five minutes."

"I'm not watching *you* right now, I'm watching television." She moved back on the couch pushing off Ryan's back with her foot.

"Stop it!" he whined as he tried to slap at her leg. "Get your cooties off me!"

"Better spray your back with cootie repellent!" Linda said in a mocking tone as she pushed him again with her foot and moved down the couch. "ABC Blackout!"

"Quit it!" Ryan said, tears welling up in his eyes.

Linda had moved behind Marvin. He could feel her knee brushing against his shoulder. "I'm not bothering you, am I, Marvin?"

"Not really."

"Are *you* afraid of cooties?" She leaned forward on the couch, her knee pressed into his shoulder. His instinct was to slide forward, but he didn't. She reached out and touched the curls on his head as if inspecting them. "Are you?"

Marvin looked over at Ryan and then back at the TV. He knew his alliances had shifted but he couldn't help it. The words just rolled out of his mouth. "No. I'm not afraid. I'm past all that kid stuff."

"That's good," she said. "You're not a pansy like Ryan, are you?"

Marvin shrugged. He felt it best to let it pass and keep silent but that peculiar effect Linda exuded pulled the answer from his lips. "No."

"That's good," she said.

Marvin could sense Ryan's attention turn from his sister and settle on him.

"Some friend you are," he said bitterly.

"What?" Marvin asked. "What did I do?"

"You did nothing," Linda replied, "He's upset because you see reason."

"I'm telling mom," Ryan said, tears ready to fall.

"Tell her what? That your maturity level is stunted? That you still wet the bed like a 3-year-old? That you're a little wuss? She knows it."

"Shut your face, Linda!" Ryan stood.

"Make me, you little baby."

"I'm telling mom about the cigarettes I found in the shed."

"Oh really? Well, big whoop!" Linda replied. "She already knows I smoke."

"I'll tell her what you and Steve Hablin are doing down in the basement when she's gone."

"Go ahead! Tell her. Like I care. If you knew half the crap *she* does when you're gone, you'd really cry."

Ryan walked to the front door."Come on Marv, let's go."

"Where do you think you're going?" She asked.

"Who cares?"

"Yeah? You better stay in here. I'm warning you!"

"You're not the boss of me." Ryan jerked open the door and pushed the storm door open and went outside.

Marvin sat for a moment waiting for the tension in the room to clear. To lift like the smoke from some fireworks. The presence of Linda's knee against his back retreated. An Alka Seltzer commercial came on. He waited until the ad folded into the next one. "I guess," he said, "I should go... out there. See what he's doing." He stood and glanced back at Linda. She stared straight ahead. The flickering images of the TV simmered in her eyes and bounced both of their shadows on the wall behind the couch. It was a commercial for shampoo. Her interest was now invested there. In what the announcer was saying. In how soft and manageable her hair could be.

It took a few blinks for his eyes to adjust to the dimness outside. The only assistance combating the dusk came from a porch light next door. A frosted glass globe housed a yellow light that warded off insects while it provided a golden glow to the lawn, bushes, and driveway. Ryan was not visible in the half-circle of amber light. Where could he have gone that quickly? Did he run somewhere?

Marvin walked down the driveway. He heard an odd sound; leaves rustling on a tree limb. It came from the large oak to the left in the opposing neighbor's yard. Neighbors that welcomed insects with a plain porch light. June bugs were crashing into it like jalopies at a demolition derby. Some missed it and pinged off the storm door and tin siding.

"Ryan?" Marvin called as he crossed the lawn toward the tree.

"What?" came an answer. The sound of his voice placed him about halfway up.

"What are you doing?"

"Climbing."

"Yeah," Marvin replied. "I could've guessed that."

"Ronnie said you can see South Center from this tree. When it gets dark, you can see the lights."

"Really? Can you see it?"

"Yeah," Ryan said. "I can see the lights of Famous Bar. You should climb up and look."

"That's all right. I'm going home now. It's getting late."

"Fine," Ryan replied. "Sure you don't want to look?" Another limb shook and a few dead limbs cracked, pieces fell through the leaves.

"No. I told my grandma I'd be home about now."

"OK."

"See you tomorrow?"

"I guess so."

As Marvin walked home he thought about Ryan in the tree and Linda on the couch. His face felt warm again. What Ryan had said about knowing what Linda was doing in the basement. What was it? What was she doing? Making out? Like those older kids at the Crest, slouched down in the dark in their seats. Linda smoked cigarettes too, like those kids in the restroom. Like Norb Stiebert. I bet Norb doesn't blush around girls. He probably makes out with them. Norb was Marvin's age. What would it be like to be friends with someone his age? Not a kid who climbs up a tree in anger. Someone who wasn't afraid of teachers, cops, or anyone. Who wore taps.

Summer's End (Get what I need and be done with it)

Marvin spent the subsequent summer days in a pool, on a bike, or in front of a television. Time spent with Ryan and Ronnie grew limited. They were obligated to attend various retreats and summer camps organized by Our Lady of Calvary and St. Gabriel The Archangel. When Marvin did see them, each had developed new interests; Ronnie wanted to stay inside and watch new shows he had been missing such as *Speed Racer* and *Ultra Man*. The family doctor diagnosed him with a laundry list of allergies, including pool chlorine so he resigned to stay inside, stay dry, and sneeze-free.

Ryan had met a kid his age on a retreat. This new friend lived in a nearby subdivision, and he spent the majority of his time there. Marvin took this as a sign that it was time to find new friends. To fill out the rest of the summer, he rode his bike, watched TV, listened to records, completed a few plastic models, and took Skippy for walks around the surrounding subdivisions. He saw Lauren a few riding her bike by herself; the sight of her caused no warm facial sensation nor did he feel awkward. He considered joining her but the urge would pass, he would smile, wave, and go back inside.

Toward the end of August, Marvin's new class information for 5th grade arrived in the mail. The long lazy hours filled with weekday TV game shows, afternoon daydreams, and bicycle meanderings were numbered. He would be in room 212 of Baymore Middle School and his teacher would be Mrs. Morrison.

"You'll need new notebooks and pencils, won't you?" Irene asked

as she placed a slice of meatloaf on his plate.

"Not yet. School doesn't start for a while."

"What?" Leonard looked up from peppering his corn. "I just talked to Frank Phegel this afternoon, he said all kids were starting back this week."

"They are," Marvin said. "They go to Catholic school. They always start earlier than us."

"Well, you know, your granddad has to run up to the Drug Store for his medicine. Why don't you ride along?"

Marvin took a bite and chewed. "Why?"

"The Variety store is right there. You can get what you need for school and be done with it. I'll give you some money."

"But I won't need that stuff for..."

"Marvin," Leonard interrupted, "why don't you do as your grandma says? Just ride with me, get what you need."

Marvin sighed and stabbed at a piece of meat.

"Maybe we'll stop by Velvet Creamery on the way back," Leonard said. "You can get a banana split or whatever you want. My treat."

When his grandfather offered a bonus destination as a reward for riding with him on an errand, it usually proved to be intriguing. A trip up to the auto parts store could include stopping by a tavern to shoot a game of pool. Going to the grocery store for pork chops could divert into a ride into the city, to visit the warehouse he managed. Marvin would get to drive the electric cart around the cavernous spaces filled with mountains of wooden crates. Later they would visit a barbecue place on the north side or stop for fried chicken at a hole-in-the-wall bar.

"Well, I wouldn't say no to a hot fudge sundae," Irene said. "What do you think, Marvin?"

He didn't want to say yes right away and appear too eager at the ice cream bribe which sealed the deal. He cut a few bites of the meatloaf with his fork, swirled one in a dab of ketchup, lifted it to his mouth, and said, "I guess... I can ride along. Get what I need and be done with it."

The Dime Store (I wanted the red one)

Morganfield Plaza was a strip of stores that branched out of the side of Shop-Rite Groceries like an arm that ended at Gerber's Pharmacy. Along the arm were a laundromat, a florist, a beauty parlor, a Variety Store, a Savings and Loan, and a barbershop. The stores were harbored by an awning-covered walkway that protected the shoppers from wind, rain, and snow. It reminded Marvin of a large front porch, similar to the Walton's house or the Ponderosa Ranch.

"I'll meet you back here at the car," Leonard said headed in the direction of the pharmacy. Marvin headed toward the white plastic sign with *5 to 10 Variety* embossed in red. He had squandered many hours in the aisles of the store when Irene poured detergent and coins into the machines at the laundromat or his mother sat under a dryer at the beauty parlor with a paperback.

In his early years, the toy aisle was his domain, specifically the space in front of the plastic model kits, and the GI Joe accessories—maybe a walk down the candy aisle--but on this visit, his attention was centered on school supplies in the *Stationary* aisle. He picked up a 3-ring binder, a package of college-ruled paper, a box of number-2 pencils, and a pink pearl eraser. With time to spare, he thought he'd look to see if there were any new model kits on the shelves. He had most of the Aurora monster kits: *The Mummy*, and *the Wolfman* but wanted *Forgotten Prisoner* and maybe the *69 Dodge Super Bee* or the *Chain Gang Chopper*.

Marvin pulled out a kit for the *Lost In Space Jupiter 2* when he heard a clicking sound just over the muzak. Some type of interference in the speakers? Is someone dropping marbles one at a time? He put the model back. He really wanted the *Lost in Space ROBOT* but they didn't have it.

The clicking grew louder. There was a scraping before the clicks. It was coming from a few aisles away. The sound was familiar; like someone wearing taps on their shoes. It could be anyone. Any kid who wanted to sound cool.

Marvin wasn't sure how long he had been looking at the model kits, or how long his grandfather would take at the drugstore, but it felt as if enough time had elapsed. He was ready to pay for his supplies so he walked down the aisle toward the front.

There were two people in the checkout line. Marvin figured there would be a few dollars left over from what he had and a few minutes to spare, so he headed to the candy aisle, grabbed the usual; licorice snaps and Indian Pumpkin seeds, and stepped back in line without losing his spot. The woman checking out had an issue, the slipcovers were supposed to be *on sale* but the tag was full price. The Muzak paused, and the manager was paged. The music came back on, it was *A Walk In The Black Forest*; one of his grandma's favorite songs. The canned store rendition was flattened by the overly orchestrated strings. The manager announced he was on his way. The line conversation drifted from the cost of slipcovers to; *wasn't it awful about those young kids up in Ohio back in May?* Blended within the talk about campus protests, the National Guard, the Black Forest, and the manager's apologies, a pair of shoes clicked up behind Marvin. He didn't turn around but kept his eyes on the flakes of dander that spotted the ladies' jacket in front of him. If he had a pen to connect the dots it may show a picture of *Kilroy*.

"Oh man, you got the red one. I wanted a red one."

Marvin turned around to see Norbert Stiebert holding a yellow binder, a package of paper, and a packet of pencils. "The red one?"

Norb lowered his head and a swath of hair fell in front of his face. He nodded toward what Marvin held and then jerked his head up which swung his hair back on top.

"Oh. My binder," Marvin said. "The red one."

"Yeah. All they had over there was yellow, black, and white ones left. I wanted a red one."

"Oh sure."

"Yeah, see man, I got some *STP* stickers, ya know? STP?"

"Yeah, I've seen those," Marvin said. "The stickers?"

"They would look cool on that red binder. Cause you know, it's got red with the white *STP* letters on it."

Marvin looked at the binder he held. "Yeah, that would look cool."

"It would look, *boss*." Norb flipped his hair back again. "Yellow is all right. I guess."

"Oh, you know what? It's not a big deal." Marvin held the red binder out to him. "Not to me. I don't care about the color, I just... I mean, we can trade if you want." He held it out. "Here. Take the red one."

"Are you sure, man?"

"Go ahead," Marvin said.

Norb took it. "Thanks." He handed Marvin the yellow binder. "Hey you know, you could put a *Pennzoil* sticker on that. That would look good. With the yellow background."

"Yeah." Marvin nodded and looked down at the floor. Brown tiles. He wanted to say something more to keep the inter-action going but nothing entered his mind. Norb opened the binder and snapped the rings a few times as if testing their dura-bility. A few seconds passed that seemed like minutes. A new song started. The one from *Dr. Zhivago*.

"You go to Baymore, right?" Marvin asked.

"Yeah."

"I've seen you there. In the halls."

The manager resolved the slipcover dilemma and the line moved up. Marvin studied the floor tiles again. Brown linoleum. Hundreds of scuff marks. Most of them were probably made by the manager running to the register. He looked at his yellow binder.

"I don't have a Pennzoil sticker," Marvin said, "but... I gotta *Dirt Bike* sticker. From the *Dirt Bike* magazine. It would look cool. It's yellow." Marvin said.

"Yeah?" Norb's eyes grew wide. He jerked his hair back again. "You gotta bike?"

"Yeah. Not a *real* dirt bike, it's just a minibike."

"Minibikes are cool. What kind?"

"Honda. A mini-trail."

"Yeah? Mini-trail?" He smiled. Marvin noticed that Norb's front teeth sat atop his bottom lip when he smiled. It's what his grandfather would call *buck teeth*. And the left one was chipped. "That's boss, man," he said. "My brother had a Ruttman Toad."

"Oh yeah?" Marvin tried to sound interested and not let on that he wasn't sure what a *Ruttman Toad* was.

"Yea. But our old man backed over it. Bent the frame. We also had a little Huskee," he said with a shrug, "but we blew up the motor."

"Young man," the cashier's voice beckoned. A considerable space between himself and the cashier had evolved. "Sorry." He moved forward, set his items down, and pulled out his wallet. A lady wearing--*Hello! I'm Jackie,* name tag-sorted through the purchases and clicked her nails across keys on the register. A torn movie ticket fell out as he pulled the cash from his wallet. Marvin picked it up and turned to show Norb; to further strengthen a connection between them--beyond being in the same store for school supplies, and the same grade at the same school, they also had been to the Crest on the same Friday night. He could mention that he had watched a cop escort Norb out just before the fireworks—but the space behind him was empty. Norbert Stiebert was no longer standing in line. No notice of him leaving. No, *see ya later. Thank you for the red binder.* No sound of taps walking away. He was gone.

Banana Split Boat (Mannix is coming on)

A good portion of Leonard's banana split had melted on the ride home. His full realization came when each spoonful left a vanilla trail on the kitchen table, pant leg, or shirt. "Son of a... beeswax! I need another napkin."

"Hold it over the table," Irene told him, "and then you won't make such a mess." She had a sundae, and even though it was topped with hot fudge, her ice cream was sturdy. Marvin had decided on bubble gum ice cream which still sat firmly in his wax paper cup.

"Why is mine melting?" Leonard asked as he aggressively wiped a spot on his shirt. "Only mine?"

"It's a little warm in here," Irene replied. "Maybe if we ran the air for a while."

"Nah. We don't need to run the air in the evening," Leonard said as he wiped the table. "Just run the attic fan. Marvin, go turn it on for a bit. Get some of this heat out."

He got up, went to the hall, and turned a dial on the wall just above the thermostat. A low roar emanated from above and a group of slats yawned open above Marvin's head. Late August air was pulled in from every opened window and crevice in the house, bringing with it the perfume of watered lawns and smoldering charcoal.

"Where's Marilyn?" Leonard asked. "It's almost six o'clock. She's usually home from work but now."

"I told you she had to stop to buy shoes."

Marvin sat back down and chewed heartily on the gum he had accumulated from his ice cream.

"Oh yeah." Leonard chopped at the banana with his spoon

which moved the small plastic dish—that resembled a boat—a few inches sideways.

"Watch what you're doing, Leonard, or you'll have that all over," Irene said and she pushed another supply of napkins toward him.

"I know what I'm doing." He tucked the extra napkins around his boat to hold it in place.

"How's yours, Marvin?" She asked.

He moved the wad of gum to the side of his mouth. "It's good. I think I'm going to save it. My jaw is getting sore from chewing and *Mannix* is coming on." He went to the refrigerator, opened the freezer, and set his cup inside. He rinsed his hands in the sink and then spit his gum into the trash can.

"You should have stuck yours in the freezer, Leonard," Irene told him. "Save it for later."

"I should have done a lot of things, but I didn't. I'll just sit here and clean up the mess."

Reruns, Taps, and Cigar Box (You must be looking for something)

It was an episode he had seen before. Joe and Peggy end up at a music club and she recognizes the criminal who happens to be sitting across the room. Mannix chases the guy outside. Gunfire erupts. Commercial comes on. Front door opens, Marvin turned to see his mother enter with a shopping bag.

"Welcome home. You missed melting ice cream and a mediocre rerun of Mannix."

"Oh well." She paused and searched her bag. "You can't win them all." She tossed a small package to Marvin. "There. I heard you've been asking for those. I saw them at the shoe store. The guy there said all the kids have been wanting them." He looked at the package; *Hi-Test Heel Plates.* Under the plastic were two small kidney-shaped objects and miniature nails.

"Oh wow! Thanks, Mom!" Marvin said.

"You're welcome."

HE GOT UP, went into his room, opened his closet, and considered his options. He didn't have motorcycle boots or waffle stompers--which would be perfect--he would have to use the loafers. He tucked them under his arm and went into the kitchen to search the junk drawer for tools.

"WHAT ARE YOU LOOKING FOR?" Leonard asked who was still sitting at the kitchen table sipping a can of beer. His banana split boat was now an ashtray as he tapped his cigarette over it.

"Nothing," Marvin replied.

"Well, you must be looking for something if you're rooting around in that mess. What are you looking for?"

"Something to put these things on my shoes."

"Put what things on?"

"These." Marvin held up the bag.

"What is it?"

"They're taps for his shoes," Marilyn said as she inspected leftover containers in the refrigerator.

"Taps?" Leonard squinted at the bag.

"Yes, Leonard. Taps," Irene replied. "We talked about the kids wearing them."

"We did?"

"Yes, you were sitting right there."

"If you say so," he said.

Marvin dug through balls of yarn, packets of sewing needles, coupon books, pencils, pens, toy cars, and old address books, but nothing useful for attaching taps to shoes.

"Do they have those tiny nails?" Leonard asked. "Best use a ball-peen on those. And you ain't going find one in there. I do have one in my toolbox. Out in the garage. You can use it if you put it back."

"Is this the chili from the other night?" Marilyn asked holding a faded cottage cheese container.

"That's the vegetable soup from Tuesday," Irene told her. "The chili is in that green Tupperware toward the back."

"The ball-peen has the round knob instead of the claw." Leonard dropped his cigarette into the boat and checked his shirt for errant ice cream drips. "But I'm sure you know that."

"Yeah," Marvin replied. "Thanks, grandpa."

<hr>

HE FLIPPED on the light in the garage. Skippy looked up from her bed which was an old chaise lounge peppered with quilts and blankets. "Hey Skip," Marvin said and walked over and scratched her head. "Sorry to wake you." He had pleaded with his grandparents--when he and his mother first came to stay--that they allow his dog to sleep inside. Leonard believed that the good Lord intended dogs to sleep outside. Only, these yapping rat-sized dogs needed to be inside because crows might carry them away. But regular dogs, like Skippy who was mostly Australian Sheppard, didn't need protection. She was the protector. She protected the home from threats outside—whatever they may be. After tears and turmoil, a compromise was reached. The attached garage could be Skippy's nighttime dwelling. She would be inside yet not all the way.

Marvin opened the toolbox on the workbench. The top tray of the Craftsmen was a hodgepodge of pliers, screwdrivers, pencils, fishing lures, matchbooks, and various-sized sockets for a wrench that was in some other drawer in some other place. He lifted the tray to inspect the lower compartment. More pliers, a few more screwdrivers, a claw hammer, and the round knob ball peen.

The surface of the workbench held a coat of sawdust from some project and a few spots where the sawdust had absorbed an oily substance from some other project. Marvin looked for something to clean off the surface to keep his shoes from getting dirty.

On the wall directly in front of him was a former kitchen cabinet mounted above the workbench. He opened it and found a stack of rags neatly folded on top of an old cigar box. He set the rags on the workbench and curiosity nudged and then asked him to open that cigar box to see what was inside. He did. More sockets, pencils, a few old Hot Wheel cars, and a packet of firecrackers.

"What the heck?" He picked up the packet. What were they doing in an old cigar box? It looked like there was about sixteen total, laced together, and still inside a plastic wrapper that was torn open at one end. Maybe they were left over from the 4th of July. The door opened and his grandfather leaned out.

"Did you find it?" Leonard asked.

"Yea. Got it." He dropped the firecrackers back into the toolbox. "It was right where you said it would be."

"Whatcha got there?"

"I saw this... old box in here. It has some of my old *Hot*

Wheel cars in there." He picked one up to show Leonard. "Ford Coupe."

"You don't still play with that stuff do you?"

"No," Marvin said. "Not anymore."

"You should hang around kids your own age."

"I would. There are no kids my age on this street." He dropped the car back in the cigar box, and shut the lid. "*Guys* that is. There are some girls around my age but..."

"Yeah," Leonard said. "There's nothing wrong with girls. They can get on your nerves sometimes. You'll find out."

"I suppose." Marvin picked up the hammer. "Found the hammer."

"If you need any help let me know."

"I will."

"Be careful of those little nails. They're bastards. If you drop one you'll never find it again."

"I'll be careful," he told him. Leonard closed the door and Marvin set about attaching the taps to his loafers. He laid the rags down and placed his shoes on top of them. He opened the package and focused on not dropping the tiny nails but all the while he couldn't stop thinking about the firecrackers in the cigar box. Why were they in there?

5th Grade, Rosa, and Lunch (Army men teetered)

The first couple of days of fifth grade were informal social forums; getting used to new faces, habits, and voices of classmates. A time for the teacher to pronounce everyone's name correctly. *It's Milstead. Not Milstone. Why is it so confusing?* Marvin wondered. *It's not even spelled that way.* A school district clerical error--never corrected--followed him for years. Stead not Stone.

Marvin waited until the 2nd week of fifth grade to introduce his tap-enhanced loafers to the floors of Baymore middle school.

A few other guys from other classrooms had also modified the heals of their footwear so, during normal excursions to the lunchroom or recess, it was difficult to tell who caused the *clicks* since there were so many of them. At times it sounded as if a poorly syncopated musical number had launched in the hallways.

The teacher, Mrs. Morrison was the first person to acknowledge Marvin's additional sounds. One day she had announced they would be watching a new *educational* program in the afternoons, PBS and the *Children's Television Workshop—who brought us Sesame Street* were premiering a new show called 'The Electric Company'. It was aimed at older students.

Murmurs and whispers of excitement spread across the classroom. *Watching TV? In class? At school? How cool is this?*

"Marvin, would you be so kind as to help me?" She pulled the large metal cart out of the corner which held an oversized box television bolted to the upper shelf. She pulled it toward the front of the room. "If you would please close the door and turn off the overhead lights?"

Sandra Wilbert who sat in front of Marvin turned around and winked. "Oh. Teacher's pet," she said with a smile.

In 4th grade, Marvin had a crush on Sandra. She had long brown hair and bangs that teetered just above her eyes causing her to blink more than unusual. She also wore go-go boots and brightly colored dresses. She reminded him of the girls on the show *Laugh-In*. He still liked her, but it was 5th grade now; time had moved on, and so did crushes.

He rose and walked down the row clicking as he moved toward the front of the class.

"What's that noise?" Mrs. Morrison asked as she angled the

TV. She rolled the cart back and forth a few times as she believed the metrical sound was produced by the cartwheels.

"It's Marvin's shoes, Mrs. Morrison," Stan Zellesky announced. "He's got taps on his shoes."

Her brow dropped down along with her head as looked toward him. "Marvin?" Do you have those *things* on your shoes?"

"Yeah," he replied. "I do. Sorry."

She uttered a sigh that carried a note of exasperation tucked inside. She blinked a few times and then said, "That's fine. I suppose it'll be like a production of *42nd Street* for a while until the next fad comes along. Maybe next year it will be... *spurs that jingle jangle jingle.* Anyway. Go ahead with what you were doing." She twisted the knob on the television and the room filled with the high pitch of the cathode-ray tube inside warming up.

Marvin flipped up the doorstop and pulled it closed. He reached up for the light switch and just before he flicked it off, he looked at the class as a final snapshot from his position in the corner of the room. Faces were excited that they were about to watch TV and whispered to each other, others stared out the window, some at the surfaces of their desks, some at the ceiling waiting for the dark, Sandra smiled and blinked under her bangs but what stole Marvin's attention was the girl in the third row from the right, second seat back, her name was Rosa Alhambra. If he wanted to apply his adolescent crush on someone new, it would go straight to Rosa. She was looking at him just as his finger touched the light switch. She smiled. He smiled back. He flipped the switch and the room went dark just before he blushed. Her face with the smile was the Polaroid image frozen in his eyes as walked back to his desk. His face felt warmer at that moment than any degree Linda Heffendorf ever made it rise to.

"WHAT'S HER NAME?" Denny Walters asked through a mouthful of cheese sandwich. Denny had been Marvin's lunchroom companion since the first grade; he sat across the table from Marvin on the first day and assumed the same spot every year thereafter. No one else wanted Denny at their table. He was short, thin, nervous, and wore thick glasses—similar to Lauren Phegel's but instead of making his eyes appear larger, they made his head look smaller. Kids called him *"Barney"* after the deputy on the *Andy Griffith Show* and often picked on him for a variety of reasons; he always carried a book with him wherever he went—*Hey Book Worm Barney!* And he rotated an endless collection of lunch boxes from *Voyage To The Bottom Of The Sea* to *Superman.* Today's selection was *Land Of The Giants.* Denny always positioned his lunch box upright so that the lid opened toward him and he had in effect a small tin barrier in which to sit behind. A tradition Denny carried from first grade was to pack two green army men in his lunch and he would place them on top of his lunch box to act as sentinels which would ward off spitballs and other projectiles.

Marvin felt sorry for Denny and let him assume a spot at this table.

"Rosa Alhambra," he told him in a soft tone. In case she was nearby, she wouldn't hear her name being spoken.

"Rosa Hammer?"

"No." Marvin cleared his throat to raise his volume a few degrees above the symphony of chatter, flatware jingling, lunch trays sliding, and exhaust fans rumbling. "*Rosa Alhambra.* I think she's new. I've never seen her before 5th Grade."

"*Alhambra?* Sounds like a Spanish name," Denny said. "Does she look Spanish?"

"What does Spanish look like?"

"I don't know. Sophia Lauren?"

"I think Sophia Lauren is Italian."

"Oh," Denny replied. "Who does Rosa look like?"

Marvin took a bite of his peanut butter and jelly and thought as he chewed. "Well, she has short brown hair. Brown eyes. Did you see the movie *True Grit?*"

"I'm not a fan of westerns."

"Oh."

Marvin took a sip of milk. Denny detecting a lull in the conversation opened his book and began reading. Marvin looked at the cover; it was called *Second Foundation.* There was a rocket ship on the cover. Denny always favored Science fiction-flavored stories. "You watch *Star Trek* right?"

"Of course."

"Remember where they beam down to a planet... that only had kids?"

"And the kids take over the Enterprise and summon Gorgan?"

"No. Not that one. The one where there's... some type of disease. When they get older they get sick and die."

"Oh yeah," Denny replied. "*Miri!* Bonk! Bonk!" He pounded the table with his fist. "Bonk! bonk! On the head!"

"Yeah, that one. You know the older girl? The one who liked Kirk?"

"Sure, that was Miri. The episode was called *Miri.*"

"Right. So the girl that played Miri, that's the same one from *True Grit.*"

"OK." Denny set his book down and peeled a piece of crust from his bread and tossed it in his mouth. "So, this Rosa looks like her?"

"A little bit. That type. But you know, only she's our age."

Denny peeled another strip of crust from his sandwich but it was tossed into his lunchbox. "If I had to pick someone from movies or TV... I would choose Miss Johnson from *Room 222*." He stuffed corn chips into his mouth. "I wish my teacher looked like her." Chip crumbs flew out as he spoke. "I used to like Penny Robinson." He pushed his glasses up. "More than Judy. I guess Penny is sort of that same type. The Miri type. So, where does Rosa sit?"

Marvin scanned the vast room which at the moment served as the cafeteria; the rest of the day--the tables disappeared into the walls--it became the gymnasium. "I don't see her. She's probably at a table on the other side. "

Marvin watched Denny stuff more chips into his mouth as he looked at his book, ready to pick it back up. "Let me ask you something when you think Miss Johnson and Penny Robinson... or any girl, you don't worry about... you know, cooties? "

Denny chewed frantically so he could clear the way for a laugh. "Cooties? Are you serious? I stopped that nonsense when I was five."

"Right, that's what I thought," Marvin said. "How about this... does your face ever feel warm when... you're around certain girls?"

"Are you referring to embarrassment?"

"Well, it's like that... but you haven't done anything stupid. All you did was, you know, look at them."

"That sounds like the early stages of puberty."

"Oh," Marvin said. "Right."

"Remember those films we had to watch last year? They had all the boys in one room and girls in the other?"

"I remember," Marvin said. "But I don't remember the part where they talked about our faces getting warm. Just stuff about our voices getting deeper and other things."

"It's all part of the process, Marvin. From a caterpillar to *Mothra!*" He laughed again and shook the table. The army men on his lunch box teetered.

"Thanks. I just wondered," Marvin said.

Denny picked his book back up and Marvin took a glance around at the faces that hovered above lunch trays, paper bags, and lunch boxes. His eyes connected with a familiar profile three tables away. It was Norbert. He had looked for Norb when school started but didn't see him. Not in the hallways, not at lunch, or recess. Maybe he had moved away, went to a different school, or was sent to a military academy. But no, he was about twenty feet away, sitting at a table by himself.

"So, are you going to talk to this girl?"

Marvin shrugged. "I don't know. I mean, I don't know anything about her."

"You know her name."

"I know a lot of girls' names."

"And you said she smiled at you. That's something." Denny pulled a stack of Hydrox cookies from his lunch box. "Do you want one?"

The last of Denny's social crimes was his cookie consumption, specifically, his lack of facial hygiene. Remnants of cookies could be spotted on his lips, teeth, and chin. *Hey Barney! Hey Cookie Monster! How's the Hydrox? Did any make it into your mouth?*

"No, thanks," Marvin replied. Denny always asked if he wanted a cookie and Marvin always declined. A lunchtime tradition since first grade. Denny resumed reading.

Marvin looked across the room again at Norb. He wondered why no one sat with him. He was one of the cool kids. He knew why no one sat at their table. "I think Raquel Welch is Spanish," Denny said looking up from his book. "I heard that on the *Mike Douglas show*." He took another bite of the cookie. Marvin could see the chocolate residue forming between Denny's teeth and the crumbs lines on his lips and chin. It was almost like watching Leonard and his banana split.

"Excuse me, I'm going to go throw some stuff away," Marvin said and stood. "I'll look around. If I see her, I'll let you know."

"Sure." Denny pushed his glasses up. "You didn't finish your sandwich."

"Right," Marvin replied, "I know."

"OK."

MARVIN MADE his way across the cafeteria and tossed his napkin toward the large bin with a *Pitch In* sticker. It landed on the floor. He sighed. He glanced around the foreign side of the lunchroom. It was mostly kids in the higher grades. He spotted Rosa among a group of Sixth-grade girls sitting at the last table on the 3-point line. He hoped Rosa didn't spot him sitting with the Bookworm Barney the Cookie Monster or standing here by the trash cans.

Marvin turned and headed back. He veered off his return path and glided toward the table where Norb sat. He arrived and stood for what seemed like days before he thought of something to say.

"You were right about the Yellow folder. My *Dirt Bike* stickers looked good on it," Marvin said.

Norb raised one eyebrow and looked up. "Yellow folder?"

Marvin swallowed. "Yeah. Folder. Yellow folder. It was a while ago. At the Variety store. Morganfield plaza. I had a red one... folder. You asked me to trade. You had *STP* stickers."

"Right." Norb smiled. "You're the kid with the Mini-trail."

"Yeah. That's me. I haven't found any Pennzoil stickers yet. For my folder. The yellow one."

"You should try *Krause's Auto*, up on Gravier road. They got a whole box of stickers."

"Really? Thanks. I'll look there."

Norb wadded up the brown paper bag that presumably held his lunch. "What's your name?"

"Marvin."

"Marvin?" Norb closed one eye while he looked at him as if sizing him up. "Like Lee Marvin?"

"Right. Monte Walsh. Major Reisman."

He opened his eye and smiled. "I'm Norb."

"Yeah, I know," Marvin said. "I heard Mrs. Pedrodski yell your name during the fire drill last year."

"Oh right. Yeah. Hey, you know she took my Uncle's Zippo lighter. It was engraved."

"Oh no. I think I remember that. I saw her."

"It was a cool lighter. It had this thing on it that said, *Fighter by day, lover by night, drunkard by choice, Marine by mistake.* They didn't want to give it back till the school year was over. My uncle got so mad, he came up here and cussed them out." Norb's voice rose in volume as he told the story. Marvin looked around and saw it was drawing attention from nearby tables.

"Did they give it back?"

"They had to. He's a Marine," Norb said as crumbled his lunch bag into a ball and tossed it overhand; it landed on a table in the middle of surprised luncheoners ten feet away. "Hey, Lee Marvin, you know what you should do?"

"No," Marvin replied. "What?"

"You should bring that mini trail over to my house. We gotta boss trail in the backyard. It goes around the garage and along our fence."

"Yeah? That sounds cool."

"It is. Sometimes the neighbors call the cops because of the noise, but most of the time, it's cool. Did you see the movie *On Any Sunday?*"

"Yes, I did."

"That's what my house is like. Like that movie with motorcycles flying all around. It's boss."

"Sure." Marvin looked over toward his table. Denny was still munching on Hydrox with his face inside his book. He looked toward Rosa's area. He wondered if she saw him here talking to Norb. "So," Marvin said, "what teacher do you have this year?"

"Ah. I got Pedrodski again."

"Mrs. Pedrodski? Isn't she fourth grade?"

"Yeah. See, it's a probation thing." Norb jerked his head to flip his hair up out of his face. "They wanted to hold me back a year. I missed too much. Said if my grades and my behavior improve, then they'll let me move up to fifth."

"Oh," Marvin said. "That's good."

"Who'd you got?"

"Mrs. Morrison. She's cool. We get to watch TV in class."

"Cool," Norb said, he jerked his head again. "Are there any cute girls in there?"

"No. Not at all."

Walking With Linda (S.E.N.O)

For a change from his usual route home after school, Marvin walked down the breezeway between the junior and senior high buildings instead of the traditionally traveled sidewalk--which was a four-block-straight-shot home, he opted to take the long way home. Behind the high school, next to the athletic fields, there was short cut; a dirt path through a small overgrown lot that dumped all travelers into a newly developed subdivision next to the Baymore boundaries.

The high school ended its academic day thirty minutes before the middle school day ended, so Marvin could ease through the demilitarized upperclassmen zone with slim chances of interaction.

He followed the blacktop until it dropped off into gravel and grass and had just cleared the left-field bleachers when he detected the smell of cigarette smoke. An odor his father and grandparents had raised him to recognize and endure. This particular aroma was a blend of both regular and menthol which meant more than one person. Probably some high schoolers loitering behind the shadows of the gymnasium. Marvin dropped his head and walked faster until a familiar voice halted his stride and arrested his path through the gauntlet.

"Hey little boy, do you want some candy?"

Marvin lifted his head and turned toward the movement in the corner of his eye. Linda Heffendorf stepped forward from a group of girls cloaked in strips of light under the right-field bleachers. He almost didn't recognize her at first. She looked different, and older, and... Marvin couldn't tell what it was. She appeared foreign in this environment outside of her place as Ryan's sister. She had on bell-bottom jeans with flower patches and a puffy white shirt that almost covered her stomach. She had a beaded macramé strap over her shoulder that held a small purse. She wore make-up and now her eyes didn't look so big, the acne was covered and her hair was shiny. Linda looked nothing like the plain-looking girl in baggy shorts and bathrobes from the Heffendorf house. She resembled Cher he thought. His face felt warm. Again.

"Are you walking home?" She asked.

"Yeah. I am. I was just... going the back way, you know."

"Me too." She said with a smile.

"Hey, Heffa-lump!" One of the bleacher girls said with a sing-song tone. "Who's your little friend?"

"Yeah." Chimed in another girl blowing smoke up through benches. "He ain't a narc is he?"

"Nah, he's cool," Linda announced. "He's my brother's friend." She flicked her cigarette away, picked up her books from the ground, and walked over to Marvin. She leaned in close; her long hair and breath of tobacco brushed against his face. "You're not telling anyone, right?"

"No. No way," he said. "Those were just candy cigarettes, right?"

"Yeah." She laughed. "That's right. Just candy." Linda smiled and nudged his arm. "Come on. I'll walk with you. We're going the same way." She turned and held up her middle finger toward the girls. "See you later, losers."

"Watch out little boy," one of the girls yelled. "She'll chew you up and spit you out."

"Ignore them," Linda told him as they walked up the steep hill behind the first base dugout and along the path beside the gym. They came to the common ground which was the no man's land between the school grounds and the residential grounds. Linda stopped at the mouth of the dirt path that lead up a slight hill through a small patch of weeds.

"Here," Linda said as she handed Marvin her books, "you carry these." She kicked off her shoes, picked them up, and stuck them under her arm. "Much better!"

Marvin noticed her toenails were bright red similar to the color his face must be. He turned his attention to the books; her binder was white and decorated with orange and yellow Day-Glo flowers. There was a peace symbol sticker—not a motor oil sticker—right in the middle. She had a paperback called *Go Ask Alice,* and a battered copy of *Earth Science.* He blended her books with his yellow binder and his *US History and Me* textbook.

"Shall we?" Linda asked as she began walking up the trail. Marvin followed her lead since the path only allowed a single-file procession. Normally he had one hand free to rake through the spindly grass as he walked this path but today didn't want to drop anything or manifest the awkwardness he felt. But if the truth be told, this day was turning out quite well. He had talked to Norb Stiebert at lunch, got a smile from Rosa Alhambra, and now was walking home with Linda Heffendorf. His confidence was growing like the weeds that surrounded him. Still, he didn't want to drop the books he was responsible for.

"So," Linda said, "what's the buzz, Milstead? What's been happening?"

"Oh, you know. Different things."

"Yeah? Different things are good," she said.

Yes, Marvin thought. Different things are good. "I didn't know you went to Baymore."

"Sure. Calvary only goes to eighth grade. I mean, if you have rich parents that will pay for you to go to Notre Dame or Visitation Academy, you know...peace be with you. If not, if you're the less fortunate, a one-poor-parent home, then the public schools... be with you. Which is fine. I prefer jeans over plaid skirts."

Marvin looked around to see if anyone was witness to this 10-year-old walking with a 14-year-old. No luck.

"So... what grade are you in now?" Linda asked.

"Fifth."

"Any cute girls in your class?"

Marvin considered his answer. This had already come up once today. "Yeah. A few."

"Really? Who?"

"You wouldn't know her. She's new."

"What's her name?"

"Rosa."

"Rosa? That's a cool name," Linda smiled and nudged Marvin with her elbow. "Have you asked her out?"

"No. Not yet."

"I bet you haven't even talked to her, have you?"

"Well..."

"Come on Milford. Tell me the truth."

"No, I haven't yet. I will."

They emerged from the weeds and were on the part of the path surrounded by regular grass.

"Well, you'd better." She reached into her purse and pulled out a pack of gum. She tore open a stick and put it in her mouth and chewed. "You want a piece?" She held out the pack of gum.

"Sure." He took a stick. "Thanks." He stuck it in his pocket.

"You know," Linda said, "even though school is not my favorite place, the one benefit... is that it's nice to be people your own age. You know?"

The dirt trail ended and they stepped out onto the fresh white concrete street.

"Old people are weird," Linda said. "Parents, you know." She opened her arm and dropped her shoes onto the pavement —they bounced around and settled. "And little kids are a pain. It's like... you need that middle area, you know? So, like... being around your own tribe is good. It's cool. The good thing about school."

"Ha! Cool school. You're a poet and you didn't know it."

Linda laughed as used her foot to upright her shoes and stepped into them. "It's like... there's no one on our street, our little Cancel drive. I mean, all you have is the little squirts like my brother." She leaned on Marvin to ease the shoes up over her heel. "And I have... well, *nobody*." She formed an overly exaggerated frown and then shrugged. "Well, there's Steve Hablin, but he's a jerk."

A jerk you spend time with in your basement, Marvin wanted to add but shook his head in agreement.

"You know what I mean, don't you?"

"Oh yeah," Marvin replied. "I got other friends. From school. A new friend my age. He's cool."

"Yeah? A *cool* kid?" She said with a smirk as she slipped on her other shoe.

"Oh yeah. Very cool."

"How cool?" she asked.

"Well, so... we were at the Crest one Friday night and he got thrown out by the cops."

"What?" Linda laughed. "You were at the Crest on a Friday night? And you were thrown out by the cops?"

"Oh no! Not me. My friend was," he said. "Well, it was before we were friends. But we are now. I'm going to his house to ride mini-bikes."

"Are you?" She reached out and rubbed his head. "Come on Steve McQueen," she said as she walked down the street. Marvin assumed a position next to her since there was room now. She stopped after a short distance and turned toward him. Was he walking too close? She looked down at his shoes. "What is *that*? Do you have taps on your heels?"

"Oh, that. Yeah. I do."

"You're full of surprises aren't you Milstead?" Linda winked, held her head back, and studied the sky as they walked in silence for a while. Marvin looked around the new neighborhood which had been a field of nothing many years ago when they moved here. The larger parent of the small field just traveled from the school. Most of the houses were complete. The area smelled like freshly cut wood. Some homes had grass that passed for lawns while others were trying with blankets of straw. No one had bushes or trees yet and that made the sky that Linda studied look very large overhead.

Gray clouds faded in over the powder blue background. A *coming attraction preview* of what the fall feature presentation would be. It was probably going to rain later today. A gust of cool wind came down the street that held a scent of rain. *I knew it*, he thought. Irene always claimed that she could predict rain based on the number of curls on Marvin's head. More curls meant more rain. Another puff of wind passed and he noticed that the cigarette odor had faded from Linda. Being this close he could detect something else besides her minty gum; a perfume or maybe the shampoo she used. On TV shows and in the movies, this would be where the guy would say; *You smell nice.* But he wasn't Mannix or Lee Marvin. It would sound like a joke coming from him. At that moment Linda laughed as if she knew what he had thought. "You know what I just imagined?"

"No," Marvin said. "What did you imagine?" *It couldn't be as funny as what I just imagined.*

Linda put her arm around his shoulder. The sudden physical contact overwhelmed his senses but his face did not feel warm. He must be getting used to it.

"I thought about you and this new, cool friend you told me about," Linda said, "I just imagined a TV show... like the *Brady Bunch*," she giggled. "You know... where the kid dumps his boring old friends to go hang out with the new *cool* kid. And then, realizes this new kid's not that cool. And then, in the end, he's back with his old boring friends and says '*I'm ever so sorry guys. I was wrong to leave you. Please be my friends again.*' You know, that story."

Marvin laughed. "I know that one."

Linda blinked a few times and took on a serious expression. "Isn't weird how we compare everything to stupid TV shows." She sighed. "Life's not like that."

"Yeah," Marvin replied. "It's not."

"Not all the time. Sometimes maybe." She took her arm down and started walking. "Let's go."

They were a block away from their street. A street filled with older homes and full lawns dotted with bushes and tall trees that blocked the sky, "There it is," Linda held out her hand. "I'll take it from here. I'm not going home yet. I'm going to my friend's house."

Marvin handed over her books. He stole a glance at her exposed stomach. She had one of those belly buttons that looked like an eye frozen in a wink. He looked away.

"Thanks for carrying my books," Linda said. "And the company."

"It was fun," Marvin said.

"And hey, if it doesn't work out with your new cool friend. You should come over. We can listen to record and watch TV."

"Sure." That suggestion made his face feel slightly warm. He looked down. He wasn't used to it yet.

"Or maybe..." she said holding the silence until he looked up. She raised one eyebrow. "Maybe... I'll see you at the Crest some Friday. I can give you cooties." She winked. He knew his face was fully flush now. If that had been Linda's goal, she succeeded. She turned and walked away.

Marvin focused his field of view straight ahead—at the white sign that occupied a place on the street pole. The *S.E.N.O* sign. A warning of what was to come. **Street Ends No Outlet**.

Marvin smiled. He thought if he ever wrote a story about his life, that would be the title. It sounded odd but it would fit. He knew there was always a shortcut to someplace. There was always an outlet.

Saturday Bike Ride (Box of stickers)

The Saturday morning cartoons were lifeless and flat. Marvin's attention wasn't held anymore. *The Electric Company* he watched in class was better than the stuff he used to find entertaining. He turned off the television and went outside. The rain had stopped overnight, the sun was out and everything seemed brighter than normal. The cedar trees and pfitzer juniper bushes in the front yard had relished the late September shower and were permeating the air with their fragrances.

The first stop was the Phegel house. Ronnie was watching *The Banana Splits* and would be out when it was over. Marvin considered walking down to Ryan's but some older kids had a game of fuzzball operating in the circle at the end of the street. Marvin felt that skirting their territory could induce ribbing and raillery—best to avoid it for now; especially since Steve Hablin and his brothers were there. No need to invite taunts from that lot. He drifted home, lifted the garage door, and went inside.

A moving blanket was draped over his Honda mini-trail. He could lift the blanket off, fill the gas tank, and putter up and down the driveway, but that was only 20 feet of unsatisfactory oscillation. His grandfather had warned him; *If the cops catch you on the street they'll lock you up in the hoosegow.* He couldn't confirm his grandfather's legal advice but didn't want to test it.

His bicycle would have to do today, he wheeled it out, pulled the door down, and pedaled away. He decided to head north toward Gravier road; he could see what movie posters were in the *Coming Soon* display case at *The Crest* and then visit *Krause's Auto* to see what stickers they had. The sound-track in his head for this ride was *Long Lonesome Highway.*

MARVIN NAVIGATED the suburban side streets taking care to avoid the puddles, branches, and other items that littered the roads. Residents were eager to remove the leaves from their lawns brought down from the rain. Some found it fun to imagine their leaf rakes were 9 irons and they could loft sweet-gum balls and acorns into the streets for car tires to destroy and kids on bicycles to dodge.

He reached the top of the street where two parallel roads curved around like a horseshoe and merged into a court. That court squirted out a small drive that lead to the major thoroughfare called Gravier. The worn gray pavement of the avenue sprouted deep into the city and ran far out into the rural counties. Marvin rode up on the sidewalk and paused under a large sycamore tree whose roots had urged a slab of concrete walk 10 degrees higher than the others. He watched the cars, trucks, and buses move by, some headed east, and some went west. To his left about 4 blocks was The Crest; he turned his bike and went west.

The Cowboys with John Wayne as the featured poster in the Now Playing display case. Coming Attractions had *Escape From The Planet of the Apes*. They were bringing that one back Marvin thought since the new one, *Conquest Of The Planet Of The Apes* was due out soon. He coasted down to the next display case; *Dracula A.D. 1972* was starting in a week—no Bruce Lee, only Christopher Lee—that was OK. He was the best Dracula by far.

MARVIN TURNED his bike east and rode down the sidewalk. A long-haired guy with a cowboy hat stood in front of the billiard hall and flashed a peace sign as he rode by. Music and smoke leaked out of the door as the cowboy went inside. Marvin had been in there years ago when Leonard brought him there to teach him the fundamentals of pool. While waiting for a table to open a fight had broken out so they left.

He glided behind a row of cars that were waiting at the edge of Krause's lot; past the double garage bays, and deployed his kickstand in front, under a large plate glass window papered with oil change specials and state inspection licenses. The smell of grease, oil, and cigarettes greeted him like an invisible welcome a foot from the entrance. The office was small. On one side sat two vinyl chairs with black burn marks on the green arms, a double-headed vending machine with gumballs on the left, and peanuts on the right. Next to the front window was a soda machine a *correct change only* sign, and under the window, a tiny table with magazines that had been orphaned from a spot in front of the chairs and never put back. On the other side, next to the doorway to the garage was a small desk with a small lady wearing a Cardinals baseball cap; her fingers tapping away on an adding machine. She looked up when Marvin walked in.

"Can I help you, kid?" She asked as she dropped her cigarette into the rubber tire ashtray. The surface of her desk was several inches thick white and pink service slips peppered with ashes.

"Yeah, a friend of mine said you have stickers... a box of stickers... like STP and oil stuff?"

She nodded toward the shelves on the back wall stocked with cans and boxes. "In that *Esso* box there... under that rack of wiper blades. Help yourself. Take what you want."

"Thanks." Marvin went to the box, and pulled it forward to allow the fluorescent light in as he peered inside. He found a few *Union 76*, *Dunlop*, *Castrol*, and *Valvoline*. No *STP* or *Pennzoil*.

"You might have slim pickings there sugar," the lady said. "One of them neighborhood kids was in here earlier and grabbed a bunch up."

"Oh. Ok."

"That Stiebelt kid. He's always in here."

"Stiebert?" Marvin asked.

"How's that?"

"His name. Was it Stiebert?"

"Yeah," she replied picking her cigarette up. "That's it. *Stiebert*. Ya know him? He's about your age."

"I know Norbert. Is that the one?"

"Could be. There's a few of 'em come in here. This one rides that damn mini-bike up here." She exhaled a plume of smoke up toward the cloud that hovered at the ceiling. "Dangerous if ya ask me."

"That sounds like him," Marvin told her. "I'll just take this *Castrol* sticker."

"That's fine. Take what you want. Saves me from pitchin' em."

"Thanks."

"Anytime," she replied.

He tucked the sticker in his pocket and walked outside to his bike. He imagined he would bring the smoky oil smell back home with him as well. A souvenir of his journey away from home, away from Cancel drive, just like the guy in *Then Came Bronson* traveling the roads on his Harley. But Marvin was on a purple Sears Spyder bike. He smiled and watched the traffic go by.

School Lunch (My cool new friend)

The following Monday in class, Marvin looked a few times across the room at Rosa but her attention was consumed by Tammy Baylor. Tammy was the class gossip and she sat across the aisle from Rosa. Tammy's nickname was *motor mouth* and her engine had been running laps all day.

Mrs. Morrison wrapped up her verb conjugation lesson and looked at the clock. It was an hour before lunch and a few minutes before the broadcast time of *The Electric Company*.

"Tammy, for the last time," Mrs. Morrison raised the tone of her voice, "unless you're giving life-saving instructions to your neighbor, could you please stop talking? You can palaver all you want..."

"I can what?"

"...*palaver*, chit chat, chatter... talk all you want at lunch or after school but here and now, in my class... zip the lip."

"Yes, ma'am," Tammy replied with an eye roll.

"Marvin? Door. Lights." His cue from Mrs. Morrison as the designated door closer and technician of light switches. Sandra smiled and wrinkled her nose at him as he rose from his desk and clicked up the aisle—she didn't whisper *teacher's pet* anymore, she let her grin speak for her. He flipped up the door stop and turned back to the room. He reached up for the light switch and shot a sideways glance at Rosa. She appeared to be watching him but Tammy was whispering to her; there was no smile this time. She was probably distracted. Or maybe the novelty was done. So, some curly-headed kid with taps gets to shut the door and turn off the lights. *So what? Big deal.*

A moment before he turned the lights off, he smiled at her and flashed the peace sign. She smiled. Billiard cowboy would have been proud.

It was pizza day and Marvin had brought lunch money and waited in line holding a tan fiberglass tray that had probably started life as brown but years of scalding had faded. He could see Denny Walters at the usual table, his lunch box propped up with the plastic green guardians at their posts. Why should he continue the tradition of sitting there watching Denny read a book? He should sit at Norb's table. If the only reason he sat with Denny is that he felt sorry that him, that wasn't much of a reason. Marvin had an inherent draw toward the underdogs. Ronnie and Ryan were the youngest kids on the block and the target of teasing. Marvin felt sorry for them.

"Pepperoni or Cheese?" a voice asked.

"Pepperoni," Marvin replied.

What if he sat at Norb's table today and let Denny catch up on his reading and enjoy his Hydrox, why not? Different things are good.

Norb was at his usual spot. He held what appeared to be a sad drooping sandwich in his hand. As Marvin got closer he could see a half-moon of baloney dangling under bread saturated with ketchup. The top portion of the sandwich had curled over his Norb's fingers.

"Is it all right to sit here?" Marvin asked.

Norb shrugged. "It's a free country, man."

Marvin put his tray down and pulled back the chair. "Thanks."

Norb studied the lunch tray and grinned. "Look at Lee Marvin's fancy lunch." He dropped his sandwich on the brown paper bag. "Pizza! Mama Mia! That'sa some nice-a lunch-a you gotta there! With the nice golden corn. Ho! Ho! Ho! Green Giant and... what's that mess?"

"That's Peach Cobbler."

"Looks like *snot* cobbler!" Norm wiped the ketchup from his fingers on the tabletop, leaving shiny red skid marks. He picked his sandwich up but only the bologna and half of the bread made the journey. The rest remained as pulp on the bag.

"You want part of my pizza?" Marvin asked him.

"Nah," Norb said. "I don't want anything that comes from this place. They only serve altar boys here."

"Alter boys? What do you mean?"

"They only serve fish on Fridays here. Try to ask for something else and they slap some peanut butter on stale bread. Here ya go! The rest is Alter boy food. Or as my old man calls 'em, *mackerel snappers.*"

"I never thought about it."

"The name of this school ain't *Saint* Baymore is it?"

"No," said Marvin.

"They can't make you wear uniforms here so they gotta get you someway." Norb flipped his hair back and took a bite. A glob of ketchup plopped on the table.

Marvin shrugged and looked around, opened his milk carton, and took a drink.

"I rode my bike up to Krause's Auto on Saturday," he told him. "They didn't have many stickers in the box."

"Luck of the draw."

"I guess," Marvin replied. "The lady who works there said you had been there. She said you rode your minibike up there."

"Yeah. I was there." Norb stared at the pizza as Marvin took a bite. The cheese was still hot. It didn't scald the roof of his mouth but he had to breathe in and out to cool it down before he began an awkward open-mouth chewing to prevent burns.

"I'd like to see that mini-trail you got," Norb said. "Where do you live?"

He had the temperature regulated to normal and was able to swallow. "Not too far from here. A few blocks down Baymore road. Do you know where Fairman street is?"

"Yeah."

"I live at the bottom of the hill. Candle Drive. It's the cul-de-sac."

"The what sack?"

"It's a street with a circle at the end."

"I know where that is. Steve Hablin and his brothers live over there."

Marvin nodded, took another bite, and sucked some air into his mouth for cooling purposes.

"I live on Rosedale," Norb said.

"Really? I rode my bike near there on Saturday."

"Yeah? You should ride your minibike over," Norb said as he gave up on the sandwich and dropped it on the bag. "Ya know, like after school... ya should go home, get it, and ride it over. We gotta trail out back."

Marvin considered the likelihood. It was not very likely at all. It would never happen. He did not let his face indicate the embarrassment that his minibike would not leave the driveway. House rules. There were a few he had broken and some he had bent. He only had taps on his shoes, no Zippos for the fire drill, or cigarettes for the bathroom. What he needed was to drive the conversation in a different direction. "Yeah, so... on Saturday, I rode over to the Crest to see what was coming. I saw that they're bringing the last *Planet of the Apes* movie back."

"I wish they would bring back *Billy Jack*. That was a boss movie. That guy could kick some ass."

"Do you like Bruce Lee?"

"He's OK," Norb said. "I'll tell ya who I really like and that's Elvis. Love his movies. He's always kissing some chick or punching some guy. Ya know, *real flippy*."

Minibike was cleared, for now, Marvin thought. "You know, I saw you at the Crest one time," he said. "It was a Friday night. *The Abominable Dr.Phibes* was playing."

"Oh yeah. He's from here you know," Norb said. "That Price guy. My dad did work on one of his cars."

"Really? Joe from the Three Stooges is from here too."

"I hate Joe," Norb said. "He acts like a pansy."

Marvin stirred the corn with a fork. "Yeah, Curly is the best one." He took a bite; the corn tasted like the can it came from. "So, anyway, yeah... at the Crest, I saw you there. And I saw that cop pull you out of the bathroom."

"Yeah?" Norb smiled. "I remember that."

"That was the night somebody set off firecrackers."

"Ah! I heard about that!" Norb smiled and flipped his hair. "What a drag that I missed the whole thing. Man!"

"It was really loud. Girls screamed. People were running around. A madhouse!"

Norb studied Marvin for a moment. "Let me ask you something Milstead, did you ever do get into trouble? Do anything... you know, wrong? Anything bad?"

"Bad?" Marvin thought for a moment. "What do you mean?"

"Just what I said. Did'ya ever get in trouble?"

Marvin thought for a moment. "Well, one time in third grade, we went on a field trip to the Science center. Mrs. Francis told us to stay with our groups, you know. Don't go wandering off."

"And you wandered off?"

"Well, some of the kids went into the woods next to the big dinosaur statues. Not sure why and I sort of... went with them, you know, to see... and we all got in trouble. We had to sit on the bus the rest of the day because we didn't listen."

"Wow," Norb said with a laugh. "You're a big time delinquent."

"Not really," he replied. "I just don't pay attention."

"Well, you got potential," Norb said. "Man, I wished I could've seen the firecrackers going off." Norb wadded up his lunch bag, ketchup and all. "Ya know, I think *that* would be fun to do, you know? I mean, really great."

Marvin delayed his response by drinking his milk. "Mm-hm."

"I wish I knew where I could get some, you know? Firecrackers, I mean," Norb said. "That would be flippy."

Marvin looked around the cafeteria. A girl that looked like Linda Heffendorf walked by but he knew it couldn't be—she was in the Junior high across the street. If it had been Linda, Marvin could have said, *"Hey Linda, this is Norb Stiebert. My cool new friend I told you about."*

"The one from that TV episode that you ditch your old friends for?"

"Yes. That's the one!"

"How cool, Marvin."

Marvin looked over at Denny Walters. Denny held his cookie up as he tried to turn the page of his book but dropped it —the Hydrox rolled across the table like a tiny cake wheel and plunged off the other side onto the chair where he usually sat. Denny stared for a moment at the vacant spot perhaps in consideration of retrieving the treat that got away. Instead, he placed his finger inside his nostril. Marvin turned back around to Norb. "I uh... know where you can get some."

"Some what?"

"Firecrackers."

"You do?"

"Yes, I have some," Marvin said.

"You do?" Norb smiled. "Out of sight! Well, partner old pal, you know what that means? We got some plannin' to do my friend."

Marvin took a bite of pizza. It was still hot.

THE REST of the day at school felt like that movie he went to see with Ryan and Ronnie a few summers back; *2001 Space Odyssey*. It seemed like a good movie but they had no idea what happened. It had apes, spaceships, and a moon base but they weren't sure about anything else.

Norb had formulated a plan, it seem like a good plan, but Marvin had no idea how it happened. After he said he could get firecrackers; it set off a series of instructions: in one week, Friday night, they would meet outside the men's room at the Crest. Marvin would bring the firecrackers and 1) they would deploy to the far back right aisle under the cover of a darkened auditorium, 2)ignite the implements of noise, 3)*Run*. Result would be the coolest thing ever just like *Bridge On The River Kwai*. Failure to bring the firecrackers and follow the plan would brand him a chicken and a wuss. Both.

"Don't be a chicken wuss," Norb said. "After all, you're Lee Marvin, right?"

"Yeah, that's me."

MRS. MORRISON TOLD the class about *Mariner 9*. It was a spacecraft launched by NASA and it was now orbiting Mars and mapping the surface. Marvin leaned forward and whispered to Sandra, "I wonder if they'll find the large black thing from *2001*?" She giggled. "Or maybe... the Statue of Liberty, surrounded by gorillas on horseback." Sandra giggled again. Marvin suppressed his laugh.

"Something funny Mr. Milstead?"

"What?"

"I said, is there something funny? Something you find amusing about space exploration?"

Marvin thought for a moment. He could say out loud everything he just silently thought and he might get a few laughs, even Mrs. Morrison might chuckle about the Statue of Liberty. "No, ma'am."

"Were you paying attention?"

"Yes."

"What was the last thing I said?"

"You said that the Soviets also launched a spacecraft that would be orbiting mars."

Mrs. Morrison blinked a few times. "So, let's try to pay attention then shall we, class?"

Marvin wanted to say that *he was paying attention. How else could he know what she said? He just repeated the last thing she said. Right?* "Yes, ma'am," he replied.

He wasn't sure what made him want to answer her in that manner. What his grandmother called *talking back, being smart,* or *sassing*. He wasn't sure what stopped him. She was the teacher after all and it was her job to keep control. Maybe she singled him for laughing because it was the standard teacher reply. Something she had learned. Something that worked. Maybe it was the best response she had at the moment. He kept quiet. He wanted to keep his job as a *light technician* and *door closer* for television time.

The class turned their attention back to Mrs. Morrison's words about space. The lesson continued and the pressure lifted. Marvin had felt the eyes when they fell upon him and now could sense them drifting away. He wondered if Rosa had looked. He turned to see and met eyes with her—she was still looking at him—he couldn't move. He froze. She smiled and held up two fingers. Marvin smiled. He knew she meant it as a peace sign but to him, it was a sign of victory.

Permission To Go (My friends are going)

That night at dinner, Irene had made pot roast. It was exceptionally gristly. Marvin chewed it down to a manageable pulp and then concealed it between his cheek and gums and save it there until he was able to transfer it into his napkin as he wiped his mouth.

"How was school today?" Leonard asked.

"Fine."

"What did you learn about?"

"Oh... some long division," Marvin said being careful of the meat packed in his jawline. "And Mariner. That's the spacecraft flying around Mars."

"Hm. Imagine that," Leonard said. "Flying around Mars."

"You know that old Hatsie Reinburg?" Irene asked.

"What about her?"

"She was up at the laundromat the other night and she was saying that's why there's been so many earthquakes," Irene said. "It's because they're sending those space rockets up into the heavens."

"I don't follow," Leonard said as he removed his glasses and rubbed his eyes. "What do rockets have to do it?"

"She said that God is punishing us for poking our noses where they don't belong. She said that's why Kennedy was killed. Because he wanted to put a man on the moon."

Leonard chuckled and then sighed. "I see. So, we send a rocket up into space... God sends a man with a gun down to Dallas?"

"That's what she thinks. She said that's why we have disasters."

"A small step for man is a giant earthquake for all mankind? Sounds like a bunch of hooey to me. Do you believe that?"

"Why of course not, Leonard. You know Hatsie believes everything she hears."

Leonard chuckled. "I think if the good Lord was worried about us peaking into the heavens he would have done something about the Wright brothers. Swatted them out of the sky. What do you think, Marvin? Do you believe that?"

"Nope," he replied. *I do believe I'm thinking about doing something that would launch me over the moon with my status as one of the cool kids. I hope it doesn't cause a disaster.* "I'm pretty sure that earthquakes are caused by the ground moving along fault lines. Another thing that I learned in school."

"How about that?" Leonard asked. "Whatever happened to good all reading, writing, and arithmetic? The things kids learn these days."

"Yeah," Irene replied. "It's a shame you can't learn to hold food over your plate Leonard, you just dropped some in your lap."

"Well... phooey!" He grabbed his napkin and wiped his pant leg. Marvin had a strong urge to laugh but held firm concerned the squandered pot roast exiled in his mouth may fly free.

"When's Marilyn getting home?" Leonard asked.

"Anytime now." Irene looked up at the clock and then at the window over the sink. The moisture and grime on the glass outside reported an orange hue from the sunset. "It's getting dark earlier these days."

"Most likely it's God punishing us for using light bulbs," Leonard said. He waited for a reaction but a knock on the back door arrested the result. "Who could that be?"

"I'll get it," Marvin said and sprang up from the table before anyone could move.

"Whoever it is, tell them we're eating supper," Leonard said.

Marvin opened the door. There was a skinny kid in an oversized Dallas Cowboys shirt with a pair of safety scissors in his left hand. "Hey, Ryan."

"Hey, Marvin."

"What's going on?"

"Not too much," he said. "My mom's trying to drain our pool. She needs another hose to connect the hose we got so that she doesn't flood the yard. Can we borrow one?"

"I guess. I can ask." Marvin leaned back in. "Hey Grandpa, it's Ryan Heffendorf..."

"Who?"

"Ryan. From up the street. His mom wants to know if they can borrow our hose. She's draining their pool and needs an extra one."

Leonard thought for a moment. "I guess. As long as they bring it back."

"OK." Marvin closed the door and walked out into the yard a few steps. He spat the wads of meat onto the grass. "Skippy!" he called to his dog.

"Gross! What was that?" Ryan asked.

"Pot roast. I hate pot roast."

Skippy trotted over and inspected the masticated morsels. She wagged her tail and quickly disposed of the evidence.

"Hey said it was alright, so long as you bring it back."

"I will."

"OK." Marvin looked down at the scissors Ryan held. "What are those for?"

"I don't know," he said. "I felt sorry for them."

"Oh. I see." Marvin walked over and loosened the hose from the spigot. "What are you doing Friday night?"

"Why?"

"*Dracula A.D.* is at the Crest," Marvin told him. "Wondered if you wanted to go?"

"I can't. I'm supposed to go on this stupid campout down at Johnson Shut-Ins."

"Oh. That sounds cool." Marvin got the hose loose and a small dribble of water ran out.

"Well, it's with the *Parents Without Partners*. Going with my mom," Ryan said. "I'm surprised your mom's not going."

"I don't think so," Marvin said. "I'm not so sure she liked those meetings. She said people just drank cocktails and were weird. Some guy kept calling her. She said he was a mortician, which is kind of creepy."

"Like Herman Munster?" Ryan asked with a laugh.

"Yeah. But she said he looked like Meathead from *All In The Family*." Marvin held the end of the hose up and walked with it, forcing the water to drain from the other end.

"My mom's had a couple of creeps call her," Ryan said. "But most just come to our house."

"They come to your house?"

"Yeah." Ryan held the scissors up to his bottom lip.

"What do they do?"

"They sit around and stare at each other. It's stupid." He squeezed his lip between the dull blades.

Marvin tried to imagine Mrs. Heffendorf in these staring contests. She always reminded him of Popeye's girlfriend, Olive Oyl. She was tall, skinny, and talked with a squeaky voice. She wasn't pretty at all. She had a pinched face, a pointed nose, and large brown eyes that bulged outward. Who would want to sit and look at Ryan's mom? He couldn't imagine. He could imagine Linda would eventually grow up and look like her mother. And guys would come over to look at her.

"They just stare at each other?" Marvin asked as he finished rolling the hose.

"Yeah," he replied and dropped the scissors down. "Some

stay real late. Sometimes... they stay up all night. Adults are weird."

Marvin didn't know what to say. He had finished gathering the hose into a large wreath and handed it to Ryan. "How's your sister?"

"Why?" Ryan tucked the scissors in his pocket and took the hose.

"No reason. Just wondered," Marvin said. "I saw her the other day at the shortcut next to the High School. Walking home."

"She's grounded again." He hoisted the hose over his shoulder. "Not sure what it was about. One of the guys came into her room while was sleeping. I think she said something to mom. Caused a big ruckus. Everybody was yelling. But she says a lot of stuff. She talks back and gets grounded."

"Yeah, she does say some stuff," Marvin said.

"I don't say stuff. I just keep quiet."

"So, is your sister going on the camp-out?"

"No," Ryan said. "She's going to stay with our dad. Mom doesn't trust her at home alone."

"Oh," Marvin said and let awkward silence float by. "We listen to records again sometime. Watch TV or something."

"Yeah," Ryan said. "We should. I gotta get this home before it gets too dark. Tell your grandpa thanks."

"Sure," he replied. "See you around."

"Yeah. See ya."

Marvin sat on the floor in the living room in front of *The Mod Squad* while his mother sat in the kitchen and recounted her day to her mother.

He could hear his grandmother running the gamut of her standard questions; *And then what did he say? And then what did you say?* It would lead to Irene's inevitable checkmate phrase, *Well, you know what I would have said...*

Marvin would have said that Denny Walters was right about Julie on the *Mod Squad.* She was better looking than Laurie Partridge.

"What on?" Marilyn asked as she came in and sat on the couch. She cradled a Pyrex bowl and a can of *Tab.*

"*Mod Squad.*"

"Oh," she replied and set her soda on the side table. "What did I miss?"

"Not too much," Marvin told her. "See that guy?"

"Yeah."

"He hates his father... so he joined this motorcycle gang. Now they're planning to rob him."

"Rob who?" She clanged her spoon around the bowl.

"The father of the guy who just joined the gang. The one that hates him."

"Got it."

"Pot roast?"

"Nope," she said. "It's the rest of the mashed potatoes. I'm trying to drop a few pounds before my Weight Watchers meeting Friday."

"OK." Marvin realized the subject of Friday was out in the open. Now would be the time to ask permission to go.

"Is that Bobby Sherman?" Marilyn asked. "The kid from *Here Come the Brides?*

"Yeah," Marvin said. "I think it is."

"He's supposed to be part of the motorcycle gang?"

"Yeah. He's the leader."

She took a bite of potatoes. "That was some crappy casting."

"Maybe..." Marvin said, "the brides weren't arriving fast enough... so he joined a gang."

Marilyn laughed. He knew this was his moment to ask. His mother's mood was good.

"Oh. I wanted to ask you... this Friday, some of the kids are going to go see *Dracula A.D.* It's the Christopher Lee, Dracula, the best one. Is it all right if I go?"

"I guess so," she said.

Marvin sighed. Getting his mother on a laugh was good and he knew that adding himself to *some of the kids* usually worked. A group would get permission over a solo effort.

"Wait!" His mother said through a mouthful of potatoes.

Marvin held his breath.

"Friday? Where is this showing?"

He let go a sigh and looked hard into the green sculptured carpet for the right words. The answer came with confidence. "The Crest."

"The *Crest*?" She scraped her spoon around the bowl which created a muffled ringing sound. "I don't know, Marvin. The Crest. You want to go there after what happened the last time?"

He looked at the television. It was an ad for a new show called *Kung Fu.* That looks pretty cool he thought. "Well, I know but... my friends are going."

"Which friends? Ryan and Ronnie?"

"No," he said. "Ryan can't go. He's going on that camping thing. These are friends from school."

"School friends?"

"Yeah. I don't think you know them. I mean, they've never been here."

"Are they from your class?"

"No. I just know them from school. We have lunch together. We sit at the same table. A kid named Denny Walters and another kid named Norbert."

"Norbert? You know a kid named Norbert?"

"Yeah," he said. "Norbert Stiebert."

Marilyn laughed. "Is he tall and lanky? And wear thick glasses?"

"No," Marvin said. "That would be Denny. Norbert is about my height. Doesn't wear glasses. Wears motorcycle boots. With taps. Everybody calls him Norb. He's cool. Kinda tough. No one picks on him."

"I bet. Growing up with a name like that. You'd have to be tough."

The conversation rested as a commercial for the *flex-o-matic* electric razor came on. Marilyn took a drink of soda. Marvin rubbed the carpet pattern etched into his elbows and cracked his knuckles.

"So, tell me this, how are you getting there?"

"Oh well, Norb just lives a few blocks from there," Marvin said. "I was going to his house and then we would just... you know, walk there."

"You're going to *walk* there?"

"Yeah," Marvin replied. "It's like... only a block or two."

"What time does the movie start?"

"I think it starts at 7:00."

She took a drink of her Tab and stared at the television for a moment as a commercial for Tiparillo cigars.

"What time is it over?"

"I'm not sure... maybe 8:45."

Marilyn stirred her potatoes. "Let me think about it."

"OK."

The commercial ended with the announcer asking *should a gentleman offer a Tiparillo to a lady.* Marvin had a memory of handing a candy cigarette to a blond freckle-faced girl on a playground a long time ago—when he lived in another place. She became his friend for the rest of the year. Wonder whatever became of her and how fifth grade was going for her?

No Lights, No Norb, No Linda

It was a cold and rainy day. It was so dark outside Marvin felt it must be late at night. They must have all fallen asleep and awoke at this moment—not 15 minutes before noon but a quarter to midnight. Someone would run into the room at any moment and announce they were on Candid Camera.

The atmosphere outside colored the mood of everyone inside. Mrs. Morrison didn't ask Marvin to shut the door and turn off the lights, she called on Stan Zellesky instead. Why? What he had down to an art, Stan turned into a comedy of errors; he couldn't get the doorstop to remain to stay up. All in all, it took 10 minutes to get the room as dark as the day outside. Marvin's personal best was under a minute.

Norb wasn't at his usual table during lunch. Marvin sat with Denny Walters and a book called *Time And Again*.

"Cookie?"

"No thanks," Marvin replied.

"I haven't seen you around."

"I've been around."

"Sitting with your girlfriend?" Denny asked as he pushed up his glasses and smiled a chocolate cookie smile.

"No," Marvin said. "I haven't been sitting with her."

"Have you even talked to her yet? Or are you still having that warm face condition?"

Marvin took a bite of his deviled ham sandwich and chewed slowly to allow the question to pass. Denny appeared to be still waiting for an answer. Marvin retrieved a paper towel from his lunch bag and wiped his mouth. Denny gave up and selected another cookie.

"Do you like scary movies?" Marvin asked.

Denny shrugged and screwed the cup off his thermos. "Some of them." Today the plastic army men were stationed on a *Lost In Space* lunch box. "Why?"

"*Dracula A.D. 1972* is coming to the Crest on Friday."

Denny poured a glob of soup into the cup, picked it up, and blew across the top. The aroma of vegetable barley flowed into Marvin's face. "Actually," Denny said, "I prefer *Count Yorga* over the present Dracula."

"Count Yorga?"

"Yes. Yorga."

"You like Yorga better than Dracula? But it's Christopher Lee Dracula."

"I know," Denny said taking a sip of soup. "Dracula is supposed to be a Romanian Count. Not a British guy."

"So... what is Yorga?"

"Just an ordinary vampire. American variety."

"American? I thought you said he should be Romanian."

"I said Dracula should be Romanian," Denny replied. "An ordinary vampire can be any nationality. Case in point, take Blacula for instance, he was an African prince and a vampire. Barnabas Collins was American."

"OK fine. So, if somebody asked you to go see a British Dracula this Friday, you wouldn't go?"

"Probably not." He pushed his glasses up. "I didn't peg you as a Dracula fan, Marvin."

"Well, I'm not really. I like the wolfman better."

"Are you sure you don't want a cookie?"

"No thanks," Marvin said. "I prefer the *Nabisco* variety."

MARVIN TOOK the shortcut home after school but didn't see Linda. He had tried for a few days to accidentally catch her with her friends under the bleachers but would only encounter the faint aroma evidence they had been there. As he walked up the path toward the subdivision he could see three figures coming up the street toward him. He couldn't see who they were from the distance but he heard the pulse of a basketball beating against concrete. Probably some high school kids coming up to the courts.

Marvin considered what sport he might pursue when entered high school. He'd played a few years of little league baseball and did quite well. Third base was his usual position but he preferred catching--like his heroes Johnny Bench and Ted Simmons.

The distance between the basketball trio and Marvin had closed enough to tie a knot in his stomach. He could identify Steve and his older brother Tommy Hablin. He couldn't identify the third stooge yet.

When Marvin and his mother first moved in with her parents, Leonard and Irene, the Hablin brothers didn't make the transition and integration into the neighborhood a pleasant event. They weren't the ideal welcome wagon committee.

Hey new kid, why are living with those old folks? Where's your dad? How come you live with your grandparents? Why's your hair like that? Do you curl your hair? Only girls have curly hair.

The space between them diminished enough that Marvin recognized the third kid. It was Freddy Kester who lived down the street. He was tall, lanky, and had bushy red hair and freckles. Kids called him *Freddy Freeloader* or *Scabbie*—years ago he would amuse everyone by peeling the scabs from his knees and consuming them. Other than that he was harmless but he was friends with the Hablins.

Marvin couldn't turn around without it being an obvious hightail move. *Hey! Where you going curly?* The nearest side street was a block away. He would have to keep walking and stay true, come what may. What was the big deal anyway? He wasn't a scrawny first grader anymore. Things were different and different things were good. He heard one of them laughing. Another one was chanting, *"Here comes the judge. Here comes the judge."* The basketball was slapping the ground harder. Would they pass each other without the usual peer provocation? What would the Hablin's pull from their bag of lines?

What's going on curly? Hey, did we see you walking with Linda last week? Did you carry her books? Did you look at her belly button? Nobody does that, you hear? You're in for it, Milstead.

How would he respond?

Oh yeah? She thinks you're a big jerk, Steve. Go soak your towhead in the toilet!

Make me, Milstead!

I don't have the recipe, Hablin!

Oh Yeah?

Yeah!

Marvin watched the pavement pass below as the scenarios rolled through his mind. Suddenly, he felt something slap his pant leg-it wasn't a fist or a foot, it was a flash of orange—it was the basketball. He glanced up and saw Steve running full tilt toward him. Marvin froze, he closed his eyes, and braced for the impact of whatever was coming; he was ready for the blow. But instead of a full-body tackle or hockey hip check, a slight breeze passed by and a voice said, "Sorry man." A voice like Steve Hablin's voice.

He opened one eye and turned his head to see Steve chasing the runaway ball as it spiraled down the street. It bounded up the curb, launched gracefully into the air, and plopped into the blond dormant zoysia of a front lawn.

"Nice goin' fart head," Tommy yelled to Steve. "I bet even Milstead here could dribble a ball without losing it."

"It was an accident," Steve replied, "It hit my shoe!" He picked up the ball.

"It ain't a soccer ball!" Freddy said. "You're not supposed to kick it." He nodded at Marvin. "What's happenin' Marv?"

"Not too much," he told Freddy. He stood still as they passed. In case a sudden movement would disrupt the calm balance in progress.

"Sorry about that Marvin," Tommy said. "You know how kids are. Can't take 'em anywhere. Can't have anything nice."

Marvin laughed.

"You grandparents doing all right?"

"Yeah. Doing all right," Marvin replied.

"Good."

Steve bounced the ball hard against the street a few times. The sound reverberated down the streets and between the houses echoing back almost sounding like gunshots. Tommy ran and called out, "Last one to the court is a rotten turd!" Freddy sprinted after him. Steve tucked the ball under his arm and shouted, "No fair! I wasn't ready!"

Marvin sighed. A shiver of relief flowed through his system down to his shoelaces. The tension that held his shoulders up let them float back down to their normal position. Maybe the ritual of tormenting had ended. Maybe five years was the limit on these things. Like a library book, you had to return. Maybe they got bored and ran out of ridicule. Whatever the reason, he decided to accept the outcome, stop wondering about it, and continued on his way home.

Homework and A Ride Down the Road (Then Came Milford)

"What would you guys like for supper?" Irene asked. "I've got some ground beef. I can make hamburgers or stuffed peppers. I can warm up the potato soup from last night."

"I don't care," Marvin replied from the living room. He was on the floor against the couch dividing his attention between *The Munsters* on television and homework. The pen markings on the back of his hand noted that 72-82 were the pages to read in *Social Studies Culture and You*.

"Isn't today Thursday?" Leonard asked from the back door. He was taking out the screen inserts from the storm door and replacing them with glass panels.

"Yeah, why?"

"Don't they have that fried chicken special up at the Granada Inn on Thursday?"

"You want that?"

"Huh?"

"I said, you feel like chicken?"

"Chicken sounds good," Leonard said.

"Hey Marvin," Irene called out. "How's chicken sound? We're thinking of going up to the Granada."

"I have homework. I have to read stuff for school."

"Bring it with you," Leonard said.

"Oh don't be silly" Irene snapped. "He doesn't want to bring homework with him."

"Why not?"

"What if he gets something on it?" Irene asked. "We'd have to pay for the book."

"I'd rather stay here." Marvin closed the textbook.

"What did he say?"

"He said he rather stay here," Irene told him.

"Don't you want some good chicken?" Leonard asked. "Mashed potatoes. Green beans. Coleslaw."

"Nah. They serve that at school."

"What do you want then?" Irene asked.

I want to ride my mini bike over to Norb's house, Marvin thought. *And then go to the Crest tomorrow night with a package of ruckus.* "Can't I just stay here?" Marvin asked. "I'll just eat cereal or something."

"You can't just eat cereal," Irene replied. "Come and go with us."

"Isn't mom going to be home soon?"

"She's going to Weight Watchers."

"I thought she was going on Friday."

"She switched it," Irene said. "She's going tonight."

Tonight? Why did she switch it? What did she need to do Friday? Marvin's stomach dropped.

"Why don't you come with us?" Leonard asked. Marvin heard the back door firmly close which was an indicator his grandfather was done. "After that, we'll go by the Velvet Creamery for dessert."

"If he wants to stay here, Leonard, let him stay," Irene said.

"Maybe he wants to go."

"I don't want to go."

"What did he say?"

"He said he doesn't want to go."

"All right. Suit yourself."

MARVIN READ about Peru and the introduction of Agrarian reform by the time Leonard found his keys—which he had set on a shelf in the garage—and Irene fixed her hair.

"You sure you don't want to go?" Leonard asked one final time.

"No. I have a lot to study."

His grandparents left the house. He heard Leonard's car fade down the street, he shut the book and went out into the kitchen. It was between *Count Chocula* and *Lucky Charms*. He ate a handful of both and chased it down with a swig of milk from the carton. He grabbed two slices of American cheese and went out the back door. The crinkle of the cellophane brought Skippy to the porch. Marvin sat down, Skippy sat attentively at his feet as he folded the squares over into rectangles.

"Here you go." He held it out. She sniffed it, plucked it from his fingers, and absorbed it in two bites. She slapped her tail once on the ground to signal she was ready for more as she watched Marvin nibble away at his share. "What should we do, Skip?" The idea that he still spoke to his dog made him smile. When he was very young, he expected Skippy to answer. After all, the animals on TV and in books were prone to hold conversations with humans. Even inanimate objects expressed their feelings. But dogs, apple trees, little engines, and Alka-Seltzer tablets in this world clammed up. Mum was the word. "What should we do? They went out for chicken and mom's not home. It's just you and me, Skippy."

A cool breeze whistled through the branches of the oaks. He looked up and watched the limbs above sway and bounce. The branches dangled different shades of leaves reflecting the conversion to autumn. They displayed more brown tints than the greens they held weeks ago.

Marvin held up his last morsel of cheese. "Here," he said to Skippy and tossed it to her. She opened her mouth and tried to catch it but it ricocheted off her nose and landed in the grass. "Sorry," Marvin said. Years ago she would have snatched it out of the air as quickly as natural instinct, but now it was easier to allow things to fall and find them in time.

Marvin heard an odd sound echo in-between the houses; similar to a small motor traveling down the street. Peculiar and familiar. He rose and went to the side gate to get a look at whatever might be passing by. There it was. It was Ronnie Phegel riding his bicycle with playing cards clipped to the wheel frame. The mingy motor. The hardly-a-Harley. The-baseball-card-carburetor.

"I know what I want to do, Skippy," he said.

———

THE ENGINE of the Mini Trail started on the second try. Marvin tightened the strap on his helmet, revved the throttle a few times, and slowly put it in gear-just like Evel Knievel. He rode down the driveway and stopped just at the curb. He drew in a breath, looked both ways and rode out into the street. Marvin had ignored conventions and broken rules before but the exhilaration of leaving the asphalt of the driveway for the asphalt of the street was thrilling. He sped up the street toward the cul-de-sac. He spotted Ronnie parked in Ryan's driveway, adjusting a few of the cards that had been jarred loose by the spokes. Marvin did a few laps around the circle and then pulled up behind Ronnie and stopped an inch from his rear tire.

"What are you doing?" Ronnie yelled as he jumped back letting his bicycle fall over. "You butt hole!"

Marvin laughed. "What? Did I scare you, little boy?"

"It's not funny, Marvin."

"I thought it was." He twisted the throttle a few times for effect.

"What? I can't hear you!" Ronnie said, his face flush with a mix of anger and embarrassment.

Marvin shifted into neutral and cut the engine. "There. Can you hear me now?"

"Yes, fine!" Ronnie said as he picked his bike up. "What are you doing with that thing? I thought you couldn't take it out of the driveway."

"Nobody's home right now. I decided to take a spin. I heard you puttering by and I thought I'd join you."

"How nice," Ronnie said. "I'm happy for you."

Ryan opened the front and stuck his head out. "What are you guys doing?"

"Nothing," Ronnie said as he went back to secure the cards. "Mind your beeswax."

"We're joining a gang, Ryan" Marvin replied. "Hell's Angels. We got a Honda and a Schwinn. Not sure if they'll let us but... wanna join?"

"Sure. Let me find my shoes." Ryan disappeared into the house and Linda appeared at the door. Marvin took off his helmet, and rubbed his hair. He hoped to appear as the likeness of Jim Bronson from the TV show, *Then Came Bronson* or even Steve McQueen, but judging by the smirk she had on her face, he must have looked like a goofy kid sitting on the type of bike you see clowns riding in parades.

"What are you kids doing in our driveway?" Linda stepped outside and walked toward them. She looked ordinary again, Marvin thought. She had on jeans and a large sweatshirt with **Mizzou** printed on the front and a design of some sort above the letters. Her face was shiny as if she had just scrubbed it raw and allowed the pink tint of acne to experience the light of day.

"What do you want?" Ronnie asked with a great degree of annoyance.

"I don't know Phegel," Linda said as she approached, "how about five bucks for parking that piece of crap here?"

"Right. Who died and made you boss?"

"I think five bucks is reasonable. What do you think Marv?"

"Sure. That's a bargain."

"What about him?" Ronnie asked looking at Marvin. "He's parked here! Why doesn't he have to pay?"

"Because he's cool," Linda said. "You're not. You're just a little fart munchkin."

Marvin bit his lip to suppress a laugh. He glanced away from Ronnie and he noticed the design on her sweatshirt was a cartoon tiger. It was wearing a hat. A sailor hat with an *M* on it. Not a friendly tiger-like Frosted Flakes tiger, this one had a fierce demeanor. Determined. It was a football mascot after all. He wondered where she got it. Who did she know that went to Missouri State? He wasn't sure how much time had passed when his eyes landed on the Tiger logo, but his trance was broken when Linda reached up and pulled at her sweatshirt. Marvin realized the tiger was positioned in an area where she may have thought his eyes had other curiosities.

"Sorry," Marvin started to say but at that moment Ryan bolted out the door and loud music erupted from across the street.

"What?" Ronnie asked looking at Marvin.

"Nothing. I was just..."

"Hey! I thought you couldn't ride that out of the driveway," Ryan said to Marvin.

"The old folks left," Ronnie told Ryan. "He gets to break the law for now."

"I'm not breaking the law," Marvin replied.

"Yeah you are," Ryan said. "You can't ride that on the street. You don't have a license."

"Are you going to call the cops?" Marvin asked.

"No," Ryan said. "But... somebody might."

The music got louder. They all turned to look. It was coming from the Halbin's house. The brothers had a hi-fi system set up in the garage and from time to time, liked to test the limits of volume and the neighbor's tolerance. This afternoon's test had loud guitars and the singer screamed something about *Space Trucking*.

"Somebody should call the cops on those guys," Ronnie said. "What is that crap?"

"It's *Deep Purple*, you munchkin," Brenda said.

"Ryan, tell your sister to stop calling me names."

"You tell her. She's standing right there."

"She's your sister," Ronnie said as he got on his bike. If things got worse, he was ready to peddle away.

"So?" Ryan said. "She doesn't listen to me."

"Some friend you are," Ronnie said.

"OK. Linda, stop calling him a munchkin," Ryan said in a very forced and dry way.

"No way," she replied.

"You see, I told you. She doesn't listen to me."

"You want me to stop?" Linda asked as she stood up straight and took a step toward Ronnie. "Make me!"

Normally, Ronnie welcomed a good insult battle and would counter the joust, *make me* with a litany of counter strikes such as; *I don't make trash I burn it*, but at this moment he remained silent, furrowed his brow, and examined his fingernails.

Marvin had considered asking Ronnie if he wanted to go to the Crest tomorrow but the thought withered. Mrs. Phegel wouldn't allow him to go unless he had a tantrum, which would take a while; and did he want Ronnie to tag along? Nope. Not this time.

"What's wrong Phegel? Cat got your tongue?" Linda asked.

Ronnie shrugged. Linda sighed and looked at Marvin.

"So, did I interrupt your cool guy pow-wow?" She asked.

Marvin wasn't sure why but he smiled. He smiled at the expectant expressions that Ronnie and Ryan had on their faces as if they waited for him to give the proper answer. He didn't have an answer, just a weak and pathetic smile born of the awkwardness of the situation. Four people hovered in a driveway while loud rock music filled in their silence. Marvin looked over at Linda and answered "Not really."

Linda walked over to Marvin. "Well, cool then. Let's split."

He heard the words but couldn't process a response other than to repeat it back as a question. "Split?"

"Yeah," she said. "Why don't you give me a ride on that thing?"

Marvin understood. He has watched this scene a hundred times on TV and in the movies. "Where to?" He asked.

"Away from these losers," she said.

"You're a loser," Ryan quipped.

"Yeah," Ronnie said as a second to the statement.

"Come on. Let's go."

Marvin pulled on his helmet, turned the key, flipped out the kick-starter, and stepped down once start the engine.

"Hey," Linda said, "scoot up."

Marvin moved forward on the seat and she climbed on behind him. She rested the edge of her tennis shoes on bolts securing the rear wheel and laid her hands on his shoulders.

"Where ya guys going?" Ryan shouted over the puttering motor that had conquered the music from the Hablin's garage.

"Wouldn't you like to know?" Linda replied. Marvin tapped the gear into first and eased the bike slowly forward and then sped up the driveway, Ryan jumped out of the way. Linda dropped her hands down to Marvin's waist to secure a hold now that everything was in motion. "Let's ride," she said.

He turned and drove across the yard, down onto the street, leaned right around the circle, and pushed all the horsepower the small engine could muster topping at least 25 miles an hour down the road. Marvin felt her arms tighten around his waist as the force of moving forward began to force them back. The space between Marvin and the tiger with the sailor cap closed. He turned his head and shouted to her, "Where do you want to go?"

"I don't care," Linda said laughing "Just go!"

Marvin sailed down the street and across to the new subdivision; reversing and retracing the path they had walked home from school that day. He could see Linda's hair floating in mad patterns out of the corner of his eye and it would occasionally swoop around and whip his cheek. It was nice. It was just like the movies. If it had a soundtrack thought Marvin, it would have to be that cool trumpet song *Grazing In The Grass*—the instrumental version, not the singing one.

THEY RODE down the dirt path through the field to the area behind the high school, and down the hill to the ball field. Linda laughed as she dragged her tennis shoes through the diamond dirt, kicking up fine brown clouds as they toured the bases. When they rode up toward the tennis courts, an official-looking man walked toward them. He looked irritated and yelled something as he pointed.

"Go! Split! Split!" Linda shouted with a laugh.

Marvin turned quickly and rode back across the ball field, up the hill, and back up the path to the street. He didn't slow down until they were back on Candle making a circuit around the circle. Ronnie and Ryan were still in the driveway as if frozen in the moment and weren't able to move until they returned. Marvin held up two fingers to them as they rode by but instead of a sign of peace he meant it was a symbol of victory, which was short-lived when Linda leaned forward and said; "Drop me off at the Hablins."

Marvin felt everything that had been set free and rushed through his system with excitement had just been snatched out of the air and thrown onto the ground. An ache rose in his stomach like the time Katy Colburn kicked him between the legs in 2nd grade.

Marvin coasted into the Halbin's driveway and stopped about a foot from the street. He could see Steve standing in the garage, bobbing his head to the music that coated the neighborhood. He jerked his head to the right, flipping his hair back. Linda patted the top of Marvin's helmet and she rose. *Good boy,* she might as well have said. *Here, have a nibble of cheese.* He turned the wheel of the bike, not looking back, and accelerated onto the street. If only the 50 cc engine had enough power to burn rubber with grievous commotion, but it didn't. It displaced a small patch of gravel near the curb. Marvin rode home. Covered the mini-trail back up with the moving blanket, went inside, and read about Peruvian land reform and Che Guevara in the Cuban Revolution.

Dino and a Nightmare

Since he had his homework completed and *held the fort down*-as Leonard liked to say-while they were out to dinner, Marvin was granted permission to stay up a little longer than usual to watch television. *The Tonight Show* with Johnny Carson was out of the question, that was much too late on a school night, but *The Dean Martin Show* would be fine. He made some chocolate milk—they were out of the powder, he had to pour it from the can--and sat down in front of the couch.

He didn't like the new opening of the show with the dancers spelling Dean's name and the large letters he walked through; it reminded him of something he would see on *Sesame Street.* A kid's show. Marvin preferred the older shows where Dean slid down the pole like Batman. Irene always said that Dean was drunk and Leonard said it was just an act, he did it because people thought it was funny.

Marvin had seen a few people in real life who were drunk and no one found it funny. When his Uncle Odell got drunk it made people mad. His grandfather told him there were different types of drunks; the kind who were funny and friendly, and the other kind who became mean and wanted to fight. If you had to meet one, you better hope you get the Dean Martin one, not the uncle Odell kind.

Dean started to sing. Marvin rose and walked on his knees to the television set. He turned the dial to find something else to watch until the song was over. Most of the time Dean was cool when he sang, holding his cigarette, other times like now, he acted goofy. What else was on at 9 o'clock? *Owen Marshall Attorney at Law.* Nope. *Thursday night movie; it* was a western. Not a good guy versus outlaws or Indians but one where they are looking for gold. Dull. There was a documentary on the PBS station about the bombing of Cambodia. A war movie on the UHF channel, a commercial for dog food, and finally back to Dean Martin.

Marvin hoped his mom would be home soon so he would know the final verdict about going to the Crest. What if she said no? Could he show up tomorrow at school to tell Norb, he wouldn't be there with the firecrackers because his mom said no? If she said no, he would stay home. Act like he had an illness, maybe a stomach ache, and avoid school. He had used that cover before. Let Stan Zellesky turn out the lights and shut the door for TV time. Let Denny Walters read his book in peace. Let Rosa Alhambra smile at someone else.

THAT NIGHT MARVIN had a dream he was sitting on his bike at the top of a very steep incline inside a stadium. Directly in front of him was a dirt path that led down to a very large ramp, similar to the kind he saw Evel Knievel use when he jumped over cars. He began peddling down the path until the kinetic energy took over and momentum increased. He could not see what he would be jumping over, the ramp was obscuring his view. Hopefully, it was cars or buses and not the fountain at Caesars Palace. That did not end well for Robert Craig Knievel and may not for Marvin James Milstead.

The falling sensation began to trickle up from his stomach and another sensation, a force was pushing down from above. It felt as if gravity was increasing and pressing down on his shoulders. It was getting difficult to keep his head up to see where he was going. Almost like a large invisible person jumped on for a piggyback ride but they were too big and you couldn't hold them.

The edge of the ramp was just a foot away and he was prepared to feel his bike start the angle of the incline and fly off into the air, but the force from above was too strong. He wouldn't be able to shrug off its weight in time. Instead of traveling up the ramp, he crashed directly into it, falling straight down into a massive dark pit. Laughter erupted from the crowd. Just below him, he heard firecrackers going off and knew he would land on top of them.

Marvin jumped violently under his covers and sat up. He wasn't in a pit but in his room, in the dark, and in bed. He could still hear the crowd laughing. Where was that coming from? He traced the sound to the floor. It was coming in under his door along with light from the living room. Someone was awake and watching television. He should investigate on his way to the bathroom.

The Tonight Show was on the TV and his mother was on the couch.

"Sorry," she said. "Was it too loud?"

"No. I had to go to the bathroom and I had a weird dream."

"Nightmare?"

"No," Marvin said. He watched the television for a moment. It wasn't Johnny Carson sitting behind the desk, it was Joey Bishop. "It was a strange dream. Sort of like a falling dream."

"I hate those," she replied.

"How did your weight-watching thing go tonight?"

"Good," Marilyn said. "I just have to stick to the plan they gave me. A lot of dull food."

"Yeah," Marvin said as he noticed that Joey Bishop just said something about *Dr. Phibes Rises Again* and he walked out to take a seat. "Oh look who it is! Vincent Price."

"Oh yeah."

"My friend, Norb, from school said his dad used to work on his cars."

"Really?"

"Yeah," Marvin replied. He knew this would be a good spot to ask his mother about the Crest. "Norb is the kid I told you about. You know, I'm supposed to go to the Crest with him tomorrow night."

"Listen, about tomorrow night," his mother began, "I don't know if grandma said anything or what she told you..."

Marvin braced himself. Usually, when her statements began this way, it wasn't good. "No, she didn't say anything. I mean, she said you switched going to Weight Watchers tonight, instead of Friday."

"That's right," she said.

Marvin prayed silently as he felt his hopes riding down the ramp about to make the leap.

"I had to switch because... I have a date."

"A what?"

"A date," she replied. "Well, not a date. I'm meeting someone for a drink."

"Oh," Marvin said. His hopes didn't crash into the ramp; they stalled at the bottom. "It's not the mortician is it?"

"No, it's someone dad knows."

"Grandpa got you a date?"

"Yes. Somebody he knows from the tavern that he stops at after work."

"Oh."

Joey Bishop said something funny and the audience laughed.

"I thought you had to go to the bathroom," she said as the tonight show band played out to a commercial.

"Yeah," he said. "I do. I just wanted to see what... you were watching. And ask about... "

"Oh about your movie tomorrow," she said, "I'm sure it'll be fine. As long as you come straight home after it's over."

Marvin felt himself soar up the ramp, landing safely on the other side. "I will. Straight home."

We exchanged smiles, peace signs, never any words

Friday morning was a movie in slow motion. Similar to the last scene in *Bonnie and Clyde* when they are gunned down. Marvin looked at the clock when it was 10:00 a.m. He was sure an hour had passed, glanced at the clock again it was only 10:12 a.m. Slow-motion.

Mrs. Morrison was highlighting current events that were important to know and have the class understand. One had to do with the *Paris Peace talks* and how they worked to bring an end to the conflict in Vietnam. Mrs. Morrison asked Tammy

Baylor if she could please pay attention and bring an end to her talking. Tammy said she *was* paying attention and had known about the Peace Talks by watching *In The News* on Saturday morning during cartoons.

"Very good, Tammy," Mrs. Morrison replied. "Tell me this, do you know where Vietnam is located? Could you point it out on the map?"

"No," Tammy said. "But I know that it's not in the United States. Is it near Paris?"

"No, Tammy," Mrs. Morrison said. "How about... Rosa? Can you point it out on the world map?"

Rosa nodded and got up and walked toward the map. Marvin felt his face getting warm. *Why?* She didn't smile at him or even look his way. Was he embarrassed for her? No. She seemed to know. She rose to the occasion. Her bell bottoms flapped as she approached the bulletin board with the world map secured by four thumbtacks. She studied it for a second. She reached up and touched an area that dangled below China, which looked like a handle.

"Very good, Rosa!" Mrs. Morrison said.

Rosa tugged at her puffy white shirt in case it had lifted and returned to her seat. Marvin realized at that moment why he had blushed; Rosa's outfit was similar to what Linda Heffendorf wore. They looked nothing alike except for the clothing that covered them. Rosa was *Miri* from *Star Trek*. Mattie Ross from *True Grit*. Linda was Cher with dishwater blond hair that smelled like cigarettes.

"We have time for one more topic," Mrs. Morrison said. "Does anyone have anything they wish to bring up for the class that pertains to current events?"

Sandra Wilbert raised her hand. She asked about President Nixon.

"What about the President?"

"My dad was saying that he read an article..." Sandra began, "that said the FBI had connected something about... the burglars and the break-in into that office in Washington to the President. I was just wondering, well, if that was true... how could they even do that to the President?"

Mrs. Morrison sighed and attempted a smile that didn't fully form. "I don't know that the President had any connection despite what some newspapers reported. Having said that... no one is above the law. Not even our leaders."

Marvin imagined a policeman escorting the President out of the White House like a kid caught smoking in the bathroom. *Come on, James Dean, let's go.*

"Thanks," Sandra said. "I was wondering about that."

"It will be interesting to see how it all develops," Mrs. Morrison said.

For the rest of the day, Marvin wondered how it would all develop tonight. Countless scenarios played out in his mind. Foremost, could there be any connection between him and the firecrackers? Could they dust for prints and trace it back to him? Could his grandfather have labeled them in some fashion? *Property of Leonard Wilson, 7404 Candle Street.* No of course not, that was stupid. This wasn't a coyote and roadrunner cartoon.

"Has anyone ever heard of the Tet offensive?" Mrs. Morrison asked.

Would Norb get caught? Would Norb tell on him? Or would he get caught?

"It was a major enemy military push staged during the Lunar New Year or *Tet* as they call it. We will learn about it next week."

His stomach growled. He felt light-headed. It was getting close to lunch.

"Marvin," Mrs. Morrison said. Marvin slipped from the murkiness of his mind back to the classroom. Sandra was turned toward him with wide eyes blinking under the awning of her hair.

"I'm not... I didn't have a question."

"That's fine," she said. "How about you get the door and the lights, please?"

"Oh. Yes."

———

AS THE FIFTH-GRADE classrooms were dismissed for lunch and meandered down the hallway toward the adjoining hallway which led down the stairs to the lunchroom. Marvin heard quite a few kids humming or singing the *Spiderman* song from *The Electric Company*. He turned to look and noticed that Rosa Alhambra was walking nearby. She would usually hang back and walk with Tammy—who was always one of the last ones to exit the class-but today, she was not with Tammy, she was by herself and she was a mere a foot or two away from Marvin.

I should say something, Marvin thought. *We've exchanged smiles, and peace signs, but never any words.* They had occupied the same classroom in the same grade of the same school for almost two months now. How could she know he liked her if he never said a word to her? They turned the corner of the hallway which led to the stairway to the cafeteria. It had to be soon. Time was running out. Marvin turned to her. She had looked away. He looked at the floor. He thought for a moment and then turned to her again. Since everyone was singing, may he should sing. But sing what? The song *How Do You Do?* came to his mind. That might be funny to sing. But what if she never heard the song? What about *Hello, I Love You?* No way! Was he crazy? He'd better not sing anything. Now, her eyes looked straight ahead. Now was the chance. He waved and nodded to get her attention. She looked at him.

"Hi," Marvin said.

"Hi," she replied.

"Sounds like everyone likes the Spiderman song."

"Yeah, I noticed," Rosa said.

"Nice job on Vietnam, by the way."

"Thanks," she replied with a smile. "Nice job on the door and lights."

"Thanks," Marvin said.

"So, that's what you said to her?" Denny asked as he chewed his cheese sandwich.

"Yeah. At least I said *something*. Even if it sounded stupid."

"I wouldn't say it sounded stupid. It sounded... political."

"Political?"

"Yeah," Denny replied. "Anytime my sister mentions Vietnam my father accuses her of being political."

Marvin glanced down and noticed there was only one plastic army man on top of Denny's lunch box. He was back to *Land Of The Giants* today. "No, it was the map, Denny," he said with agitation. "She knew where it was and pointed to it. It would be geographical more than political. I don't know how saying good job for pointing to a place on a map could be political. That doesn't even make sense!"

"Sorry. Jeezo Peezo."

It wasn't anything Denny had said even though he could be annoying. It was because Norb wasn't there again. That fueled Marvin's tension. Did he even remember about tonight? Would he be there? Marvin slid his sandwich from a paper bag followed by a bag of chips. It was Fritos today. Every time

Marvin brought them, Denny would sing; *Aye yah yah yahye! I'm dee the Frito Bandito!* but today he refrained. He sat silently and chewed with an open mouth.

"Well, it's good that you said something to her," Denny said. I mean, now, you've broken the ice. The possibilities of conversation are endless."

"I suppose," Marvin said. "I almost considered singing at one point."

"Singing? What were you going to sing?"

"I don't know."

"What? Tell me!" Denny said.

"Did you ever hear that song, *How Do You Do?*"

"Who is it by?"

"I think they're called Mouth and McNeal."

"Mouth?" Denny chuckled. "Don't think I've heard of them. They all have stupid names now. Edison Lighthouse. Iron Butterfly. Stupid."

Marvin pointed to the top of Denny's lunch box. "What happened? Did you lose one of your soldiers in an enemy military push?"

"No. I got some potato salad on him and I had to wash him off. While he was drying on the sink, Snooks, our schnauzer, got a hold of him and... put him out of commission."

"Sorry to hear that. Skippy chewed up my *Major Matt Mason*, you know the astronaut guy. He lost an arm and a foot."

"I had a Major Matt Mason. My little brother took some rubber bands and five bottle rockets, he wanted to send him into orbit. But.. he just caught on fire in my neighbors' rosebushes."

"What a shame," Marvin replied as unwrapped his sandwich. Deviled ham. A one-time staple of his lunches until someone told him it looked and smelled like cat food.

"What are you going to be for Halloween?" Denny asked after a considerable silence.

"I haven't thought about it. Not sure I'm going out this year." He took a bite of the sandwich. He could tell his grandmother made it. It had the right ratio of mayonnaise to deviled ham. His mother would suffocate it in mayo.

"I was thinking of going as Colonel Neville from *Omega Man*," Denny said. "Did you see Omega Man?"

"I saw it," Marvin replied. "So you would go out as Charlton Heston?"

"No, Denny said, "as one of the Albino mutants." He took a bit of his sandwich. "My other idea is probably better. My mom has a Styrofoam wig head that she doesn't use anymore. I can get one of my dad's old work shirts, cut a hole in the shoulder, and then fasten the head on it. I would be the *Incredible 2-Headed Transplant*."

"That's a good one," Marvin said. "That would be great. People would get that. Not too many would know who Omega Man is. Unless you wore a sign around your neck. *I'm the Omega Man*. And then they still might not know.'""

"True." Denny signed. "If you remember I was Dr. Zaius from *Planet of the Apes* last year, and nobody knew who that was. They thought I was either Cheetah from *Tarzan or Lancelot Link*. People around here a very shallow." Denny poured out apple juice from his thermos and took a sip. "Plus, *Omega Man* was just a remake of the one with Vincent Price."

"Do you know who Norbert Stiebert is?" Marvin asked.

"Yeah, I know Norbert. He was in my fourth-grade class. Mrs. Penrodski's. I heard he's still in her class this year." Denny took a stack of Pringles from a plastic bag. "Why?" He set the chips carefully on his tongue and closed his mouth.

"Well, we were going to see a movie tonight..."

"*Dracula A.D.?*"

"Right." Marvin sighed.

"I didn't know that Norbert was your friend."

"Well, he's not a... full friend, I mean, I just got to know him." Marvin set his sandwich down as a glob of the ham oozed out onto his thumb and dropped onto the lunch table. He got a paper towel out of his lunch bag to wipe it up. "I was supposed to help him do something tonight."

"Help him do something? I thought you were going to the movies?"

"We are," Marvin said wiping his thumb. "He wanted to... play a prank."

"A prank? At the movie?" Denny's eyes grew large behind his glasses. "That's funny."

"Why is that funny?"

"Because my older sister and some of her friends did that at the South County Cinema during the movie *Willard*."

"What did they do?"

"You know that one scene where Willard commands his rats to attack the bad guy?"

"Sure. Ernest Borgnine had it coming."

"During that scene, my sister and her friends unleashed a bunch of tennis balls to roll under the seats."

"What happened?"

"Some people screamed. Some laughed. One lady passed out when a ball rolled over her foot. They got into so much trouble."

"How much trouble?"

"A Policeman brought her home," Denny told him. "She was grounded for a month. It was bad." Denny stacked another mouthful of chips. "So, what are you guys planning? Squirt guns with red food color? That's what I would do," he said as he crunched his chips.

"Something like that."

Marvin stood at the crosswalk and considered whether he wanted to take the shortcut behind the high school or walk along Baymore road. Everyone walked home along Baymore. Clumps of kids floated along the sidewalk with about 4 steps of concrete and fresh air in between the strolling packs. He usually trailed behind the kids who lived on the other streets near Candle drive. Streets that held illumination names. Lamplighter court. Lantern drive. Beacon way. Most of them dead ends.

The crosswalk light changed and flashed *Walk*. He took a step off the curb just as he heard a familiar voice behind him.

"Hey! Lee Marvin!"

It was Norb. He was flanked on each side by two taller kids with long brown hair. One wore an army coat and the other sported a jean jacket. They looked like they belonged on the high school side of the street.

"Hey, Norb," Marvin said. "I tried to find you at lunch today."

"Yeah, I had to eat in the principal's office today. Somebody drew a big peace sign inside the crapper stall. I got blamed."

The two long hair kids laughed.

"This is Marvin. The kid I was tellin' you about. The one with the Mini Trail." The kid with the army coat nodded. The other kid in the jean jacket shrugged as if Norb had asked a question.

"This is my brother, Langford," Norb said and flipped his hair back. "This cretin is his friend, Carl."

"Nice to meet you," Marvin replied not sure which one was Lance and which was Carl.

"Hey, we're still on for tonight, right?" Norb asked as he reached into his coat pocket and pulled out a cigarette.

"Yeah... what time? Where should we meet?"

"I dunno," Norb said. "Say about seven or so. We'll just find each other. It ain't that big." He punched the army coat on the shoulder. "You gotta light, man?"

"Sure." Army coat dug into his pocket and pulled out a book of matches.

"You headin' home?" Norb asked Marvin.

"Yeah," Marvin said. He looked up and saw the crosswalk had changed to *Don't Walk*.

"We're headin' up to *Booger* Chef." Norb stuck his finger up his nose to illustrate his joke.

"I'm starvin'," Army Jacket said.

"You're always starving," Denim Jacket replied.

Marvin noticed their eyes had a reddish tint that was similar to Christopher Lee's Dracula. His eyes would turn blood red when he attacked a victim.

"Wanna come with us?" Norb asked.

"Uh... Oh no, no thanks," Marvin told him. "I have to... uh...Go."

Norb struck a match and flicked it at jean jacket who jumped back. "That ain't cool, Norbert!"

The crosswalk light had not changed but Marvin noticed the persistent swish of passing cars ceased to pulse in his ears. There was a lull in traffic. Time to go. "So, anyway," he said as he stepped off the curb. "I'll see you tonight. Seven." He sprinted across the street. "Somewhere inside."

"Right!" Norb called out. "Bang! Bang!"

MARVIN DIDN'T STOP his sprint until he was halfway down the breezeway between the junior and senior high buildings. So much for walking down Baymore with the clumps of kids. He was taking the shortcut. Plans change but the plans for tonight were still in motion. The Sonny and Cher song *Bang Bang* played in Marvin's head as he walked home. It was the sound-track for the shortcut and for the plans.

The Sleeping Bag, the basement and the back way

White smoke curled up through the branches of the oak trees behind his grandparent's house. Marvin saw the blend of brown and gray in the air as he stepped on the street from the shortcut path. As he got closer—and was a few blocks from *Cancel* drive —he could smell the sweet scent of roasted leaves and twigs. Leonard must have come home early, grabbed a rake and the perforated burn can, and set about to liberate the lawn from the dead foliage.

Odds were high that his grandmother would subtly suggest that Marvin lend his grandfather a hand with the yard work; but he only had so much time--maybe three hours--he was good for gathering a few piles of leaves but that was it. He entered the house as silent as possible and made his way to his room.

"Marvin?" Irene called out from the kitchen.

"Yeah?" He answered as he opened a dresser drawer to retrieve the sock that held his allowance.

"When you get a minute," Irene said, "if you're not busy with homework or anything... your granddad could use a hand out back."

Marvin pulled his hand from the sock and it only held .75 cents. Two quarters, two dimes, and a nickel. Admission on Friday night was $1.25. This is not good he thought. Not at all.

"His back has been giving him fits," Irene said. "All that bending over out there isn't good for him."

He submerged his hands below the underwear and socks in

the drawer. His fingers explored the paper liner at the bottom; he found a ticket stub from when he went to see *Patton*, a guitar pick he caught when he and Ryan saw Mac Davis at Six Flags, and a Frito Bandito eraser that slipped over a pencil. Digging further back he felt something round, maybe a quarter. No such luck. It was the Snoopy commemorative astronaut coin.

"Maybe you'd like to go out and help him a little while. Before dinner."

"Yeah," Marvin replied. Maybe his mom would be home before he left, before her date, and he could ask her for fifty cents.

"If you help out, I'll buy you an ice cream tonight," Irene said.

Marvin dropped the coins in his pocket, shut the drawer, and walked to the kitchen. "The thing is... I'm supposed to go to the movies tonight. With some friends from school. So, maybe instead of ice cream... do you think I could get just fifty cents instead?"

"What show?"

"The show at the Crest. To see the new Dracula movie. Mom already said I could go."

"Dracula?" She made a face as if something foul had wafted into the room or she had tasted something spoiled. "Why don't you see something nice? Something decent?"

"Dracula is decent. So, could I just get fifty cents instead? "

"I don't know why anyone would want to see all that blood and nonsense." Irene slid a cigarette out from the pack that lived near her elbow on the table. "What about that *Wonka* movie? They say that's pretty good."

"That was last summer," Marvin told her. He watched her light the cigarette, take a drag, and then blow the smoke up at the ceiling where it mushroomed.

"Well, Marvin, I'd give you the change but..." She reached

into her purse that was hooked on the back of her chair and got out her rubber coin purse. She squeezed it open. "...Mrs. Phegel came around collecting for Catholic Charities. I'm afraid I gave her have her all the change I had. Not a cent left."

Melvin sighed. "That's OK. Did mom say what time she was getting home?"

"The usual time, I imagine. And she didn't say anything to me about you going to the show tonight. Is she supposed to take you and your friends?"

"No," Marvin said. "I'm meeting them there."

"Meeting them? How are you getting there?"

"I going to walk."

"Walk?"

"Yeah. I've walked up there before. Ronnie, Ryan, and me walked up there lots of times."

"When?" Irene asked.

"We went to see the Pufnstuf movie, remember? It was on a Saturday afternoon. It's no big deal."

"But that was in the daylight hours. Not at night. It's not safe walking up there at night. You could get hit on the head."

"But I'm not going into the city, I'm walking through perfectly safe neighborhoods." Marvin tried not to whine but it happened when he spoke. He needed to sound mature and responsible. He tried again. "I'm going to be with kids my age. Nothing will happen to us. No one will hit me on the head."

"I don't know Marvin." Irene took another drag. "I don't think you should be out walking at night. You never know what kind of crazy person is waiting for some kids by themselves. Remember that poor Greenlease boy." She often brought up the boy who had been kidnapped and murdered in Kansas City. The kidnappers hid and were caught in St. Louis. This story was used to instill fear; it meant that others could be hiding in the shadows. Child kidnapping was the spirit of St. Louis.

"I will be fine. I'm not a little kid," Marvin said. "I'd better get out there and help. Before it gets dark." He walked to the back door. "Before some crazy person jumps out of the trees and kills us."

LEONARD HAD three leaf mounds gathered around the burn can. Skippy was busy inspecting the piles with her nose, having all this material in one area was a bonus; it saved her time and energy from having to sniff it all spread across the yard.

"Heard you could use some help," Marvin said.

"Ah, not much to do now," Leonard said scooping up a lump between his gloved hand and the rake. "This is just the start of all this crap." He dropped the batch of leaves into the conflagrant can. He pointed with the rake handle up toward the canopy of the trees, "See that? There's three times as much up there waiting to come down. Damn oaks are stubborn. I've seen them not fall till the following spring."

"Yeah? I guess they're not in a hurry."

They stood in silence for a moment. The crackling of the burning leaves drew Marvin's attention. He could see the glow through the holes grow brighter, refreshed by the last delivery of fuel, and the pale smoke billowed upward and released a new breath of campfire perfume.

"So, I was wondering," Marvin said, "do you think maybe I could get part of my allowance, in advance, like just fifty cents? I need it for the movies tonight."

Leonard chuckled. "Don't have anything smaller than a twenty. Your grandma took all my change."

"Oh, OK. That's all right."

"Say, there was something I was wondering... I was talking to Harlan, next door," Leonard said, "told me he saw something the other day." He turned the rake around and plucked off leaves that had been speared by the tines.

"Yeah?" Marvin's stomach tightened. "What did he see?"

"Said he saw some kid riding a minibike down the street out here."

"Really?"

Leonard handed the rake to Marvin. "You wouldn't happen to know anything about that, would you?"

Happen to know? Marvin considered as he took the rake and turned to locate an area that may need attention. *Would I like to confess? Would I like to be grounded to my room starting now and for the foreseeable future? No.* "When was this?" Marvin asked.

"Few days ago."

Marvin raked as he considered his answer. If only the Hablin's had a minibike. He would gladly pin it on them.

"Do you know who it was?" Leonard asked. "I sure as hell hope it wasn't you."

"No," quickly said as he scooped up leaves and dropped them in the can. "It wasn't me. It was Norbert Stiebert"

"Who?"

"A kid from school."

"Norbert?"

"Yeah. He has a Ruttman Toad. Rides it everywhere. All over the streets around here. Even goes up to Krause's Auto to get Oil stickers. He came by the other day, he wanted to see my mini-trail. I told him... you know, I couldn't leave the driveway. He said, you know, that's fine, he just wanted to see it. I showed him. I removed the blanket and let him see it. He wanted to ride it but I... I said no."

"Is that right?"

"Yeah. He... he asked if I wanted to ride *his* bike and I said no. So, yeah, he... just, rode his bike around. Up and down the street a few times... and that was it. He left."

Marvin could sense his grandfather's eyes were studying him as he dabbed the rake at a few leaves that had blown from the pile. He felt it was best not to make eye contact yet. It was better to look natural and continue working. It would hopefully sell the story.

"I don't know about this Norbert fella," Leonard finally said. "Think it's best to stay away from kids like that. He sounds like trouble."

"Right," Marvin replied. "He does tend to get into a lot of trouble."

"I knew a kid like that when I was your age. He was always up to some sort of shenanigans." Leonard pulled a cigarette from his jacket pocket. "He was always getting himself into all sorts of scrapes." He lit the cigarette. "Chet Swanson."

"Chet Swanson?"

"Yes. That was his name."

"What sort of stuff did he do?"

"Well, bunch of us went over to Knox College one night. Stood out in front of the girl's dormitory..."

"Dormitory?"

"Yeah," Leonard said. "It's a building where all the college gals live. Like an apartment." He took a drag from his cigarette. "Some of the fellas started tossing things up at the windows. Trying to get a rise out of the girls. Sticks and things." He blew out the smoke. "I found a small rock by the street. I guess I threw it too hard. It hit a window on the second floor and it shattered. Girls screamed. Lights came on. Everybody ran."

"Oh no!" Marvin replied as he looked up from the leaf pile to his grandfather. He expected to see a jovial grin, a smile but Leonard held a serious countenance. The look he wore when he was trying to make a serious point which was a smirk on the bottom of his face and a squint on top. A squint like Clint Eastwood in a western just before he draws his gun.

"You want to take a guess at who got blamed for it? Who had to pay for it?"

Marvin knew the answer was simple. Why would he ask this question unless it would be easy but have a twist? He decided to try the obvious response. "You?"

"Nope," Leonard told him. "Chet Swanson. He had to pay. Chet took the blame for a lot of things I did. Things we all did."

A few sticks in the can released steam that had been trapped with a loud pop. Marvin saw that the answer wasn't simple but he felt it was obvious where the subject was pointed. He looked down at the can, the fire was catching up with its load now, and the holes looked like menacing red eyes. The burn can beast was alive. Irene's voice cut through crackling.

"Marvin? Phone call!"

An exit. Whatever moral lesson was about to be taught had to wait. Whatever further evidence, if any, some neighbor may have submitted about a kid on a mini-bike would have to wait on the back burner. Perfect timing he thought as he turned and walked toward the back door.

"Hey! Hold on there!" Leonard spoke up. Marvin stopped. Here it comes. The moral of the story. He turned around slowly. "The rake."

"The what?"

"Are you taking the rake inside with you?" Leonard asked.

"Oh," Marvin replied. "I wasn't thinking." He stepped forward and handed the rake back to his grandfather.

———

"Hello?"

"Hey, whatcha doing, Marv?"

"Not much, Ryan. Raking leaves and burning them."

"Cool."

"I thought you were going camping with your mom."

"I am," he replied. Marvin could hear Mrs. Heffendorf's raised voice in the background.

"Do you have my sleeping bag?" Ryan asked.

"Why would I have it?"

"Last summer when we camped out in your backyard, Think I left it there."

"Oh yeah," Marvin replied. "But we went over to Ronnies' the next day, remember? His mom let us air everything out on her clothesline."

"Oh yeah." Marvin could hear Linda yelling now. "Could you go over there and get it for me? Please!"

"Me? Why don't you get it? It's your sleeping bag."

"You live closer and I have to pack stuff. And... another thing, they're all mad at me."

"Who? Who's mad?"

"Well, pretty much the whole Phegel family."

"What did you do?"

The line fell silent. No one was yelling in the background, only Ryan breathing in the foreground. Finally, he spoke, "I called Lauren, *Clarence the cross-eyed lion.*"

"Why did you do that?"

"Cause she called me a *turd-eating tard.*"

"What?"

"It's a long story, would you just go and see if it's over there? Please?"

Marvin sighed and let his moment of silence pass. "All right. I'll do it.

"Thanks, Marvin!"

"For fifty cents."

· · ·

He told Irene he would be back soon, that he had an errand. He went out the front and ran across the street, two houses up to the Phegels. It was a long-standing tradition in the neighborhood for kids to stand outside and '*call*' a friend's name. Normally, Marvin would stand on the front lawn and sing out "Ooooooh Ronnie!" But he didn't have time for tradition. He went up to the door and knocked.

Ronnie's mom opened the door. "Well, hello Marvin!"

"Hello, Mrs. Phegel. I was wondering..."

"Ronnie just went up with his father to get dinner," she pushed open the storm door. "Yeah, they just ran up to get us some fish sandwiches from that Burger place on Gravier."

"Oh, that's fine. I didn't come to see Ronnie..."

"Come on in," Mrs. Phegel opened the storm door further to allow Marvin entrance. He stepped into the living room. Lauren was sitting on the floor in front of the TV, still wearing her school uniform, her homework spread out in a fan formation in front of her.

"Hey Marv," Lauren said. "Ronnie's not here."

"Yes, I heard."

"What?"

"Lauren Ann Marie, why don't you turn that down?" Mrs. Phegel said and nodded at the TV. The news was reporting a plane that had crashed in France. Lauren rose, went over to the television console, turned the knob, and John Chancellor's voice faded. Marvin heard music coming down the hall from one of the back bedrooms. It sounded like the song from the Temptations, Four Tops, or one of those groups. He was confident it came from Joannie's room because Janey only listened to The Osmonds or The Monkees. The teenie bop bubble gum stuff. Joannie listened to everything else. Lauren returned to her place on the floor.

"Would you like a soda or something?" Mrs. Phegel asked. "Would you like to have a seat?"

"No, thanks," Marvin replied. "I just came by to uh... see if you... by chance... may have found an extra sleeping bag? See, when we all camped out that one time and hung up our stuff in your backyard. I think one of the sleeping bags got left behind."

"Oh my," Mrs. Phegel said, "I don't recall that." She gripped her chin in thought and squinted at the floor. Mrs. Phegel was the oldest of the mothers that Marvin knew, but that was based on the manner she carried herself; she moved slowly, hunched forward, and had more gray hair than brown. She seemed to be closer to his grandmother's age than his mother's. "Well, if it's here, it would be with that stuff in the basement."

"I can take him down to look," Lauren said. "Come on, I'll show you." She sprang up, holding her pencil, and headed toward the basement door in the kitchen. Marvin followed her.

"Thank you, Mrs. Phegel," he said as went down the stairs. At the bottom he watched Lauren pull strings above her head that created a path of illumination below around a workbench, a washing machine, a ping pong table, and a roll-top desk.

"There," Lauren said as she looked toward a series of shelves hovering above a row of cardboard boxes and suitcases. "It's probably in that corner with the other camping stuff." She pointed with the pencil she had brought. "Sorry, the bulb doesn't work over there. Ronnie broke it with a soccer ball."

"Thanks," Marvin said and he stepped over a rolled-up carpet. He studied the various folded forms on the shelf. He should have asked Ryan for more details; *what color was it? Did it come in a bag?* Everything in the corner looked like a rolled-up sleeping bag. Everything was gray or olive drab in the minimal light.

"Do you see it?" Lauren asked.

"Um, I think... maybe." He took a few steps closer. *Was it*

Red? Green? Blue? Should he just grab one and hope for the best? Why did he agree to do this?

Lauren hopped over the rug and stood next to Marvin. "The red one is dad's. That blue one is Joannie's. Mom and I don't have one. Ronnie's got ruined on the last retreat, so that leaves the green one. That must be yours."

"Right. Probably so, " Marvin said. "I couldn't see yet. My eyes weren't adjusted to the... basement." He took a step forward and pulled the green bag out. "Got it." He stepped over into the area beneath a light bulb and brushed off the dust. He could sense Lauren standing near. He turned the sleeping bag over which displayed a patch with the name *Heffendorf* printed in marker. Marvin stuffed it up under his arm quickly and looked at Lauren. A smirk was forming across her face. Did she see the name? Why was she standing so close? "Thanks for your help."

"Sure." She said. "That's not really yours is it?"

Marvin was frozen. He wanted to bolt up the stairs and leave her in the light bulb basement, but he didn't. Kids were mean to Lauren, he wanted to be an exception. He studied her face while he prayed for the correct response. He could see every freckle on her face. Yellow flecks on her lips that came from biting her pencil. Her lazy eye was magnified but holding steady on him.

"No," Marvin replied. "It's not. It actually belongs to..." He chewed his bottom lip in thought. He needed a good answer. Lauren pushed her glasses up. "...it belongs to a turd-eating tard that lives down the street."

Her eyes grew larger behind her glasses. A few seconds of silence disguised themselves as minutes. Lauren let out a peal of laughter that made his ears ring. She bent over in laughter.

"Thanks again," Marvin said. He took advantage of the moment and turned to leave, taking each step two at a time. He moved quickly through the kitchen, and into the living room, "Found it!" he said to Mrs. Phegel. He could hear Lauren's footfalls coming up the stairs. "Thanks again. I better get home."

"Oh. Okie Dokie," Mrs. Phegel said. "You sure you don't want a soda or something? They should be back anytime now."

"No thanks. I was helping my grandpa with the leaves. His back was bothering him. I need to get back."

"Sure thing," she replied.

Lauren entered the room and Marvin looked over at her, her face was flush from laughing. Instead of a smirk, she wore a smile. She sat back down in front of her homework. The secret of the sleeping bag was safe.

"See you around, Lauren," he said and walked to the door. "Tell Ronnie hello for me."

"I will do," Mrs. Phegel said.

Marvin pulled open the front door and placed his hand on the handle of the storm door. He needed to walk across the street toward home in case Mrs. Phegel watched him. He couldn't turn right and walk up toward the Heffendorf's house because it might look odd.

"If you see Ryan," Mrs. Phegel said. Marvin suspended all motion. The latch on the storm door handle snapped back across his knuckles. "You tell him that I need to see him. I have a bone to pick with him."

"Oh yeah. Sure, I will," Marvin replied. "I don't see him all much anymore, but... if I do... I will defiantly tell him." He heard Lauren giggle and a new song echoing down the hall. It sounded like the Beatles. How long had he been standing in the doorway trying to leave? "Bye now," he said and pushed onward.

. . .

As Marvin crossed the street he saw the garage door was open. His grandfather must be in there, maybe putting away the rake or some other grandfather business. He needed to get the firecrackers from the cigar box but not while Leonard was present. *What are you going to do with those things? And why are you holding that sleeping bag?* He needed to get it to Ryan without being seen walking up the street. He had to travel *the backway* which meant climbing five chain link fences and crossing four backyards without being noticed by the neighbors. He and Ryan had accomplished the back-way trials several times for fun, but this day it was a mission. One Mr. Phelps on *Mission Impossible* might appreciate.

Marvin moved quickly by the garage and opened the back gate. Skippy trotted over to inspect what he held. "It's just a stupid sleeping bag. Please don't start barking when I make the run. OK?"

All the yards up to the Heffendorfs' looked clear. He tossed the bag over the fence, climbed over, picked it up, and ran across the lawn to the next fence. He repeated it three more times until he got to Ryan's yard. He only heard someone yell once, but he didn't stop to clarify what they said. He was focused. For the most part. His mind only wandered once as he considered the show *Mission Impossible*--how did Mr. Phelps know where the tape recorder was located at the start of each show? Who told him where to go?

He landed in the final yard and to keep his cover, Marvin went to the back door and knocked. After a few minutes, he saw the kitchen curtains move as Mrs. Heffendorf peeked out. Six taps of his tennis shoe later, the door opened and she stood there swaddled in a large Terrycloth robe and a white towel crown on her head.

"Well, hey there Marvey," she said in her usual drawl that was based from somewhere in southern Illinois. "I couldn't imagine for the life of me who'd be knocking at the back door."

"Hi, Mrs. Heffendorf. I just came by to drop off Ryan's sleeping bag. He said he needed it. He left it over at the Phegels. I got it for him."

"Oh, well sure enough." She opened the door while calling out, "Ryan, honey! Marvin's here!"

"No, uh... actually, I have to get back home," Marvin told her. "It's almost dinner time. We're having... hamburgers from that place up on Gravier." Marvin could hear Ryan yelling "*What?*" from somewhere in the house.

"Well, fiddlesticks. You sure you don't want to come in for a minute?"

"No. I just wanted to drop it off." Marvin stepped forward and put the bag down next to Mrs. Heffendorf's flip-flop feet. "I'll see Ryan when he gets back. When are you getting back?"

"Sunday night," she replied. "Wish you and your mom were going with us."

"Me too," Marvin said. "But... you know. She does have a date tonight."

"Oh does she? Well, that's just super."

"Sure is," Marvin replied. "I'd best be going. Thank you Mrs. Heffendorf. Have fun at the... thing."

"We will and thank you, Marvin," she said as she stepped back inside.

He stepped off the back porch and hesitated for a moment; he realized it would look odd for him to climb the fence and run across the yard instead of going around to the front. Thankfully, Mrs. Heffendorf never asked why he came to the back door. Why push his luck? The coast should be clear for him to walk down the street. Marvin opened the gate and proceeded to the front. A voice called out when he was a few steps down the driveway. "Hey, kid!" He froze. "What are you doing sneaking around my house?" He turned to see Linda sitting on the front porch huddled in Peacoat with bell bottoms blooming below.

"Oh! Hi there," Marvin replied, "I had to drop off something for your brother."

"How did you sneak by? I've been sitting out here for a while, waiting for my ride."

"No, I came the back way. Through the yards."

"Hiding from the fuzz?" She asked with a smile. "You're busted!" She pointed her finger and cocked her thumb back like a gun. "Hey, you don't happen to know what time it is, do you?"

Marvin remembered the Phegle's clock in the kitchen—when he looked at it--had been 5:15. Adding the time he spent crossing the yards and talking. "5:30 maybe or so."

"5:30?! Come on people!" Linda said. "Time is money!"

Money. Marvin suddenly remembered. He was supposed to collect fifty cents from Ryan. *Should he go back and knock? Was there time?*

"It's about time!" Linda stood up. There was a low roar like a train rumbling in the distance. Marvin turned to see an orange Plymouth Barracuda coming up the street.

"Who's that?"

"That is my dad," Linda said as she crossed the yard. The car eased into the driveway. The man behind the wheel looked like an adult version of Ryan; same blue eyes and dark brown hair. He smiled and waved. Marvin waved back but realized Mr. Heffendorf had waved to Ryan who was coming out the front door.

"Mopar!" Ryan shouted as he ran to the driver's side of the car and Linda climbed into the passenger side.

Marvin watched the scene unfold for a few moments and smiled. His father, Dutch, used to drive a blue Dodge Charger. It was a cool-looking car with a long rear window. Marvin loved to lay in the back and watch the clouds float by overhead. That was many years ago. He wondered if his dad still drove that car. He smiled, turned, and walked toward home.

He had no cares and no fifty cents; which meant no movie. Chances were good that Leonard was still in the garage so he couldn't get what he needed. *What was the point of it all anyway?* Marvin wondered. *Why was it a big deal? To be liked and accepted? Who would even know he had a hand in the incident? What kid set off the firecrackers last time?* Marvin shrugged. *What was his name? Who knows? When it was all said and done he would be a plain 11-year-old like before. Just baseball cards tucked into the spokes. Just the mini-bike and not the motorcycle.* Why should he bother?

A low rumble of thunder came up behind Marvin. He moved over to the side and walked along the curb. "Hey, little boy," a voice sang to him. He turned and saw Linda hanging out of the window. She had her arm outstretched and her clenched fist held something. "You want some candy?"

Marvin didn't feel like playing this game. He put his head down and kept walking.

"I am serious Milstead!" Linda yelled. "Come here, right now!" Her voice carried a tone and intensity that cut through the rumble of the Barracuda and caused Marvin to turn and look at her.

"Sorry." Marvin walked over to the car. She shook her hand at him as if to say, *here.* He held his hand under her fist and she dropped two quarters into his palm. "There! From Ryan. I'm supposed to give you that."

"Thanks!"

"You're welcome," she said with a wink. "See you later."

THE GARAGE DOOR was open but no Leonard inside. Marvin ran in, opened the cabinet, reached into the cigar box, and got the package of firecrackers. He went to the front of the house, set them far back under the pfitzer juniper bush by the lamp post, and then went inside to clean up.

"Do you want me to fix you something to eat?" Irene asked.

"Not sure," Marvin replied. "What time is it?"

"Quarter to six," she told him. "Your granddad wants eggs and sausage for supper. Do you want a couple of eggs?"

"No thanks." He stepped into the bathroom and turned on the faucet. His fingers smelled like gunpowder. "I'll just have bologna and cheese."

"You don't want a couple of eggs?"

"No."

"I can scramble them. I could make a bird's nest for you."

"No thanks," he dipped the washcloth in the warm water and rubbed his face. "Bologna and cheese is fine."

"You don't want more than that?"

"No thanks."

"Mayonnaise? Mustard?"

"Just mayo," Marvin said. He went to his closet and grabbed his brown pants, and yellow sweatshirt, and changed into them. He slipped off the loafers and put on his tennis shoes. No one on the *Mission Impossible* team wore taps to the job.

He sat at the kitchen table and ate his sandwich Irene monitored the sausage links in the frying pan on the stove. "So, what did Ryan need?"

"His sleeping bag. He left it over at the Phegels."

"At the Phegels?" She opened the refrigerator and got out a carton of eggs. "Why did he call you?"

"He wanted me to go and get it. He needs it for the camping trip."

"Why did you have to get it?" She cracked an egg against the pan and let the yoke find a place near the sausages.

"He made fun of Lauren's lazy eye. They're all mad at him."

"Why that little stinker," Irene said. "You should have told him to take a flying leap."

"Well, I got fifty cents out of the deal."

"Fifty cents?" Another egg went into the pan.

Marvin looked at the clock. It was 6:03 "Oh man! I've got to get going." He folded the last bit of the sandwich into his mouth and stood up.

"I forgot you were going to that monster picture," Irene said as she rolled the sausages. "Don't you want to wait till your mother gets home and have her run you up there?"

"No," Marvin replied. "I'm meeting... my friend... at his house."

"How are you getting to your friends?"

"My bike."

"After dark? You're not riding a bike at night."

"Why not?"

"You don't have lights," Irene said over the increased sizzling. "You'll get yourself hurt. Somebody could be driving along, not see you, and run you over."

"I'm riding in the middle of the street." Marvin got up from the table.

"Why don't you just wait till your mother gets home and she can take you." She went to the cabinet and got a plate. The back door opened and Leonard came in bringing with him the scent of cooked leaves.

"No, she has a date," Marvin said. "It's fine. I'll walk. It'll take twice as long but... fine."

"What's going on?" Leonard asked.

"Nothing." Marvin went to the hall closet and got his coat.

"Where's he going?" Leonard turned the faucet on to wash his hands.

"Up to the show," Irene said. "Your supper's almost ready."

Going To The Show

The way there was simple. It was the same way he had been many times on his bicycle but this time he was walking; it was getting dark, and colder, and he had miniature explosives in his pocket. When Marvin had left the house and walked to the pfitzer bush; the neighbor who had told his grandfather about the kid on a minibike was outside raking leaves from under the hedges. Marvin waved. The neighbor waved back and then turned away to look at something. Marvin ducked down to get the firecrackers, stuffed them in his coat pocket, and then pretended to examine one of the branches of the bush; in case the neighbor turned back and needed to report to Leonard his observations about the kid in the front yard. *He was doing something to your juniper bush.*

Marvin sprinted across the street and cut through Franzini's yard to Fairman road, ran up the hill to Baymore avenue, and then stopped to catch his breath before he continued. He kept a brisk pace, feeling the breeze from the passing cars tug at him to walk faster. Tonight he thought, the soundtrack should be something cool, with a saxophone; like the music he heard late at night on the radio. Music played by a disk jockey who called himself the *Man In The Red Vest*. A jazz song like *Take Five* would be a good tune for this night. Ryan and Ronnie hated jazz music. That's fine. Forget them and their stupid kid songs. They aren't walking with him tonight. It was just Marvin and could imagine any song he wanted.

Finally, he came to the side street that joined as a horseshoe, the first one was Rosedale—he recalled that Norb lived on that street—but he had no idea what the address was. All the houses were the same, small brick bungalows with pointed front archways. It was getting too dark to see if any of the homes had a dirt bike track in the backyard. There was no time. Maybe he would find Norb walking up to the Crest but he couldn't see anyone else walking.

He jogged to the top of the street where it curved around into the court. Marvin spotted some silhouettes moving along the sidewalk. One of them might be Norb. He would wait until they walked under the streetlight and follow at a distance. He could hear the bustle of traffic on Gravier growing closer. The sidewalk figures entered the cone of light, Marvin saw it was a young couple walking a dog.

Instead of strolling down the street that poured out onto the sidewalk along Gravier, he went down an alley that ran parallel to the street, behind businesses and homes to an old brick pathway-it would shave off 10 minutes. The timeworn bricks led to concrete steps down to the parking lot of the Crest. Marvin and his friends had used the shortcut many times, during the day, but during nightfall, it was a new experience for him. The dark of the alley is where Irene would insist child kidnappers were hiding—they would jump out of an imperceptible crevice, hit you over the head, and initiate the *I Told You So* from your grandmother along with a ransom demand.

Marvin made it down the steps to the parking lot without lumps, in one piece. There were some cars in the lot but it wasn't full. Not many Dracula fans on Friday night. He walked around to the front of the cinema. Different clusters of kids loitered under the brightly lighted half-moon canopy that was coated with hundreds of small white bulbs. The marquee stood at attention above the canopy with most of the plastic letters in place and the green neon ribbons that outlined the whole thing buzzed like a giant mosquito. The entire luminous aura cast a glow across both lanes of Gravier avenue and reflected off the cars as they drove past.

Marvin looked around but didn't find a familiar face except for the girl who was a library helper at school. Friday nights at the Crest must be her liberation from sorting books all week. He walked over to the box office and waited in line. He felt his stomach grumble as he stood there. Perhaps he should have eaten more than a bologna sandwich and given his waves of nervousness a little more to work with, but at the same time a sense of excitement he felt, evened it out. Excited that he was doing something by himself. Something slightly dangerous.

"How many?" the lady asked through the round vent in the glass.

"Just one."

"1.25, please."

Marvin reached into his pocket and carefully pulled out his change of four quarters, two dimes, and a nickel, and placed it on the counter. He reached up and patted his coat pocket to make sure the secret package was still there. The last thing he needed was to find that he had lost it somewhere along the way or back in the dark ally—snatched up by head-thumpers and kidnappers—but they were still in his pocket.

"I'm sorry kid but we don't take these," the lady said through the vent.

Marvin looked up and she was holding a coin. A coin that looked like one of the quarters but it wasn't—it was his Snoopy commemorative Apollo coin.

"Oh!" He dug back into his right pants pocket and found nothing. Left pocket, nothing. Right coat pocket, nothing. No way it could be in his left coat pocket. He slipped his fingers in carefully, under the cellophane wrapper, nope. He was certain he had the change. Could he have lost a quarter somewhere? Maybe bending down under the pfitzer bush? On the street somewhere? The parking lot. Someone in the line behind him sighed. *Hurry it up, kid.* He plunged his hand back down into his front right pocket and there folded over in the lining at the bottom was a coin. Marvin twisted to get it free and rescued the smothered quarter.

"Sorry. Here it is." He slid it toward her and she slid back his Snoopy coin. She pressed a button and a ticket spit out of a metal slot. He grabbed the commemorative coin, and his ticket, and walked to the entrance.

At The Crest: Faces in the Light Friends in the Dark

The first person Marvin saw when he entered the lobby was the police officer that had escorted Norb out at the last Friday night firecracker fest. He was leaning on the concession counter sipping a soda through a straw. Marvin looked down at the well-worn maroon carpet, made his way to the doorman, and held out his ticket. He took his half of the ticket and walked inside the auditorium. He noticed a few things upon entering; it was very warm inside—the heat brushed your face as soon as you stepped inside, more people were milling about than he judged by the cars parked outside—many were probably dropped off, and finally, it did indeed smell like a dirty sock.

He walked toward the restrooms. No Norb loitering around that area at the moment. Marvin decided to find a seat and wait it out. He walked down the aisle and sat in the same section he and his mother had sat for *The Abominable Dr. Phibes*. His stomach growled again. He was nervous but wasn't sure if it was the precarious act that was planned that caused it; what he owed a new friend to do this evening, or perhaps the price he might pay if they were caught by a soda-sipping policeman.

Caught 'em red-handed Mrs. Milstone... sorry, Milstead. Your son and that other juvenile delinquent detonated a small package of tightly wrapped gunpowder in a public facility. The package as I am to understand was taken without proper permission from a cigar box located in a cabinet in the garage of a Mr. Leonard Wilson on Candle Drive. I'm afraid it's the hoosegow for both of them. Or maybe his fate would be similar to Denny Walter's sister and they would just drive him home. He would prefer home over the hoosegow.

Marvin tapped his foot to the music that made it through the clamor of kid voices. He smiled when he recognized the tune as *A Walk In The Black Forest*. They must use the same Muzak system as they use at Variety Store, Marvin thought. He heard it the night he traded his red folder for the yellow folder. Maybe the song was an indication that Norb was here now. He looked around at the various figures who meandered the aisles; kids of all shapes and sizes, guys who had the same hairstyle as Norb, with long hair drooping on one side so they had to jerk their heads back to clear the overflow from their faces. Each sudden movement caught Marvin's eyes, *no that's not him, nope neither is that one.*

It was like watching an old rerun from a Friday long ago but this time he was watching it alone. Kids wandering aimlessly around rows and aisles of the local cinema. It was just as entertaining as any feature presentation. And then a familiar flash caught his attention; short brown hair which he was used to seeing in a different environment. She walked down the aisle as if on her way to point out a location on the map. It was Rosa Alhambra. She was here. At the Crest. Marvin watched as she sat down in a seat five rows from the front, one seat from the end. By herself. He felt the instinct to move. To rise out of his seat and walk down the aisle and... say hello. The thought of doing that made his face warm. It was the thing that Denny Walters talked about. Those films they watched last year. The same force that urged him to get up and speak to Rosa Alhambra was the same one that made him feel warm and clumsy. Dealing with cooties was easier. You had your imaginary spray and that took care of it. Or you declared ABC Blackout and touched something black and you were cured. But this puberty business was difficult. Marvin stood up, stretched, and stepped out into the aisle. Maybe he could casually walk by Rosa. *Hi Rosa, what are you doing here?* No, that is a very stupid common question. *Oh hi, Rosa! So, you like Dracula? Yeah? I was wondering if you..."*

"Excuse me, Marvin," a voice snapped from behind him. He turned and saw Tammy *Motormouth* Baylor holding a soda and box of Milk Duds.

"Oh, hi Tammy. Sorry." Marvin stepped out of her way. Tammy continued down the aisle. He sighed, turned, and walked up the aisle. *Wonder if Norb is here yet.*

The usual crowd of High schoolers started to take their place along the back partition wall. Most of them wore Baymore Letterman jackets and a look of anticipation; like the B team waiting to be called into whatever game that might unfold in front of them. Only a few people were lingering outside the restroom area and Norb was not of them. Maybe he was inside smoking a cigarette. Marvin took a deep breath and walked inside. He glanced around; one person standing, one person sitting, and no one was smoking so he washed his hands and walked back out.

Go back to his seat and wait? Stand around the restrooms and wait? He had no one to ask what he should do but himself. A few girls walked past and giggled. Maybe he should look around for Linda. She said she would see him or perhaps he would find someone else he knows. What are the chances someone from his class was here? Stan Zellesky? Sandra Wilbert? The best course of action Marvin decided would be to join the ranks of nomadic kids who roam the auditorium landscape in search of their uncharted rewards. He would pick a friendly-looking group and follow behind as they explored the aisles.

The group he chose to tailgate explored the outer perimeters of the auditorium therefore it was easy to get a panorama of everyone. Marvin spotted a few kids that he knew. He wasn't sure whether to wave or simply nod and keep moving. There was Tim Goggins recognized from first grade. And there were the Sanderman twins who lived around the corner. They didn't see him, so he didn't need to choose a wave or a nod. He just followed.

The caravan reached the front and proceeded across no man's land between the first row and the sullied screen. Since he was so close, Marvin looked up at the screen and could see the tiny perforations that allowed the sound to pass through. Sound which was considerably louder at this location. A Henry Mancini song blasted from behind the screen. Marvin tilted his head to the right and shrugged up his shoulder to muffle the jarring sound of the organ.

Some of the teens Marvin followed would spot someone and break off or join a different wandering group. As they paraded along the front, he scanned the stationary faces in the seats. Some faces looked excited. Some looked bored. None looked like Norb or Linda. One face wore a familiar scowl. It was Tammy Baylor. She had her soda and milk duds but she wasn't seated with Rosa. She was next to an older couple. It had to be her parents. That probably explained her scowl.

The music stopped suddenly and the lights started to fade.

The main aisle was about ten feet away so Marvin made a beeline to find a seat. He moved past a few rows just as the lights went out and in the dark, all he could see was a ghost imprint of the last thing he looked at--the carpet, gold paisley patterns on the maroon background. He wondered who was their technician of light switches. He did a good job.

A white cone of light poured through the projection booth window accentuating a haze of smoke near the ceiling. It gave enough glow for Marvin to find a seat on the end. The coming attractions filled the screen. There were no surprises about the films *coming soon to this theater!* He had already seen all the preview posters out front.

His eyes adjusted to the cinema light, and he looked around to get his bearings. He assumed he landed somewhere maybe six or seven rows back. There were not a lot of people who chose the intimate distance. Parents warned kids that sitting too close would ruin their eyesight and play havoc with their hearing. Same rules transferred here.

A slow realization took hold as he turned and looked up the aisle toward the area where he had first sat down. His face became warm. He recalled watching someone walk down the aisle and sit five rows from the front, one seat from the end. He sat up to peer over the seats. There she was. Across the aisle, two rows up, and by herself. Rosa Alhambra. Instead of migrating toward the back to look for Norb, Marvin decided to stay where he was for a while.

He watched the previews for *Conquest Of The Planet Of The Apes*, and *The Valachi Papers*. The feature presentation started. An eloquent English man said the year was 1872. The final confrontation between Van Helsing and Count Dracula. Peter Cushing and Christopher Lee are fighting on the top of a horse-drawn carriage. The horses broke free, and Cushing is thrown clear just as the carriage crashed into a tree. Dracula has somehow been impaled by the spoke of a wheel. Van Helsing pushed it deeper into Dracula's heart. At that moment, Rosa turned her head, not wanting to watch the implied suffering and gore. She could have cast her eyes in any direction but she looked right at Marvin. Marvin looked right at her. Dracula turned to dust as recognition set in for her. She smiled. Marvin waved. Rosa waved and turned back to watch the movie.

It's now or never Marvin thought. The same gumption that lead him across the lunchroom to Norb's table, that lead him to ride out of the driveway and down the street, moved him from his seat, across the aisle, and into the seat behind Rosa Alhambra. The opening credits started. It was present-day London, 1972.

Marvin took a deep breath and leaned forward. "Glad to know there's another Dracula fan in class," he said.

Rosa giggled. "He's OK."

"Do you like Yorga better?"

"No," she said. "I like the wolfman better."

"Me too," he said as the theme music started.

She turned. "What?"

Marvin considered repeating himself but let it pass. "Nothing."

She smiled. "Do you want to sit up here?" She nodded to the seat next to her. Marvin was certain his face moved to a new shade of red based on the heat he felt radiating from it.

"Ummm... sure. If it's all right?"

"Sure," Rosa said.

Marvin considered climbing over the seats, as if scaling a backyard fence, but instead, moved up to her row from the aisle. He saw that her purse occupied the seat beside her, so he took the next one over. He thought it was probably better to play it cool. If she wanted him to sit next to her she would have moved it. While it may be important to learn about Peruvian land reform and Tet offenses, knowing where to sit was important also.

He took his seat. Rosa leaned over and said, "Now, I'll be able to hear you."

Marvin wondered if the only reason she asked him to sit there was for the purpose of hearing him. Well, it was a start. He then wondered--since she could hear him--should he repeat what he said about the wolfman or something more relevant?

"Did you see that Tammy Baylor was here?" Marvin asked. "She's sitting with her parents."

"I know. But she talks too much. I had to sit here or else she would talk through the whole movie."

"Right. I will be quiet. I promise."

She smiled. "No, you're fine."

"Thanks."

Suddenly, the movie cut to a party scene with loud music and people dancing. If he had anything more to say, he would save it. He would need to be closer to her to compete with the volume. Marvin sat back and watched the people on the screen moving to the music. Rosa raised her arms as if she were dancing along. Marvin laughed and joined in, flailing his arms wildly. Rosa laughed as she scooted down in her chair and planted her shoes on the seat in front of her. Marvin smiled to himself. He recalled that a summer ago he was content sitting in front of a condenser fan drying off after a swim with his friends. Now, here he was at the Crest, content to be sitting one seat away from Rosa Alhambra. Content that he made her laugh.

It was a pivotal scene in the movie; the groovy people from the party were now conducting a ceremony inside an old church. A ritual that was guaranteed to bring Dracula back from the dead. Rosa started to fidget in her seat. Something frightening was about to occur. Marvin knew this is where a cool guy would make a girl feel secure by putting his arm around her or by holding her hand; he had seen it in the movies and at the movies. Steve McQueen would do it. Steve Hablin would do it. Should he? Was he a cool guy? Or just pretending to be like Bobby Sherman pretending to be a tough biker on TV? Sure he wore taps on his shoes but so did guys who could dance.

Smoke was rising in the Church cemetery. Rosa moved down farther, pulled her legs in, and put her hand up to cover her eyes. There wasn't anything Marvin could do, cool or not. He couldn't stop Dracula from rising from the dead, he couldn't hold her hand because he was one seat away and too unsure that he had the confidence. What he did have was a need to go to the bathroom. His thought about sitting outside in front of the warm air of the a/c condenser made his system believe he had to pee. He tried to convince it otherwise but to no avail.

Dracula emerged from the smoke into present day. Not very scary still Rosa turned her head as Christopher Lee approached his first victim. Marvin waited until the demise was over and leaned toward Rosa, "I'll be back. I have to... go do something."

"Where are you going?"

He didn't want to say where he was going, bathroom functions seemed a bit personal to announce at this point. "I uh... I have something for a friend. I need to give it to him."

"Oh. OK." She turned back to watch the movie.

That was easy, Marvin thought. Irene or his mother would have a litany of follow-up questions. *Who is your friend? What are you giving him? Would he like some chicken?*

"I'll be back," he told her.

Rosa shrugged and kept her eyes on the screen. He couldn't tell if she was disappointed, indifferent, or something in-between. He got up and instead of squeezing past her, walked down the opposite way to the far aisle. *I guess that went OK for the first time. I sat near her. We talked. We laughed. I didn't hold her hand or anything but I told her I would be back. Just go to the bathroom, find Norb, give him the stupid firecrackers and... then what? What am I supposed to do? I don't even know. All these guys in the back row making out with girls, how did they get there? A hypnotic stare like Dracula, step from the smoke, open your cape, and move in for the kiss? Make out? He didn't know how.*

Marvin reached the top of the aisle and thought he heard someone call his name but he kept walking. Norb was not in sight. He went on into the men's room. The soda-sipping policeman was rising his hands in the sink. Marvin did what he needed to do and prayed the officer didn't ask what he had in his coat pocket. The policeman dried his hands and left. Marvin waited a twenty count and then went to the sink, rinsed, and dried his hands. He checked himself in the mirror. He looked alright. His hair was a little on the wild side but that came with curly hair, it did whatever it wanted to. If he could follow that example and do whatever he wanted to, he would toss the fire-crackers in the toilet and forget this whole Norb business, because obviously, Norb forgot about the plan. Maybe Linda was right. It was like some episode of some show; Norbert Stiebert was not the cool kid.

As Marvin came out of the Men's room he almost expected to see Norb standing there, that's what would happen on TV or in a movie, but instead, Linda was standing there, her arms crossed. *This must be a new episode*, Marvin thought.

"Didn't you hear me calling you?" Linda asked.

"I thought I heard someone call me. I didn't know..."

"What were you doing in there? Smoking?" She walked over to him and rubbed his hair.

"Yeah, sure," Marvin said.

"So, are you here with your new cool friend?"

"No. I haven't seen him."

"What a drag," she replied. "I'm here with some of my friends. You can sit with us. I think you met most of them under the bleachers that one time."

"Actually, I..." Marvin started to say

"Actually you what?"

"I was sitting with... someone."

"Really? Who?" Linda's eyes widened as she smiled. "Is it that girl from your class?"

"Yeah, I mean, it's not like a date or anything... I didn't know she was going to be here... and..."

"And what?" Linda asked.

Marvin looked around. They were standing in the middle of the cross-flow of both restrooms. "And it's a little busy right here."

"Come here." Linda grabbed his hand and lead him into a corner near the rear exit doors. It was more private and slightly darker than anywhere. "Ok. Now what?"

Marvin could hear Peter Cushing's soothing voice. He explained to someone how vampires attack.

"Well, I..." Marvin said to Linda. "I don't know... what I'm supposed to be doing."

"What do you mean, *what you're supposed to be doing? What do you wanna do?*"

"I... I don't know. I see other guys here with girls and..."

"You mean, making out? I see." Linda laughed. "OK. Let me show you something." She looked around and then said, "Lean in a little. Tilt your head to the right."

"Why? What are you..." Marvin didn't understand how he could get much closer. Linda slipped her fingers up behind his head and pulled him forward and planted her lips firmly against his. Everything melted at that moment. He felt as if his face were about to burst into flames. Every scene from every movie he had ever watched with two people kissing fed an unrevealed instinct and he knew what to do. He was Clark Gable, Humphrey Bogart, Burt Lancaster, Ryan O'Neil, and Captain Kirk. It was strange and magical. He could taste chapstick, cigarettes, toothpaste, and soda. He felt light-headed. Was he supposed to breathe? Was this what she and Steve did down in their basement? And then it stopped. He opened his eyes. Linda was a few inches away.

"There," she said. "That's what you do and how you do it. Got it?"

"Umm... yes."

"Listen to me," she said in a serious tone. "Two things. One, I did that because you're a friend. That's it. Don't get all weird about it. This was between you and me. That's it. And two, most important, if you try this with a girl... and she isn't cool with it? She turns away? You stop. Don't push it. You dig?"

"I dig I won't."

"Promise?"

"I promise," Marvin replied.

She gave him a quick kiss. "There. Now you have cooties. You'll never get rid of them." She rustled his hair. "See you around. Stay cool."

He watched her fade into the darkness of the auditorium. He felt strange—as if he were floating—or maybe drunk like Dean Martin. The happy drunk. He needed to sit. He aimed toward the section where he first landed. He maneuvered through the people milling about, past the kids leaning on the partition wall who made their odd noises at him, but he didn't care, it didn't matter now. He found his place and sat down.

The Plan, The Good, and the Problem

Marvin couldn't focus on the movie. The plots were the same. Same as *Taste The Blood Of Dracula,* and *Scars Of Dracula.*

Dracula is nothing at the beginning. Ashes. Someone performs an act or ritual of some sort, brings him to life, and spend the next 45 minutes trying to kill him for the next movie.

Marvin's head cleared. It was time to resume his place near the front. He told Rosa he would be right back. He stepped out into the aisle.

"Hey! Lee Marvin!" A voice called from behind. He stopped. Who knew *that* name? "Hey, Mini trail." Marvin turned. Norb stood at the top of the aisle with a grin. Marvin sighed. He wanted to turn and walk away but didn't. He walked up the aisle toward whatever fate waited for him there. "I thought you forgot."

"I would've been here sooner," Norb said. He nodded toward the kid in the army jacket who was slouched against the back wall. "But *dip wad* over there forgot to prop the exit door so I could get in."

The kid in the army coat shrugged.

"Did ya bring the goods?" Norb asked.

"Yeah, got them right here." Marvin reached into his coat pocket.

"Whoa Silver! Not here. Be cool." He nodded to his left and walked away. Marvin assumed he was supposed to follow. They walked to a dark corner. It was the corner directly on the opposite side of his Linda corner. He'd much rather return there.

"So, let's see it. Show me. Show me."

Marvin reached in his coat and withdrew the package. Norb squinted to see. "How many are in there?"

"Sixteen. I think."

"Boss! That should make some noise. Right?" Norb took them and felt them through the cellophane. "Hey. What about matches?"

"Matches?"

"Yeah kemosabe," Norb said. "To light 'em, right? How else are we going to do it? Rub some sticks together?"

"What about your Zippo lighter?"

"What Zippo?"

"The one from last year. The one that belonged to your uncle."

"Ah. I lost it somewhere. It's gone."

Marvin sighed. He was only responsible for the firecrackers. Sneaking them out of the garage and barging his way to be here tonight. Coming up with ticket money. Matches were never discussed. "What about your friend over there?"

"Who? My brother?"

So army coat guy is your brother, Marvin thought. Langford. Who was responsible for naming you and what century were they from?

"Nah. Langs, ain't got nothing."

"OK," Marvin replied. He thought for a moment. They could ask one of the adults sitting in the smoker's section, but there weren't many adults here tonight, and it was doubtful they give matches to a kid. "What about the bathroom?" Marvin asked. "You know, the smokers? Get some matches from someone in there."

"Good idea, chief." Norb punched Marvin on the shoulder. "Hey, how's that Honda running? You been ridin' it?"

"Yeah. I have. I did. I rode it the other day," Marvin said. "Gave a girl a ride."

"Yeah?" Norb smiled and flipped the hair out of his face. "A girl huh? Real flippy." Suddenly Norb looked beyond Marvin and traded his amused expression for one of painful annoyance. He turn away and stuffed the firecrackers into his jacket. Marvin felt a firm hand on his shoulder.

"Excuse me, gentlemen." Marvin turned to see a policeman standing behind him. "I recommend that you young fellows find a place to sit. Management doesn't want kids gallivanting about."

Marvin attempted to move but the officer's hand had no give to it. It held him firmly in place.

"I know you, don't I?" the officer asked Norb. "Have I seen you in here before?"

"No sir," Norb replied using a strange southern accent. "This here is my first time. My pal here and me was lookin' for the... gentleman's facilities. See, we drank too much sodie pop, and well, seems we got ourselves turned around."

"What's your name son?"

"Me? It's... Vince Everett," Norb replied without blinking an eye.

Marvin glanced at the badge on the Policeman's shirt. It was just like the one his dad wore; a crest in the center with two bears standing on either side. The name *Heilbronn* was on his name tag. Wonder if they knew each other? Not that it mattered at this moment.

"What about you son?" He looked down at Marvin. "What's your name?"

"My name's... Steve."

"Steve, what?"

Marvin wanted to say *Hablin* but didn't. Steve Halbin turned out to be OK. And now, he and Steve shared something in common. They knew which flavor chap-stick Linda wore. "Mannix," Marvin said. "Steve Mannix"

"Swell, Mr. Everette and Mr. Mannix, why don't you fellas go and find a seat?"

"Sure thing," Norb replied, "That sounds flippy. Right after we enjoy your restrooms." He grabbed Marvin's arm and pulled him free from the hand of the law.

They walked with a hurried purpose toward the hovering red letters on a small lighted sign in the distance that spelled

Restrooms Marvin glanced over his shoulder, and only Langford followed, Heilbronn addressed the teens along the partition wall. The pleasant feeling Marvin had earlier dissolved into dread. He felt his heart beating in his ears. His adrenaline raced. "That was a close one."

"Cops, man," Norb replied. "Can't stand 'em."

They stopped on the border where the worn carpet of the back aisle switched to the grimy ceramic tile of the restroom entrance. Norb stood where the ambient light from the doorway split him down the middle. He could move into and out of the shadows with one step. He jerked his hair back. "Ok we need to find some fire and then lay low," he said. "The fuzz is pretty active tonight. We need to be cool. Tell you what, we'll let things simmer and then meet up back up here in a little while. Sound cool?"

Marvin wasn't clear on what more he needed to do. He brought what he promised to bring and he gave them to Norb. Why did he need to meet back up in a little while?

"Marv, come here for a sec." Norb nodded to the spot next to him outside of the light. Marvin stepped into the shadow next to him. He heard the crinkling of cellophane. "Here. Take 'em for now."

"Why?"

"Cause. If I get busted trying to score matches and they find *those* on me... the jig is up."

Marvin sighed and stuffed them back into his coat. "When should we meet back here?"

"Half an hour," Norb said looking around. "Scram for now." He walked on into the men's room.

Peter Cushing was trying to find his granddaughter on the screen and Marvin was trying to find Rosa in the seats. Since they cracked down on kids standing around, many of the empty seats were now occupied. He found a seat off to the side and waited for a bright scene to light up the rows so he could spot her. She had been five rows from the front and one from the end but now she wasn't. The seat was empty. Maybe she went to the bathroom.

Cushing was now in a struggle with Dracula's minion who had been the main groovy young man that brought the count back to life. The groovy young man wanted to be dark, dangerous, and drain blood from the necks of mortals like his hero - but presently was wobbly, weak, and losing the fight to a frail older man. It was laughable, not frightening.

The decrease of excitement--in the movie and at the movie-- curtailed the energy Marvin had floated on most of the night. The pulsation in his ears was gone. What he had expected here at the Crest had taken a different path altogether; he imagined a daring, slightly dangerous--but exciting--prank that would lift his self-esteem onto a new and different level. But it wasn't a risky caper that elevated him, it was sitting one seat away from the girl he liked. It was learning how to kiss in a dark corner.

Peter Cushing had found Christopher Lee and the showdown would commence. Good would ultimately triumph over evil. Marvin didn't want to stay for the rest. It was time to go. He would hand the firecrackers over and call it a night. If Norb was there, fine, if not, he would return them to the cigar box.

The only person waiting in the agreed meeting spot was Langston. "Hi there," Marvin said to him. "Where's your bother?"

"Dunno. Around somewheres."

Marvin reached into his coat. "Can you give him something?"

"That reminds me," Langston said, "He said to give this to you." He held out his hand and pinched between his thumb and finger was a book of matches. Marvin's studied the matchbook. He was confused. This plan kept changing.

"Take it, man," Langston said.

He took it and glanced down at the cover. It looked like it said *Musical Piggies*. It had one match tucked outside for good luck. He wanted to say *Thanks, but no thanks*, and hand everything over to Langston, but when he looked up he was gone.

MARVIN WALKED into the men's room. Peter Cushing yelled out *Count Dracula!* and the sound reverberated around the ceramic tiles. Someone stood inside the stall next to the wall just below the vent in the ceiling. Strands of cigarette smoke floated up but before they could curl into a cloud they were sucked through the slats to join other foul odors inside the ventilation.

The next stall was vacant. For a moment he thought about tossing it all into the toilet but had concerns about it all being able to flush. He thought about the walk home. He should probably take advantage of his present location and crossed to the urinal to create relief for the journey.

Even though the cigarette odor was being escorted out--to who knows where--he could still smell it. Even though he wasn't watching the final battle between Dracula and Von Helsing, he could still hear it and imagine it was amusing. Marvin finished, went to the sink, and washed his hands.

"Who's smoking in here?" asked a familiar voice. Marvin glanced in the mirror and saw Heilbronn behind him. He nodded toward the occupied stall. Heilbronn looked that way and nodded. He strolled over, the soles of his shoes smacked on the tiles with each step, he stopped and tapped on the stall door. "All right, ditch your butt in the can and come on out here, kid."

Marvin skipped the towel dispenser and wiped his hand on his pants. He walked out as quickly as he legs could move. Just outside Norb and Langston were waiting. Norb had an eager expression on his face like a small child on Christmas eve.

"Go time! Go now!" Norb said. "Last chance, best chance. Last row! Go now while the fuzz is in the can!"

"But wait! I thought you were..."

"No time. Less talking, more walking. Go, Lee Marvin!"

Marvin wanted to ask, *What are you talking about? But he knew exactly what Norb meant.* He hadn't considered the possibility of being more than a secret accomplice. Should he do it? Be the talk of the Baymore lunchrooms on Monday? Who would believe Marvin Milstead set off firecrackers at the Crest? Ronnie? Ryan? Linda? Lauren? Rosa? No one would know but Norbert and Army Coat Stiebert. It would be a great story might tell one day. *But that's all it would be,* Marvin thought. *A stupid story. A story no one would believe.*

He could see someone was standing at the partition wall. Someone Heilbronn had not chased away. If Marvin was going to do this, he would need to sneak past this person, move around to the last row, light the fuse, toss them under the seats, and go out the side exit door. It would be just like the end scene in *The Dirty Dozen* where Jim Brown had to run under Nazi gunfire and drop the grenades down the vents. Only this would be without the Nazis or the gunfire.

He looked down at the floor as he walked. The battle between good and evil was reaching its peak on the screen. How many times he had reached into his coat pocket this evening but this would be the final time. Marvin glanced at the screen, Dracula had been stabbed but was not dead. Yet. He held his breath as he walked behind the person at the wall. He squinted from his peripheral to see if they noticed his sneaking presence. He saw the person was a lady. An older lady standing there at the wall, not one of the usual teenagers. Marvin recognized the clothes she wore. His mother's clothes. He froze for a moment. He took another step and looked again. Enough light from the screen confirmed his suspicion. It was. It was his mother. She was standing there watching the movie.

He moved toward her. "Mom?" he called. The music swelled as Dracula had been dosed with holy water and fell to his doom in a grave, she didn't hear him. Marvin walked up beside her and reached out. "Mom?"

She jumped. "Oh criminetly! You scared me, Marvin."

"What are you doing here?"

"I thought I'd pick you up. Save you the walk," she said. "Why are you up walking around?"

"I wasn't. I went to the bathroom."

"I see. Well, the nice manager let me come in here and wait for you."

"But... I thought you had a date," Marvin said.

"Well, I did. It was... kind of a drag. I was over early."

"Oh. OK." Marvin was sure what to say or do at this moment. His final plan had been halted. He looked around with no expectation of seeing Norb and his brother. They were no were in sight. He wasn't disappointed. He knew they would disappear. He was relieved. "We can go if you want."

"Don't you want to see the end?"

"This is the end. Christopher Lee is done. He fell on a stake again. That's pretty much it. They'll just stand around and pat each other on the back and drink brandy. Just like in the other Dracula movies."

"Well, sure. If you want, we can go," she said. "Before all the people and traffic."

"That would be good."

Going Home

Marvin waited outside by the front doors of the Crest. His mother wanted to tell the manager *Thanks* and purchase a few candy bars for Leonard.

Kids roamed under the lights as they waited for rides, yelled dialogue from the movie at passing cars, or played a crude version of tag that involved a punch to the arm. Marvin walked to the corner of the building to see if he could spot his mother's red Ford Maverick in the parking lot.

"Hey look Heffendorf, it's your little boyfriend," a voice taunted loudly. Marvin turned around to see a group of girls strolling by. Amid the cluster was Linda. Their eyes met and then she looked away. If he didn't know any better Marvin was certain her face displayed a red coloration that overwhelmed the makeup she wore. One of the girls held a cigarette up, "Hey! You got a light sailor?" The girls laughed.

"Why would he have anything, Lynn? He's a kid!"

"Actually, yeah I do," Marvin spoke up as he dug into his pocket. He pulled out the book of matches. The girls laughed harder. Linda stared at something down the street. Lynn placed the cigarette between her lips and walked to Marvin. He held up the matches and just before she snatched it from his fingers he saw the cover read *Musial and Biggies.* Not *Musical Piggies.* The matches were from the steak house owned by the famous baseball player Stan Musial.

"Ooh fancy-*schmancy*," Lynn said before striking the match. "Is this where he takes you to dinner, Linda?"

"Every night," Linda said with a wink.

The girls giggled and Lynn handed the matchbook back to Marvin.

"It's OK. Keep them," he said. "You can have them."

"Well, thanks! He's a keeper, Heffendorf."

Marvin heard the familiar rumble of the Barracuda as Mr. Heffendorf pulled up.

"Shotgun! I called it," Lynn yelled and flicked her cigarette into the air as she ran toward the car. Only Linda hesitated a moment as she looked back at Marvin.

"You doing all right?" she asked.

"Doing good," he said.

"Good." Linda smiled. "Stay cool." She ran to the car, climbed in, and pulled the door closed.

For the amusement of the crowd outside and the girls inside, Mr. Heffendorf punched the accelerator and let the tires scream out as they headed down the street.

What was taking his mother so long? He saw Tammi's mother and father come out followed by Tammi who was busy talking to someone. It was Rosa. They were coming toward him. He wanted to get Rosa's attention. He wanted to explain. But Tammi had her attention. As they walked by, Rosa glanced at him. And smiled.

EVERYTHING WOULD BE ALL RIGHT. Except for Leonard's candy bar. The concession stand had closed for the night and Marilyn couldn't negotiate a prize.

On the drive home, Marvin considered asking his mother why her date was a drag, but that might lead her to ask him about his night. His night wasn't fully realized yet. There were avenues he didn't want to travel down, and secrets he didn't want to share.

"Shame about the candy bars," Marvin said. "I know how grandpa can get when he has his heart set on something."

"It's fine."

Marvin thought about turning on the radio but the drive was so short by the time he found a decent song they would be home. "What about *Velvet Creamery?* They should be open," Marvin said. "I know he likes banana splits. That might make up for the candy bar."

"That's true," she said. "Let me think... isn't there a shortcut here somewhere. One of these side streets. Maybe by the pool hall?"

"Yeah. I think so." Marvin thought for a moment as he looked out the window. "But you know, after all the turns and other streets you have to go down, it's not worth it. If you go the regular way, it works out better, sometimes."

"Does it now?"

"I hope so."

About the Author

Lee Mueller was born in St. Louis, Missouri. For over thirty years he has been involved in the performing arts, from acting, directing, improv/sketch comedy, and most notably as a playwright. His first one-act play, "In Between Days" was produced during a national writer's conference. His second one-act, "The Favor" was a finalist in a short play competition in St. Louis.

He has specialized in comedy murder mystery plays that have been produced all over the world. His play "Death Of A Doornail" won "Best Original Comedy" at the 27th Annual "Arty Awards" in Fairfield California. "Murder Me Always" ran for a month at the Laugh Factory in New York.

Lee also hosts a Podcast on creativity called "And So The Mind Reels" and has published a collection of short stories called "Idle Essence: Tales Of Marvin".

Also by Lee Anians-Mueller

A Medley Of Murder Mystery Plays

Idle Essence - Tales Of Marvin

Basic On Stage Survival Guide For Amateur Actors